Secrets TO A GENTLEMAN'S Heart

SAMANTHA GRACE

SECRETS TO A GENTLEMAN'S HEART

First edition. October 20, 2015.

Copyright © 2015 Samantha Grace.

ISBN: 978-1518640636

Written by Samantha Grace.

Dedication

I'm blessed to have many amazing and supportive people surrounding me who encourage me to believe in my vision and see it through to the end. I'm so grateful to my family, friends, and talented fellow authors, but this book is dedicated to *you*, my reader. Thank you for laughing, crying, fanning yourself, and smiling along the way. And thank you even more for reaching out to me and sharing what my books mean to you. I am truly touched by your generous spirits.

Coded Message

Received in London on 22 February 1820
jtfqghugsigmksxlrymuetrkuivkxrxzmwmdvviwkfxzvpwgtwwrq
lfyxrmhamiveklwghpwchlmoppxlmksqcndghfivzsweiliupwkew
ejpigaviuwwltpcjhdxrppjwmisplvdlhfbivymksxrthuragvzyieicec
hftnsvzdivrthzetxsdyifmilpgvgbaeteioqgaakzhzlalivnizopruzqm
ntwjhlaibffdzwahlzsjhuchwrzvyevlvqtmisjdqetdxyhqllpruwwfo
gvfzigdwsghbhhpzvwpbssigowkaqpvwilkqiylvwmtekoiltxjzvph
uahghzbswmewpxlxrvrnwuiczzqelwscgiilpgviwkydyzqpxlalzvut
jtwkb'aeonecvmkvprkvqkjdrrwptnwetnjxrgc

Deciphered Message
Upon your orders, I have been tracking Wedmore for five
months, and my investigation has led to Algiers by way of
Tripoli. Wedmore has managed to stay several steps ahead of
me ever since my arrival in Alexandria. A credible source placed
the earl in Algiers a week ago and witnessed him board a ship
bound for Cyprus. I am to sail to the island tomorrow and
hope to have this deplorable task behind me at last. If I should
perish in the line of duty, I will hold a place for you in hell.

His Majesty's loyal servant,
Sir Jonathan Hackberry

One

It is with great joy my dear Matthew and I have welcomed our first child. She is the most beautiful creature I have ever beheld. Matthew says it is impossible to determine a child's redeeming qualities when she is only days old, but it should be obvious to anyone with eyes that our daughter is meant to lead, not follow. Therefore, with my loving husband's blessing, I have bestowed upon her the name Regina, in honor of the Queen of Angels.

From the diary of Isabelle Darlington
November 1797

April 1820

In Regina Darlington's third and final Season on the marriage mart, she'd discovered a most unfortunate fact. When Uncle Charles was away, the rakehells came out to play.

Her guardian often traveled in his quest for antiquities, leaving Regina and her two younger sisters under their elderly great-aunt's care, but he hadn't met them in London as planned, and he hadn't missed a Season since before Regina's debut.

Despite Aunt Beatrice's reassurances that her nephew had likely forgotten to consult the calendar to insure his timely arrival, Regina was worried. Or she would be if the scoundrels sniffing around her skirts would allow her a moment of quiet to work herself into a proper dither. They were sorely trying her patience, none more so than the deplorable rake leering at her from Uncle Charles's favorite wingback chair.

Lord Geoffrey sprawled on the furniture with the insolence born of a duke's second son, stroking the ivory damask upholstery with his long tapered fingers. His eyes narrowed at the corners and glinted with amusement when she sat up taller on the settee beside her aunt and squared her shoulders.

Only the clicking of Aunt Beatrice's knitting needles disrupted the tense silence. The cur hadn't spoken beyond the obligatory exchanging of pleasantries upon his arrival, not that he needed to utter a word. Regina knew the reason he'd called, and he wasn't searching for a wife.

Last night during the waltz, he'd tried to shock her by whispering the vilest words into her ear. A lady with less fortitude might have required smelling salts. Regina simply had abandoned him mid-dance and given him the cut direct in the park this morning. Nevertheless, here he was, imposing his unwelcome company on her and her aunt.

Untroubled by Aunt Beatrice's presence beside her on the settee or Regina's glowers, Lord Geoffrey leisurely swept his gaze over Regina's body. He paused on her bust line and squeezed the arm of the chair a few times.

She cleared her throat in censorship, and a cunning grin spread across his face. He was proving to be wretchedly hard to discourage—at least by the usual means available to a lady. She would love catching him by surprise with one of the ancient warrior moves she'd learned from Uncle Charles. Perhaps then Lord Lewd would think twice about attempting to shocking young ladies at the assemblies or fondling unsuspecting furniture.

"I detect a rare smile from you," he said, victory lighting his pale blue eyes. "I will accept it as evidence of your pleasure to see me."

"I would expect nothing less of you, my lord." Regina remained stiff-backed on the edge of the settee and schooled her expression. Her smile had not been intended for him, but for all the innocents she would save from his loathsome company if she were allowed to humble him with a well-placed kick to his person.

Just as he'd ignored her previous rejections, he glossed over the pointed reminder she found him insufferably arrogant. "I expect I could win more smiles on a stroll through the park."

"I expect you could *not*, my lord."

His blond brows arched in challenge. "It sounds as if we are on the verge of a wager."

Regina notched her chin, ignoring the whispers of her competitive nature to prove him wrong. She had no desire to engage with him in whatever game he seemed to be playing.

Lord Geoffrey leaned forward as if anticipating her acceptance. "What is your answer, dearest? Will you allow my escort through the park?"

Aunt Beatrice looked up from her knitting as if just now hearing any part of the conversation and blinked in Lord Geoffrey's direction. "A breath of fresh air would do you good, young man," she said to the marble bust on the pedestal to his left. "I've never seen such a pasty face in all my life. Allow me to retrieve my walking stick and bonnet, and we may be on our way."

Regina swallowed the half-laugh, half-groan rising at the back of her throat. Aunt Beatrice had her heart set on finding Regina a husband, and a duke's son, no matter how boorish he was, would be considered a good catch by many. She refused to accept Regina would be happiest following her example. Aunt Beatrice had never married, but she seemed perfectly content with her life. And so was Regina. She saw no reason to make a change, especially when her great-aunt and Uncle Charles would both need someone to care for them eventually.

"Regina?" Aunt Beatrice smiled fondly at her and reached to pat her knee, underestimating the distance. At the slight widening of her aunt's eyes, Regina captured her hand where it landed on the velvet pillow and pressed it reassuringly between her own palms.

"I am here, Auntie."

"Yes, here you are, my darling." She raised Regina's hands to place a kiss on her glove. "You should run along to engage in your exercises while Lord Geoffrey and I take a turn around the park."

"Oh?" Either Aunt Beatrice was up to no good, or she was losing her mind as well as her eyesight. "You and Lord Geoffrey alone?"

"Of course, dear. I hardly require an escort at my age." She pulled her hand free and made a shooing motion. "Now, do run along. I am anxious to see how many smiles the young man can win from me."

Lord Geoffrey sputtered. "I believe there has been a misunderstanding, Mrs. Allred."

"*Miss* Allred. I never married, but I promised myself long ago if the right man came along..." Aunt Beatrice waggled her eyebrows in his direction—or perhaps she was flirting with the sculpture at Lord Geoffrey's shoulder.

Lord Geoffrey shifted on the seat, tossing a wide-eyed look at Regina as if begging for assistance as she fought to control the laughter bubbling up inside her. When he found no help forthcoming, he surged to his feet. "Miss Allred, please forgive my sudden change of plans. I've only now recalled an appointment with my solicitor."

As he dashed for the door, he collided with the housekeeper coming through the threshold. Mrs. Cox, red-faced and glistening with sweat, spared a brief scowl for Lord Geoffrey before appealing to Aunt Beatrice. "Ma'am, you must come quickly. Cupid is loose in the square, and Mr. Burgess has twisted his ankle giving chase."

"Oh, dear. Not again."

Regina popped up from the settee. "I will retrieve him."

"No, he will think having you chase him around the mulberry bush is a grand amusement." Aunt Beatrice wiggled to the edge of the settee and rose with an exasperated huff. "He will come to me if I call for him."

Cupid, Aunt Beatrice's incorrigible black toy poodle, had the run of the house. And the neighborhood. He was quick to come to Aunt Beatrice because she always rewarded his naughtiness with a piece of fatty ham. Not that Regina and her sisters spoiled him any less. It was impossible to resist his adorable black eyes and heart melting whimpers.

Aunt Beatrice bustled from the drawing room with Mrs. Cox leading the way. Regina hurried to the open window behind the settee to see if her help was really needed and discovered their butler seated on the grass with his leg drawn up to inspect his ankle. Cupid zipped from under the bush, bit Burgess's pants leg, and shook it. Burgess yelped and flailed his arm side to side, trying to catch the fur ball, but Cupid ran in a fast circle out of his reach.

Burgess bared his teeth. "You blasted hound of hell!"

Cupid followed suit, baring his own teeth before launching into a high-pitched bark.

Regina sighed over the antics outside. "Just another day at Wedmore House."

"It's a damned madhouse."

Regina startled at the sound of Lord Geoffrey's honeyed voice at her ear. She spun toward him. "My lord, I thought you were leaving."

"So did I, but *Cupid* saw fit for us to be alone." He leaned closer, a lascivious grin easing across his face. "At last." His breath smelled strongly of spirits and made her nose wrinkle.

"I have no desire to be alone with you." She backed away to put distance between them. "You should go."

"Don't be coy, Miss Darlington. I am twice the man Neil Lawrence is."

Regina blinked in confusion. She'd danced with Mr. Lawrence twice last Season on two separate occasions. What connection could the bashful young man possibly have with the rake prowling toward her? "You are making no sense, and I have asked you to leave."

"Did you believe Lawrence was capable of keeping a secret, dearest?" The feverish gleam in Lord Geoffrey's eyes caused an icy shudder to pass through her. She took another step away, her muscles tensing in anticipation of a fight. "Word has spread about your kiss, and he assured the gents you approached the endeavor with great enthusiasm."

Anger flared inside her. "If Mr. Lawrence said we shared a kiss, he is a liar. You and your cohorts are fools to listen to him."

"I always knew you had hidden passion waiting to be discovered."

She rolled her eyes, not caring that her behavior was rude. Lord Geoffrey had crossed the line of propriety the moment he walked into Wedmore House with the intention of seducing her. When he took another step in her direction, she held up a finger in warning.

"You have outstayed your welcome, my lord."

He halted his pursuit, as any well-bred gentleman should.

With a relieved sigh, she turned her back to lead him from the room. "Allow me to show you to the door."

"I decide when I go. Come here." He threw his arm around her neck.

Regina's instincts leapt into action. She grasped his forearm before he could get a good hold, ducked low, and flipped him around her body to knock him off balance. He landed on his side with a grunt and started flopping like a fish.

She wrenched his arm behind him just enough to get his attention, but if he moved an inch, he would feel a stab of pain in his shoulder. "Be still before you hurt yourself."

"Go to the devil!" He gasped, quickly discovering movement was ill advised.

She frowned down at his red face. In some circles, she supposed he was considered handsome, but his soft features were too boyish for her tastes, not to mention his morals were on par with an earthworm's.

And he *cursed* like a sailor.

"Language, my lord. A lady is present."

He snarled. "I see no lady. Do you know what I see?" The tips of her ears began to burn from the fount of nasty insults that followed.

"Regina, darling," Aunt Beatrice called from the foyer.

"Quiet," Regina said. When a litany of curses continued to pour from Lord Geoffrey, she placed her foot against his neck, effectively convincing him to fall silent. "Behave and I will release you in a moment."

Aunt Beatrice entered the drawing room with Cupid cradled against her chest and bumped her shoulder into the doorjamb.

Regina hissed in sympathy. "Are you all right, Auntie?"

Her aunt flicked her hand dismissively and didn't acknowledge that she had misjudged the location of the doorway. "The good boy came to me just as I predicted."

Regina flashed a smile from her place behind the settee and held tightly to Lord Geoffrey. Wisely, he remained silent. "And Burgess?"

"He threatened to resign again, but I expect he will come around in a day or two." Aunt Beatrice frowned and looked around the drawing room. "What happened to Lord Geoffrey? Did he take his leave?"

The settee blocked Aunt Beatrice's view of him, although Regina's aunt might not see him even if he were laid out at her feet. "I am afraid so. I don't expect he will be returning either."

Aunt Beatrice's grin was positively wicked. "Excellent news. We have no use for his kind at Wedmore House. Was it a trick of my eyes, or was he the palest lecher you have ever seen?"

Regina glanced at Lord Geoffrey's crimson face. "I didn't notice."

Cupid's curly ears flattened on his head, and a guttural growl rumbled in his small chest. Clearly, he hadn't missed the strange man lying on the carpet. The little dog scrambled to break free of Aunt Beatrice's hold.

"No, no." Aunt Beatrice shook her finger in his face. "You have been a naughty boy today. Let's see if there is a piece of ham in the kitchen."

Cupid perked up at the mention of his favorite treat, and Aunt Beatrice carried him from the room without incident.

Regina looked down at Lord Geoffrey with no hint of mirth. "I am going to release you in a moment, but allow me to reassure you, it is no accident you are in this position. If you attempt to accost me again, I'm afraid I will be unable to practice the same level of restraint."

She removed her foot from his neck, released his wrist, and moved to a safe distance. Lord Geoffrey winced as he unwound his body and pushed to his feet. He glowered once more. "If anyone hears about this..."

No doubt, he meant to sound threatening to ensure she kept quiet about their encounter, but his bark lacked bite at this point.

"I will not utter a word." She smiled pleasantly. "As long as you keep your distance from my family and me."

"You and your kin are insane," he spat, jabbing a finger in her direction. "Keep your mouth shut about today, or I swear to you, I will ruin you all."

Lord Geoffrey's threat sobered her. His father, the Duke of Stanhurst, was an influential man. She might not care about making a marriage match for herself, but her youngest sister had dreamed of her wedding day since she was a girl.

Regina swallowed hard. "I promise to tell no one, my lord."

He hurled another insult at her and stomped from the drawing room. Regina's stomach twisted in knots. She hadn't meant to jeopardize Sophia's future, but she'd needed to defend herself.

"Ludwig!" Regina collapsed on the settee and sank into the plush cushions. Now that she knew the reason for the rakes dogging her heels, the Season had gone from merely a bother to a nightmare. She'd done nothing wrong, and yet the thought of confiding in her sisters or Aunt Beatrice caused her cheeks to burn with shame.

Her fingers curled into fists. How dare Mr. Lawrence tell false tales about her? If she crossed paths with the blackguard any time soon, she would be sorely tempted to throttle him in full view of the *ton* at large. If someone was going to ruin her reputation, she preferred to do it herself. Unfortunately, she wouldn't be the only one to suffer, which left her in a bit of a bind. Not only did she have Mr. Lawrence's lies to contend with, she had to figure out how to avoid Lord Geoffrey.

It was fortuitous she and her family were planning an evening at home. The quiet would allow her time to think of an acceptable excuse to bow out of Lady Eldridge's annual ball tomorrow night. It remained to be seen if she was creative enough to fabricate an excuse to miss every other event of the Season.

Two

In the middle of Xavier Vistoire's morning exercises, the old rooster began crowing in the farmyard outside. Even with the window boarded in his prison cell, he couldn't avoid the obnoxious sound.

Lamplight illuminated the slanted walls of the attic. He couldn't stand upright in some parts, but it certainly wasn't the worst place Xavier had ever spent a night. Nevertheless, he'd welcome the chance to wake in an alley with a terrible case of cottonmouth, a skull-splitting headache, and the freedom to make bad decisions all over again.

Xavier paused in his exercise, holding himself parallel to the plank floor. "Benny, wake up" he yelled to his gaoler who was snoring just outside the attic door. "It's time to milk the cow."

A drawn out groan filtered under the door, and he imagined Benny stretching his massive frame to release the kinks he must have from spending the night on the stairs. "I'm not asleep," he mumbled.

Xavier lowered his body toward the floor and raised it again. Routine had become his sanity and keeping his strength was necessary as he planned his next escape. "I could do the milking for you, if you like."

"No, thank you, Mr. Vistoire."

It had been worth a try. He supposed he would have to break out of the attic just like every other place Benny had tried to hold him.

Earlier in the week, Xavier had kicked loose the boards nailed over one of the farmhouse's bedchamber windows and climbed down the drainspout. He'd almost been free, but

Benny returned from his monthly excursion to the village early and caught him in the meadow. For a large man, he was fleet-footed.

Now, Xavier was back in the attic. From his previous stay, he knew the window lead to a four-story drop to the hard packed ground, and the moth-eaten clothes kept in the trunk weren't strong enough to fashion a rope. Benny had repaired the door, and Xavier was not supposed to break the lock this time. Even if he ignored his gaoler's request, Xavier wouldn't make it past Benny now that he spent most of the day guarding him.

The stairs groaned under Benny's weight. Xavier pushed to his feet and approached the door. "*Mon ami*, today you will allow me to go, no?"

"No," Benny said. His lumbering footsteps sounded on the stairs, growing quieter as he moved farther away.

Xavier sighed. Nothing ever swayed his unlikely companion.

Other than the beginning of his incarceration, Xavier had no contact with anyone besides Benny, which suited him fine as long as he was stuck here. The other gents who'd grabbed him outside the Den of Iniquity and brought him to the farmhouse had been unable to hear, or else hadn't wanted to listen. No matter how many times he'd denied being a French spy, they'd kept hitting him and asking the same question. Eventually, they must have decided he was telling the truth, because they left and hadn't returned.

Yet, a little over two years since he was snatched from the alley leading to the gaming hell, he was still a prisoner.

When Xavier was reasonably certain Benny had left the house to see to the morning chores, he grabbed the lamp from the primitive bedside table and hurried to the weak spot he'd discovered in the floor last night. The board bent slightly under his weight and crackled. Xavier bent down to investigate. He pried up the edge of a plank and a piece of it broke away. The wood beneath the surface had begun to crumble.

He smiled. "Dry rot."

Standing, he slammed his boot heel against the floor and heard the sweet sound of splintering wood. He stomped the spot repeatedly until the board gave way and fell in pieces to the room below. A beam of light poked its way through the hole, and he crouched to determine what room was located beneath this part of the attic. Debris littered a large bed covered with a faded blue-stitched quilt. Once he'd created a hole big enough to climb through, he would have a soft and quiet landing.

He returned to stomping the floor to make as much progress on the hole as possible while Benny was outside. By tomorrow, he hoped to have his escape route ready. He would leave after nightfall when he heard Benny snoring and make his way back to London. The farmhouse was north of the city, or so he had gathered from his nightly conversations with Benny, which often were one-sided since Xavier's gaoler was not a verbose man.

How far from London, Xavier didn't know. He'd been in and out of consciousness for the trip there. Benny didn't know either. The man barely recalled living anywhere else. He was six when his mother died, and he was sent to the old farmhouse. Benny had never gone any further than the village ever since. After the caretaker and his wife passed away several years ago, Benny had been without regular human contact. It was a wonder he wasn't chattier.

Xavier abandoned the hole in anticipation of Benny completing his chores and dragged the trunk filled with the tattered clothes over it before he returned to the house. As he had discovered the first time he was locked in the attic, there were an abundance of useless items stored here.

He grabbed an overhead rafter at the highest point in the attic, made sure it could hold his weight, and continued his exercises while he waited for Benny to bring his breakfast. A loud clacking sound from the lock tumbling interrupted his last exercise. He finished pulling himself up so his chin was higher than the board before he dropped to the floor and moved toward the door.

"Porridge again, my friend?" he asked as the door swung open.

Benny grunted in reply and ducked to enter the doorway. He was empty-handed.

Xavier frowned. Benny thrived on routine, too. No porridge, or *any* morning fare, alerted Xavier that something was wrong.

Benny pursed his lips, which seemed to be permanently stained burgundy from eating an unusual amount of pickled beets. "Come to the kitchen."

The hair on the back of Xavier's neck stood on end. Occasionally, Benny brought him below stairs for companionship, but his voice never quivered when he spoke. Something was definitely out of sorts. "Why?"

Benny lunged and clamped his burly hand around Xavier's upper arm. "Please," he hissed. His breath smelled of vinegar.

Xavier allowed Benny to pull him toward the stairway. He couldn't ignore a possible opportunity to escape, even if he didn't know what he would find below stairs.

In the kitchen, nothing appeared to be afoot. A fire burned in the red brick hearth blackened with soot. Steam rolled from the spout of the heavy kettle hanging over the flames, and a tin of porridge and a large bowl sat on the wide-plank table.

Tension drained from his body. "You could have just said you were lonely. You had me worried for a moment."

"As you should be," someone said behind him.

Xavier spun toward the sound, and his pulse ripped through his veins. The man responsible for his abduction and interrogation was standing in the pantry doorway with a pistol pointed at him.

"What do you want, Farrin? Nothing has changed. I am still not a French spy."

A leisurely smile spread across the blackguard's thin lips. His rust-colored hair lay slick with pomade against his head. "Benny," he barked.

Xavier's gaoler grabbed him from behind and slammed him onto the wooden bench at the table. His meaty hands gripped Xavier's shoulders to hold him in place.

He gritted his teeth. "Benny, what did we agree about not manhandling me?"

"Sorry, Mr. Vistoire." The man loosened his grip and bent forward, bringing his round face into view. Xavier could see the gaps where he was missing teeth. "You have a visitor," he whispered.

"So I see," Xavier drawled.

Even though his heart was pounding, he wouldn't give Farrin the satisfaction of knowing he'd caught him by surprise. Before the interrogation could begin, he recited the story he'd told the blackguard two years ago. It hadn't changed in the weeks following his abduction when Farrin ordered his henchmen to beat the truth from him, and it was the same now.

"I am an *American*. I hail from New Orleans, and I'm not a bloody Frog, as your countrymen have so cleverly dubbed the French."

He cared nothing for either country's politics. He only wanted to go home.

"I know who you are, Mr. Vistoire, and what you are not. At the moment, you look like something the dog dragged in." He made a show of leaning toward Xavier and sniffing. "And *pissed* on."

Benny bent forward to sniff him too. His unruly brows angled toward each other in confusion. "I don't smell anything. No dogs have been around for a long time now."

Farrin cocked a hip on the edge of the table, ignoring Benny's observation. Xavier took in the richness of his navy blue coat and the perfect tailoring. His clothing suggested wealth, but the deep lines of his face told another story. He wasn't a pampered son of nobility. He had seen a good many days of labor in his past.

Xavier scowled. "If you know who I am, why are you still holding me?"

The man didn't acknowledge his inquiry, and instead, passed an assessing glance over Xavier from head to toe. His top lip curled as he found him lacking.

Xavier's fingers twitched with the urge to smooth his unruly dark hair. Vanity had an odd way of rearing its head when his appearance was the least of his concerns. Farrin's brown eyes gleamed, revealing the pleasure he took in his discomfort.

Xavier sprawled insolently on the chair. He'd perfected indifference years ago. "Had I known I'd have a visitor, I would have summoned my valet first thing."

Farrin reached inside his coat and retrieved a piece of paper. "I am in need of your services."

Xavier accepted the sheet he held out and unfolded it. There were primitive ink drawings of the interior of a house and an address written on the page. "Do I look like I am a servant? Do you mistake me for a bloody footman or butler?" He flicked the paper back at him. It floated to the floor.

The man sighed as if he were dealing with a child then bent to retrieve the drawing.

"You should hear Tommy out," Benny said in his ear. His fingers were still digging into Xavier's shoulders to keep him immobilized.

Farrin nailed Benny with a scathing look, and Xavier felt the tremor pass through the larger man.

"I'm not supposed to call him Tommy any more," Benny whispered in his ear. "He is Mr. Farrin now. Listen to him, because this is your chance to go home."

The mention of home caused Xavier's eyes to narrow. Was this a new means of torture? Dangling what he wanted most in the world in front of him just to snatch it away, or did Farrin hope to use Xavier's longings to manipulate him? He'd sooner trust a snake than the blackguard.

Farrin's keen gaze bore into him. "You do wish to go home again, do you not?"

"What do *you* want?" In Xavier's experience, no one did anything for another person unless they wanted something in return.

Farrin imitated a sheepish shrug. The hardness to his eyes said he wasn't ashamed in the least. "An interested party is willing to pay handsomely for a map kept at this address. I want you to search for it tonight while the residents are attending a ball."

He slid onto the bench across from Xavier, spread the paper on the table, and touched his finger to the diagram. "It is likely to be in one of three rooms. The library, study, or the master's chambers. I will tell you how best to search for the hiding spot to make quick work of it."

"A map?" Xavier gaped at the drawing then at the lunatic sitting across the table. "Like a treasure map? As in pirates with buried gold, or leprechauns and rainbows?"

"Like a bloody *map*," Farrin snapped, his face flushing crimson. "It is the key to you leaving England. That's all you need to know. Retrieve it, hand it over to Benny, and you will be on the next ship sailing to America."

Benny grunted in surprise. "I can leave the farm? Can I go to America too?"

Farrin's icy gaze darted to the man standing behind Xavier. He could feel Benny shrinking back.

"If you want it," Xavier said, pulling the man's attention back toward him, "why not retrieve it yourself? Or use one of your men."

"Because if you help me, I will help you in return. Tonight you could be a free man."

The devil, he would be free. He knew a liar when he saw one. Drumming his fingers against the table, he pretended to give Farrin's offer serious consideration. "If I agree to do your dirty work, how do you propose I go about it? I cannot fathom the butler will grant me entrance to search the premises while the residents are away."

"Wedmore House is between butlers, which I've come to understand is a common condition."

"And the other servants?"

"There is a housekeeper, cook, coachman, and a lady's maid. The maid has been visiting her sister and her newborn nephew on the evenings the ladies are away. The cook and housekeeper return to their own homes at night, and the coachman has quarters in the coach house."

"You seem to know a lot about the goings-on around there."

"The streets have eyes and ears, Mr. Vistoire. I know a good many things about a lot of people."

"Again I ask, why me?"

Farrin's eyebrows rose on his forehead as if he was bewildered by the question. "How many times have you almost escaped, Mr. Vistoire? You are harder to contain than water in a bucket full of holes. I have no doubt you are capable of getting away if you are about to be discovered."

Oh, Xavier would find a way out. If Farrin believed he would return with or without a map, the man was a fool. Once Xavier was out of sight, he would be on the next ship home.

"Besides," Farrin said, "if you are captured, no one will care what happens to a French spy who has escaped from custody."

"I am not a bloody spy," Xavier said through clenched teeth.

Farrin flashed a sly smile. "You are if I identify you as one."

In other words, if Xavier was caught, he would never see home again. Hell, he might even be executed, which settled the matter quickly in his mind. He wouldn't be caught.

"Prove you intend to release me after I bring you the map. I'll need decent clothes and money for my fare."

"And a bath," Benny added.

Xavier frowned up at him. "You said you didn't smell anything."

"You always ask for a bath. I thought you'd be pleased."

Farrin growled under his breath, and Benny snapped his mouth closed. "I will find clothes for you," Farrin said. "Benny can see to the bath. We leave at dusk."

Xavier lifted the paper to study the drawing once more. "Wedmore House. I don't believe I had the honor of meeting Mr. Wedmore during my time in London Society."

"Earl of Wedmore." Farrin's reddish brow arched. "Nor do I expect you ever will, Mr. Vistoire."

Several hours later, they were headed to London. Xavier was clean, well attired in clothes only slightly too large for him, and wedged onto the same bench with Benny in Farrin's travel coach. The blackguard had only kept part of his word.

"Where is the money for my passage to New Orleans?" Xavier asked. "That was part of our agreement."

Farrin flicked a disinterested look in Xavier's direction before pulling his hat over his eyes and reclining in comfort on the spacious side of the coach. "You must think I'm a fool, Mr. Vistoire. What is to stop you from running to the docks as soon as you are out of my sight? You will receive your money when you deliver the map."

Xavier bit back a curse. His time in London had been fruitful before he was abducted. Large wins at the gaming tables would allow him to return home a wealthy man once again, but he couldn't access his bank account at this hour. And he had no proof of his identity. No shipmaster with a head for business would allow him passage without a guarantee of payment. He had to rethink his strategy for paying his fare, because he wasn't coming back to collect it from Farrin.

Merde! A rather distasteful idea came to mind. Before he found a quick exit from Wedmore House, he must take a piece of jewelry. Xavier had committed many sins in his life. He'd gambled, drank his weight in rum, and cavorted with paramours, but he had never been a thief. It hardly seemed like the best way to begin his life as a reformed man, but he was out of choices.

Three

The evening of the Eldridge ball, Regina joined her two sisters and aunt in the drawing room while they awaited their escort. Cupid had wormed his way between her sisters on the settee and was catching up on his sleep.

Sophia and Evangeline were dressed in gorgeous gowns made from silks Uncle Charles had brought back from one of his excursions to the Far East. Sophia wore her favorite color, blue, and Evangeline had chosen a rich yellow that highlighted the subtle copper color of her hair.

Aunt Beatrice had donned a more vibrant emerald green gown. As she was fond of saying, even though she had never married or bore children of her own, she had managed a household and raised three girls. She'd earned the privilege of wearing whatever she pleased.

"You all look lovely," Regina said.

"Thank you, dearest." Aunt Beatrice took up her yarn and needles from the sewing basket at her feet. After years of knitting, her aunt could create a shawl in her sleep, and she liked to keep her hands busy.

Sophia smiled, revealing a dimple in her right cheek. "I wasn't certain which gown I should wear. Octavia said the Eldridge ball is the most prestigious social event of the Season, and I didn't want to be underdressed."

Octavia was Sophia's best friend, and they hadn't stopped chattering about the ball for days. "You've chosen well," Regina assured her as she dropped onto the wingback chair across from her sisters.

Sophia leaned forward, her blue eyes sparkling. "Octavia said Lady Eldridge only chooses diamonds of the first water to attend her annual ball."

Evangeline snorted softly. "I think Octavia might have wool for brains. I am hardly a diamond and *I* was included on the invitation."

"Of course you were," Sophia said. "You are one of the Darlington Angels."

Regina shook her head slightly when Evangeline met her gaze. She didn't want to spoil Sophia's pleasure by revealing Crispin Locke, Viscount Margrave—an old family friend—was responsible for the coveted invitation.

"Regina, I truly don't understand how you can miss the ball." Sophia tossed her hands in the air as if she was aggravated by the whole affair. "This could be the most important night of your *life*."

Regina shrugged one shoulder. She still hadn't told her family about Lord Geoffrey or what the other men were saying about her. "I am feeling a bit tired. That is all. A restful evening will likely have me back to my usual self tomorrow."

"Are you certain you don't want me to send my regrets and keep you company?" Evangeline asked.

"You should go. Crispin might need your help keeping the husband-hunters at bay."

Regina hadn't wanted to impose on Crispin by asking him to escort her aunt and sisters to the ball—he unequivocally detested the marriage mart—but he was forever reminding Aunt Beatrice to call on him any time Uncle Charles was abroad. Regina was slightly surprised he hadn't posed an argument when she saw him in the park and made her request that morning.

A knock sounded at the front door, and the lady's maid answered. Crispin could be heard announcing himself and his purpose in calling.

Regina hopped up from the chair. "There he is now. Let me see you to the door."

Crispin stood inside the foyer; his strong dark blond brows were drawn together. "Your lady's maid is answering the door now?"

"Of course not."

Regina discreetly shooed Joy away before Crispin took it upon himself to question the help. Because he was Uncle Charles's godson and had spent much of his young adulthood at Wedmore House, he had a tendency to think he had authority over the ladies of the house. They neither wanted nor needed a caretaker. Regina was already fulfilling the role, and she would see that a new butler was hired soon—although she feared there might not be anyone left who wanted the position. Between Uncle Charles's suspicious nature, Aunt Beatrice's tendency to speak her mind, and Cupid's general dislike of strangers, it had been difficult to keep a butler.

When her sisters and Aunt Beatrice came into the foyer, Crispin seemed to forget about the oddity of the lady's maid manning the door and came forward to greet them. Cupid tore into the foyer, dashing between Evangeline's and Sophia's skirts to reach him first. The little dog adored him. Unfortunately, the love affair had been one-sided ever since Cupid ripped the viscount's pant leg in an overzealous bid for attention. Crispin commanded him to sit, but like all the other residents at Wedmore House, he didn't believe he had to obey the viscount.

Regina scooped Cupid into her arms then kissed her sisters' and aunt's cheeks. "Enjoy yourselves and don't worry about me. I will be retiring early."

Once her family and Crispin were in the carriage, she closed the front door and turned the lock. Joy walked out of the shadowy corridor where she'd retreated to wait until everyone left.

"Would you like to change into a nightrail, miss?"

"I can manage on my own," Regina said. "Go help your sister with the baby. Your plans shouldn't be altered because I've decided to stay home. I had Deacon ready the carriage earlier, so you won't need to hire a hack tonight."

Joy nibbled her bottom lip, a nervous habit that made her seem younger than six and twenty years. "I'm afraid your aunt wouldn't approve of me leaving you alone. My sister will understand."

When Cupid began to squirm, Regina placed him on the marble floor and he dashed back into the drawing room. The poodle had a short memory. He would spend the next half hour searching the house for her aunt and sisters.

"I insist you go," Regina said. "You will return before Auntie, and I will be fine on my own." She held up a finger when Joy started to argue. "*Please.* If you refuse to leave me alone, I will feel obligated to attend the ball, and I would rather not. You only see your family when we are in London. I know you must miss them."

Joy sighed. "I do. I miss them terribly sometimes."

"It is settled then."

"At least allow me to loosen your corset before I go."

Regina agreed, although she could remove it herself if needed. Joy accompanied her above stairs and helped her strip down to her chemise. "I want to wash up before bed," she said and playfully nudged Joy toward the door. "Run along to your sister."

Joy smiled, ducking her head shyly. "Thank you, miss." She slipped from Regina's bedchamber, pulling the door partially closed behind her.

When Regina was finally alone, she took a cleansing breath. She would have to return to the ballrooms soon, but tonight she welcomed the peace and quiet. Stripping her chemise over her head, she moved toward the washstand to fill the basin with water from the pitcher. She kicked off her slippers before removing her drawers and stockings.

Her door swung open when Cupid nosed his way inside. His black curls glistened in the candlelight as he crossed the thick carpet en route to her canopied bed.

"You little rogue," she chided. "Don't you know better than to disturb a lady during her toilette?"

The poodle paid her no mind and hopped on the mattress, turned several circles to find the most comfortable place on the luxurious counterpane, then plopped down to nap while Regina prepared for bed.

She wet a cloth and drew it over her bare skin. When she reached for a sliver of her favorite soap, she accidentally bumped the dish and knocked it off the stand. Cupid jerked awake with a yelp. His large round eyes were like wells of ink. He snapped his head from side to side as if searching for the culprit responsible for disturbing his nap.

"It is all right, sweetheart," she cooed as she retrieved the soap and unbroken dish from the carpet. "I didn't mean to startle you."

She held the soap to her nose to draw in the spicy orange scent. It was the most delicious smell in the world, and she hated that it would be all used up soon. If she was lucky, Uncle Charles would bring back a whole crate when he returned. He never arrived home from his travels empty-handed.

Cupid continued to stand at attention with his floppy ears twitching. First his right, then left, then right again. Before she could utter another word to soothe him, he leapt from the bed and tore out of her chamber.

"What has gotten into you, you silly dog?"

She dipped the soap in the water then scrubbed it against a cloth to make suds. Just as she touched the cloth to her cheek, the loose tread on the servant's staircase creaked.

Regina's heart bolted into her throat and she froze.

"Joy," she called softly. The maid didn't answer. Regina strained to listen for evidence she was not alone in the house until the high-pitched ring of silence vibrated in her ears.

Cupid's sudden deep-throated growl outside her door caused goose bumps to rise along her arms.

A muttered curse carried on the air.

Cupid's growl grew more ferocious.

Regina's heart pounded so hard she could barely hear anything over its drumming. She snatched a bath sheet draped over the dressing screen and covered herself, debating if she had time to grab a wrap from the wardrobe before the intruder reached her doorway. Her gaze landed on the fire poker next to the hearth. Making a hasty choice, she hurried to grab the iron weapon and tiptoed toward the doorway.

"There, there. You seem like a reasonable pooch," the man crooned in a thick accent. "Could I trouble you to move aside? You are blocking the path."

A snappish bark made her jump.

"Damnation. That was unnecessary."

Cupid whimpered as if truly contrite for making a fuss.

"There. That is better." The man's deep, smoky voice washed over her, leaving her slightly breathless. "You should know, I like dogs under normal circumstances, so do not take offense. But nothing was said about a dog."

Regina furrowed her brow. He was uncommonly chatty for a thief, not that she'd met many. It just seemed counterproductive to be talkative when one's success depended on his ability to sneak into homes unnoticed.

Cupid apparently tired of the man's nonsense and renewed his efforts to deter the man. His barking grew more frantic and he dashed into her chamber a second before tearing back into the corridor.

Faith!

In just a few steps, the intruder would be at her door. She tightened her grip on the poker and held it aloft. The element of surprise was on her side, but for some unfathomable reason, she hesitated. Perhaps the way he spoke to the little dog as if he were a person gave her pause. Or maybe it was simply curiosity over what ridiculous thing would come out of his mouth next.

Before she could sort it out, Cupid dashed back into her chamber, and the man lunged to grab the door handle to shut him in the room. He spotted her standing just inside the threshold with the poker raised.

His jaw dropped. Vibrant green eyes locked with hers and her breath froze in her lungs. He looked nothing like she'd pictured. He had the appearance of a gentleman, except for the unruly dark curls ringing his rugged face. But his eyes were most unexpected. They were clear and kind and filled with... regret? No, her mind was playing tricks, and she couldn't afford to be fooled.

He was here to steal from them, plain and simple—his gaze slid to the bath sheet draped around her and his eyes darkened—or *worse*.

She clutched the bath sheet tightly and adjusted her grip on the poker with her other hand, brandishing it. "Leave here or I'll—"

She couldn't bring herself to utter what she'd do if he took one step closer. She *would* defend herself, but he wouldn't fare well if she struck him with the iron poker. In all the years she'd prepared to protect herself and her family, she'd never considered what it would mean to be called to action. It was one thing to discourage a persistent rake, tarnishing his pride and perhaps leaving him with a bruise or two. But the reality of hurting someone—possibly fatally injuring another—caused her stomach to pitch.

Cupid was barking like a rabid beast now, snapping the air close to the thief's ankles. The man's gaze never strayed from her, however. He released the door handle and held his hands up in surrender. Deep creases appeared between his thick brows. "I beg your pardon, miss. There has been a mistake."

A mistake seemed like too mild a term for breaking into someone's home.

He backed into the corridor with his hands still raised. "Please, don't be alarmed. I am leaving."

She held her breath as he kept his word, retreating without turning his back to her. He was almost to the servants' staircase when Cupid flashed his needle-like teeth with a harsh growl and attacked. The dog latched on to the man's pants leg, tugging with all his might.

"Cupid, no!" Regina lowered the poker and hastened into the corridor.

The intruder blurted a string of words she couldn't understand as he shook his leg to dislodge the poodle. Cupid refused to relinquish his prey, planting his paws on the carpet runner and jerking harder while the man hopped on one foot and increased his efforts. The heel of his boot came down on the edge of the stairwell. His eyes flared wide. He tipped backward and grabbed for the railing. His fingers grazed the polished surface, but he couldn't hang on.

Regina stood rooted to the carpet, helpless to stop his fall. Cupid released him before he, too, was dragged down the stairs. The impact of the man's body shook the floor beneath her bare feet. More bumps and a loud boom broke her trance, and she rushed to the stairs. He lay crumpled in a heap against the landing wall. A muffled moan came from him.

"Oh, thank God!" She dropped the poker and scurried down the steps. He was alive. Kneeling beside him, she held the bath sheet together with one hand and grabbed his shoulder. "Can you move?"

He slowly rolled to his back; his face twisted in pain. A large, shiny knot was already peeking through the curls lying on his forehead. His glassy gaze wandered around the stairwell as if he couldn't locate her voice.

"Sorry I frightened you," he muttered between gasps.

His dark lashes fluttered. He was losing consciousness.

"No, wait." She gingerly patted his cheek, fearful of causing further harm, but he didn't open his eyes. "Sir, you cannot die here. Wake up!" Emboldened, she smacked him harder.

His eyes opened to slits.

She grabbed the front of his jacket to shake him. "I say, you cannot *die* in Uncle Charles's stairwell."

"I understand. The scandal..." His eyelids drifted shut.

She frowned. Since when did thieves concern themselves with causing a scandal? "Sir, please wake up. I don't know what to do. Is there someone I should summon to come for you?"

He gripped her hand. "I cannot go back. *Please*. I need...rest. Then...then I will leave."

His fingers relaxed and he dissolved against the floor.

"This week couldn't get any worse," she grumbled. Cupid sat at the top of the stairwell with his tongue flopping from the side of his mouth.

"I hope you are pleased. This is another fine mess you've made for me to clean up."

Only this wasn't a shredded pillow or puddle on the marble floor. This was a man. Battered and bruised. She turned back to him, flummoxed. His inky lashes fanned against olive skin, and his chest rose and fell with regular breaths. He was no longer gasping, much to her relief.

She sighed, her shoulders slumping forward. It seemed she would get no help deciding what to do with him. If she could rouse him, perhaps he could climb to the upper floor with her assistance. The closest bedchamber was only a few feet from the stairwell. The unused room was small and likely smelled musty from being closed up, but he wasn't a guest and he wouldn't be staying long.

Clutching his shoulders, she shook him until he opened his eyes again. "I need you to sit up. Can you climb the stairs? There is a bed where you may rest a short while to catch your breath, but then you must go."

He nodded and struggled to his elbows. With Regina's arm behind his back, they managed to get him upright. More effort was required to help him to his feet and support his weight. The bath sheet slipped, and she frantically grabbed for it to cover her exposed breasts.

"*Magnifique*," the intruder murmured. His eyes were open *now*.

She scowled up at him. He was no different from the scoundrels that had been plaguing her all Season. "Stop looking at me."

His gaze lingered a moment longer then he glanced away. "I beg your pardon, mademoiselle."

With a tighter grip on the bath sheet, she helped support his weight as they climbed the stairs. When they finally reached the bedchamber, he collapsed on the bed.

"*Merci*," he said on a breath and succumbed to unconsciousness with his legs draped over the side of the bed.

She shouldn't trouble herself with his comfort, but he might be in worse shape when he woke if she left him that way. And she needed him to leave as soon as possible. He couldn't stay past an hour at most. She visited her own bedchamber to don a wrapper before returning to tug off his boots and wrangle his legs onto the bed. He was lying on the coverlet, so she couldn't draw it over him, but the room was stuffy anyway. She moved to the window to throw up the sash with the hope fresh air would help to revive him.

There was movement in the hedge below. A large shadow shifted and a stick cracked. "Who's there?" she called out. Likely, it was an accomplice, another thief stationed outside to keep a lookout for anyone passing by on the street. "I have your man."

Her tone sounded taunting even though she hadn't intended it that way. Or perhaps she had. She'd tolerated quite enough foolishness this week.

"A Runner has been summoned," she lied. "You'll be tossed in gaol along with your partner before the hour is out."

The hedge parted, and the bulk dashed across the lawn, moving much faster than she would expect for someone so large.

"Are you sending me to gaol?" Her captive's rough whisper tugged at her heart even though he didn't deserve her sympathy. In his condition, however, he wouldn't fare well in gaol.

"No." She returned to the side of the bed and looked down into his glassy green eyes. He really didn't appear well at all. "Your accomplice needn't know I am taking mercy on you though."

He blinked, his brow creasing. "Why?"

"That is none of your concern." Her reasons were self-preserving. If anyone learned she had been alone with a man, her reputation would be ruined. The fact that he was an intruder made the situation worse, because everyone would assume he'd had his way with her.

"You promised to leave after you rest, so try to sleep."

A weak smile eased across his rugged face, and he closed his eyes, slipping back into oblivion.

When Regina checked on him half an hour later, he was sleeping too deeply to rouse. The subsequent times she tried to wake him were no more successful. Eventually, she had to face the truth. He wasn't going anywhere tonight.

She changed into an apron front gown and waited in the dark drawing room for her sisters and aunt to return from the ball. As she'd predicted, Joy arrived home first. Regina could hear the maid hurrying up the servant's staircase to turn down the beds and light the oil lamps as she did every night.

The mantle clock chimed at half past midnight. When she heard the clopping of horses' hooves on the street, she went to the window to peer out. The carriage stopped in front of Wedmore House. Regina didn't alert anyone to her presence when Crispin saw her family to the door and bade them a good evening.

Cupid yipped as he raced down the stairs to greet Aunt Beatrice.

"There you are, my good boy," her aunt crooned. "Cupid and I are off to bed, girls."

"Goodnight, Auntie."

Once Regina was certain Aunt Beatrice was out of hearing range, she came out of the drawing room.

Sophia gasped. "Regina, what were you doing sitting in the dark?"

Evangeline took one look at her, and her mouth set in a firm line. "Something is wrong."

"One might say that, yes." Regina held her hands out toward her sisters with her palms up. "There has been an unusual development this evening, and I don't know what to do."

She ushered her sisters into the drawing room and lit a lamp. When she told them about the encounter the day before with Lord Geoffrey and the thief in the bed upstairs, they were appropriately appalled.

"Perhaps he is awake now," Evangeline said. "If so, we will sneak him out the backdoor once Aunt Beatrice has turned down her lamp."

Sophia tugged on the fingers of her gloves to remove them. "And if he is not?"

Evangeline's gaze locked with Regina's. "I am afraid we will be forced to allow him to stay overnight."

Regina nodded. They often spoke of Sophia's aims to marry, and Evangeline or Regina would do anything to see that their little sister was happy. A scandal of this magnitude would certainly hurt Sophia's chances of marrying well. None of them would be received any longer.

"Please," Regina implored, "I don't want Aunt Beatrice to know about Lord Geoffrey or the man upstairs. I cannot stand the thought of disappointing her."

Sophia pushed from her seat to embrace her. "Oh, Gigi," she said, reverting to the moniker she'd given Regina when she was too young to pronounce her name. "Auntie would never be disappointed in you. We will sort this out. You will see."

"If he must stay," Evangeline said, "it would be wise to keep Aunt Beatrice in the dark. She has never been good at keeping secrets."

Regina smiled at her sister's attempt to lighten the mood. Aunt Beatrice was infamous for presenting them with Christmas gifts weeks early, so she wouldn't have to worry about spoiling the surprise. Regina and her sisters suspected in reality, she derived immense pleasure from making gifts for them, and she was too excited to wait. Her enthusiasm and devotion to Regina and her sisters were just two qualities that made her dear to them.

"What will we tell Joy?" Sophia asked. "We wouldn't want her to get a shock if she decides to clean the spare room."

Regina exhaled slowly. "We will tell her the truth. Joy can be trusted."

Four

Benny hunkered in the dark several houses down from where Mr. Vistoire was being held. No one had come to take away his friend yet, but it couldn't be much longer.

A carriage had stopped at the house a while ago, but only ladies with pretty gowns and a man in fancy clothes had climbed out of it. The man left alone, so Benny knew he couldn't have been the Runner.

He sighed and glanced in the direction of the park. Tommy—*Farrin*—was waiting for him to deliver Mr. Vistoire and the map. Benny had to remember not to call his brother by his real name anymore. Tommy got real mad when he did, and Benny didn't want to end up like the men his brother brought to the farm before Mr. Vistoire. Tommy had said they were bad men, and Benny shouldn't care what was happening in the cellar, but he had. He didn't like to remember the screaming.

Mr. Vistoire wasn't a bad man, though. Tommy thought Benny didn't understand much so he usually spoke freely in front of him. An important man had accused Mr. Vistoire of being a spy, and he wasn't. When Tommy realized the truth, he'd smashed a glass in the kitchen hearth and said no bloody noble was going to manipulate him into doing his bidding. Benny didn't know what manipulate meant, but he'd understood the man told lies about Mr. Vistoire, and his brother had been in a temper about it.

While Tommy had been debating what to do with his prisoner, Benny had shored up the courage to ask if Mr. Vistoire could stay with him. It was lonely on the farm during the long stretches between his brother's visits. Benny almost withdrew his request when Tommy's icy gaze had locked onto him. He said if Benny ever set the prisoner free, he would watch while his men skinned him alive.

Benny knew from experience Tommy was telling the truth.

Now with the threat of Mr. Vistoire going to gaol, Benny wished he'd been brave enough to defy his brother. His friend wanted to go home. He spoke about it often, and Benny had hoped Mr. Vistoire might take him to America, too.

He glanced toward the park again. He didn't dare arrive without Mr. Vistoire or the map. He'd never been a smart man, but he was no fool.

Xavier buried his fingers in the goddess's gold-spun hair. It was like the finest silk he'd ever touched. She reached to release the toga fastened at her shoulder, but he stopped her. "Allow me."

Her teasing smile as she dropped her hands to her sides heated his blood. She moved closer as if to kiss him, but at the last second, her tongue shot out and she licked his nose. Xavier sputtered and tried to turn his head, but she lapped at his mouth, his cheek—even across his eyelid—making a wet mess all over his face.

"*Sacre bleu!*"

What the devil was happening? Slowly, he came to realize the goddess had merely been a dream, but something very real and annoying was launching a slobbery attack against him. He cracked an eye open, and bright light split his head in two. Groaning, he squeezed both eyes shut and blindly tried to fend off the persistent little tongue.

"Cupid! Stop that," a feminine voice said.

Xavier blinked to bring the room into focus.

A slender young woman stalked to the bed and snatched a small black dog off his chest. She tucked the drooling bundle under her arm and brushed a strand of golden auburn hair away from her face with the back of her wrist. "I'm sorry he woke you. Somehow he keeps nosing his way inside, no matter how many times I try to secure the door."

A rosy pink blush dusted her cheeks as if she'd come from taking exercise, or perhaps she was simply put out with the dog. Whatever the cause, the result was breathtaking. She was one of the most beautiful women he'd ever seen. And he had no bloody idea who she was.

Xavier eased up to his elbows to glance around the unfamiliar room. The square chamber was half the size of his dressing room back home in New Orleans. A faint musty scent hung on the air even though the window was open. A slight breeze stirred the sheer curtains, causing the miniature Egyptian sphinxes on the wallpaper to undulate. Queasiness welled at the back of his throat.

"Oh, dear. He's going to be sick."

The woman thrust the dog toward another young woman he hadn't noticed earlier and grabbed an empty bucket from the floor. She sat beside him, sliding her arm beneath his shoulders to help him sit up.

An icy wave of nausea churned inside him. He clutched the bucket. Panting to stave off the urge to toss up his accounts, he closed his eyes, willing the sickness away. When it passed, his hands went limp on the bucket. His nursemaid took it from him before helping him lower to the bed and adjusted the pillows behind him.

"Evangeline cornered Dr. Portier at the lending library yesterday and questioned him about knocks to the head. You might be ill for a few days until you are healed."

Nothing she said made much sense, but the raspy quality to her voice soothed him. The bed shifted when she stood, and his stomach roiled again. An involuntary moan slipped through his lips. He couldn't remember ever being this incapacitated.

The dog whined.

"Shush, Cupid," the younger lady scolded.

Xavier stole a peek in her direction. She was another beauty with pale blond hair and an air of naiveté, whereas his nursemaid exuded confidence and seemed very capable. Neither struck him as the type to work for Farrin, but he couldn't lower his guard.

When his nursemaid returned to the bedside, she placed a cool wet cloth over his forehead. Something about her seemed familiar—the soft curve of her cheek, slightly pointy chin, and the elegant length of her neck. His breath caught. She resembled the goddess from his dream.

"Joy prepared a restorative broth," she said. "When you are able to sit up without becoming sick, I will help you take a sip."

Joy, Evangeline, Dr. Portier... Xavier didn't recognize any of these names, and he couldn't comprehend how he'd come to be flat on his back under their care, but he was relieved to wake to new faces. *Pretty* faces. After too many mornings of staring at Benny's ugly mug, Xavier had almost forgotten the pleasure of gazing upon the fairer sex.

A cart rattled over cobblestones outside, and a gravel voice announced the approach of a vegetable seller. He had to be in London, but he didn't know where he was being held. He recalled arriving in Town after dark and Farrin threatening him if he tried to escape. He'd been charged with the task of breaking into an earl's house and stealing a map, but he didn't remember arriving at the town house.

Xavier's gaze darted toward the bedchamber door to look for Benny or one of Farrin's men guarding him, but the corridor appeared to be empty. "Was there an accident? Where are the others?"

His nursemaid crossed her arms. "If you are well enough to talk, so be it, but you are in no position to lead this interrogation, sir."

"Interrogation?" His pulse skipped. He tried pushing to a seated position and collapsed against the headboard as another dizzy spell slammed into him. How was he to endure an interrogation in his condition? "How many men?"

There had been three when he'd been questioned in the beginning of his incarceration. Two to hold him while the other drove his fist into Xavier's gut.

The ladies exchanged a look he couldn't decipher.

"Never you mind how many men we have for protection. It is enough," the goddess said with a slight pinch to her mouth. "Don't even consider trying to overpower us."

He bristled at her insinuation. "I would never hurt a lady, Miss— uh... Miss...?"

"Regina Darlington." She spoke in clipped tones. "But I suspect you already know my name. The question is who are you?"

Her name didn't spark any recognition, nor did he follow her logic. How was he to know the name of a lady he'd never met?

The other young woman stepped forward with the dog. "I'm *Sophia* Darlington, her sister, and this is Cupid." She lifted the poodle's paw and waved it toward him in greeting.

The elder Miss Darlington frowned. "Sophia, this is not a social call."

"I know." She snuggled the little dog against her cheek. Her pale blond hair was a sharp contrast to the poodle's black coat. "But he has been here for three days. He no longer seems like a stranger."

Three days? How could that be? Now that the nausea had passed, he began to notice details that had evaded him earlier, such as the caress of soft fabric against his skin. He lifted the bedcovers to discover he was wearing a lightweight ivory linen tunic and pants that were baggy in the hips and tapered to hug his calves.

"These are not mine. Where are my clothes?"

Sophia looked to her sister. "Didn't you hang them in the wardrobe after you removed them?"

"*Sophia.*" A furious crimson flush invaded Miss Darlington's cheeks, but she held her head high and refused to look away.

He smiled; she frowned. She was definitely the goddess from his dream. He was certain of it. He must have woken briefly when her hands were on him, because he vaguely recalled the rush of arousal in response to the gentle touch of a woman.

The poodle twisted his small body in an attempt to break free of Sophia's hold, his pink tongue flopping about as much as he was. "Be still." She hugged him, and he released a shrill yip that nearly shattered Xavier's brain.

"Please take Cupid downstairs," Miss Darlington said. "Aunt Beatrice will look for him when she and Evangeline return from shopping."

"You mustn't worry about Auntie. We will keep her occupied." Sophia headed for the door but tossed another smile over her shoulder. "Could I trouble you for a name, sir? You know ours."

Under different circumstances, he might have refused, but good manners dictated he comply with the lady's request. "Xavier Vistoire, miss. It is a pleasure to make your acquaintance."

"Thank you." Sophia closed the door as she went.

Miss Darlington sighed. "You've been talking in your sleep, but you have told us nothing useful. Tell me who you are, and I do not mean repeat your name. What were your intentions when you broke into Wedmore House?"

"Have I been talking in my sleep?" he asked to cover the shock of learning he had made it into the earl's town house and remembered nothing about how he'd gained entrance. "Did I say anything else of interest?"

"I am uncertain the word interesting applies. Perhaps entertaining fits better." Her full lips curved into a wry smirk. "You've been referring to our aunt's dog as a goddess and whispering loving words to him."

"*Absurde*! I would never—" Heat flashed up his face. He'd been dreaming of Miss Darlington before he woke to the little dog licking him. "Please, tell me I didn't."

"Oh, I am afraid you did." Miss Darlington laughed. "For what it's worth, Mr. Vistoire, your efforts to woo Cupid have worked. He seems to have forgotten all about your altercation. I, on the other hand, remain on my guard."

Xavier pinched the bridge of his nose to ease the ache behind his eyes. "Have I truly been out for three days? You said this is Wedmore House, no? This is your home?" He didn't want to admit to breaking into the town house when she could still summon a Runner and he was too ill to move. "Why does it feel like I've gone several rounds with a prize pugilist?"

"You don't remember anything, do you?" Miss Darlington released a noisy breath and smiled. She seemed relieved, although he didn't know why she should be happy he'd lost his memory. "Dr. Portier said when people bump their heads, they often cannot recall the accident or events leading up to it. Do you remember anything about breaking into our home?"

An enticing vision of Miss Darlington in a bath sheet invaded his memory. Her hair hanging loose, the wet ends a deeper gold and curling around her shoulders. Pink skin glistening in candlelight as the flame flickered. Slender arm lifted as if performing an exotic dance. And elegant fingers wrapped around a... fireplace poker!

His eyebrows shot up. "Did you hit me?"

"No! You fell down the stairs."

"But you had a poker. And, and a bath sheet around your—" He motioned to his chest. His blood soared through his veins as vivid memories of her bare breasts flooded him, arousing him all over again. "You were prepared to *strike* me. Don't deny it."

She bolted from the bed to stalk over to a tray resting on a chest of drawers. "I thought you didn't remember anything," she grumbled.

No wonder she hadn't wanted him to remember. She didn't want him picturing her half-dressed and as enticing as sin. Well, that was too bad. He couldn't stop thinking about her now.

Her back was to him as she poured a cup of the restorative broth. "You *fell*, and it was your own fault for breaking into Uncle Charles's town house." She carried the cup to the bed and frowned down at him. "You are lucky I didn't have you hauled to gaol."

He rubbed his forehead where he was sorest, wondering if she was telling the whole truth about the fall. "I suppose you were well within your rights to bash me over the head, but I assure you, it was a mistake. I wandered into the wrong home. I was looking for a friend. What were you doing at home alone?"

"I owe you no explanations," she snipped. "And I don't believe you." She lowered to the bed beside Xavier. When she met his gaze, the lines on her forehead deepened. "Do not think because we are helping you that we won't still summon a Runner."

He shook his head cautiously so as not to set off another bout of nausea.

"Are you feeling well enough to try the broth? You've had nothing but a few sips of water since Saturday."

"*Oui.*"

She slipped her arm around his back and held the cup to his lips. After the first sip of savory broth went down easily and didn't threaten to come back up, he tried another. Miss Darlington encouraged him to keep drinking until he'd finished the cup.

A whiff of citrus teased his nose. She not only looked like summer with her glorious sunset hair, she smelled like heaven. He handed her the cup and angled away from her, not wanting to be distracted. He needed to focus on leaving Wedmore House and finding his way to the docks.

"I promise to answer any questions you pose to the best of my ability," he said. Gaining her trust would be imperative if he hoped to escape. "But may I ask one more question of you?"

She nodded sharply and scooted from the bed.

"Has anyone come looking for me? Does anyone know I am here?"

"That was two questions, Mr. Vistoire, and why would anyone look for you here if you wandered into the wrong house?" She returned to the tray to pour another cup of broth.

Damnation. She had the advantage of having her wits about her, and his head was pounding.

"No one has been around asking after you. I imagine your accomplice believes you've been taken to gaol. I saw him hiding behind the hedge, and he ran off when I threatened to summon a Bow Street Runner."

She brought him another cup of broth without asking if he wanted one. "Now it is my turn." Her sculpted brows rose as she waited for him to take the cup.

"*Merci.*" He took another drink of broth, feeling his strength returning bit by bit, and studied her over the gilded rim.

"Why are you truly here, sir?"

"What do you mean?"

She crossed her arms. "You don't expect me to believe you are a common thief with the way you were dressed, unless you stole the clothes you were wearing. And your story about walking into the wrong house is ludicrous. I will ask once more. What is the real reason you broke into Wedmore House?"

He wasn't sure what his choices were—thief or what, exactly? Unsure of the correct answer, he held his tongue.

"Because if you came here believing I would welcome you into my bed," she said, "you have been listening to the wrong people. Mr. Lawrence is a liar. I never kissed him nor do I plan to allow any other man liberties, and if you tell anyone you stayed at Wedmore House or make up tales about what happened between us, my sisters and I will find a way to make you pay."

Xavier gaped. He could either be a thief or a lecherous rake? Neither choice was acceptable, but men were not locked away for being libertines. "I won't say a word. I am sorry. I was deep in my cups and Mr. Landry—"

"Lawrence."

"*Oui*, Lawrence. Mr. Lawrence challenged me." He hung his head in real shame. Mistreating ladies was not part of his repertoire. He had a sister, for pity's sake, and a female cousin who was as dear as a sister. He was a champion for the fairer sex. Before his abduction, he'd been helping an actress plan her escape from her abusive benefactor. He looked up and held Miss Darlington's gaze. "This is not who I am. I swear it upon my mother's grave. I made a mistake."

She dropped her arms to her sides. "I don't know that I have any choice except to believe you."

Her quandary was understandable and stirred his sympathy. If she alerted anyone to his presence, she and her sisters would be ruined. He'd been their guest for three nights.

Her tongue darted over her lips. "Your friend in the hedges. Will he tell anyone where you are?"

"No." She had to be referring to Benny. "He is my servant. He doesn't know anyone, and he is not a chatty type. We are leaving for New Orleans as soon as possible." Once his head stopped spinning every time he moved. "You will never see either of us again. I promise. Please, allow me to rest a little longer, and I will go."

She hesitated before granting permission. "You must stay in this room and you cannot make a sound. Our great-aunt doesn't know you are here."

"I see. And what about your servants? Do they know?"

"Only Joy. She is our upstairs maid, and she acts as a lady's maid when we need her. She has been with us since she was a girl. She has never given us reason to doubt her loyalty."

"Are you still between butlers? A household full of women should at least have a butler."

She released a forceful exhale as if his questions were trying her patience. "I didn't realize it was common knowledge. I will place an advertisement after you are gone. We cannot bring on a new man now."

"Humph." He drained the cup rather than speak his mind and risk angering her. The ladies were in this trouble because they had no manservant. Farrin had seen an opportunity and seized it. And he would probably send someone else for the map once he realized Xavier had escaped without searching.

Even though he barely knew the women, they were showing him kindness in nursing him back to health. He owed them one as well. "Miss Darlington, please don't delay in placing the advertisement. A home with no man in residence is vulnerable."

"We can take care of ourselves, Mr. Vistoire. If you attempt to take liberties while you are recovering, you will discover for yourself."

She turned on her heel and marched from the room.

Xavier closed his eyes, knowing he needed rest to heal. It wouldn't take long before Farrin realized Miss Darlington hadn't actually summoned a Runner, and Xavier wanted to be on a ship bound for New Orleans before the blackguard did. He hadn't yet decided if he had it in him to steal from the young women to pay his fare. Now that he'd made their acquaintances, he had a difficult time thinking of them as nothing more than a means to an end.

Five

"Are you sure you want to do this, miss?" Joy stood at one end of the copper tub in Regina's bedchamber, gnawing her lip as she awaited Regina's response.

"No, but a warm bath might help ease Mr. Vistoire's aches and pains. The sooner he feels better, the sooner he can go."

In the two days since he'd regained consciousness, he had been nothing but respectful, polite, and charming toward her and her sisters. She'd begun to soften toward him, which was exactly what she feared he wanted. Once she stopped watching her back, he might pounce just like Lord Geoffrey had. Nevertheless, she'd had to relax her vigilance a little. She'd become tired of dissecting every word he spoke and searching for meaning in every look. As long as he continued to act like a gentleman, she could be amiable.

Taking a deep cleansing breath, she grabbed the edge of the tub and nodded toward Joy. "Let's do this before Aunt Beatrice returns."

Sophia and Evangeline had coaxed their aunt into taking Cupid for a walk with them and promised Regina they would draw it out as long as possible. Fortunately, Aunt Beatrice was a social being and would engage in conversation with most anyone passing on the walkway. Some might say she was a bit too chatty at times, but Regina and her sisters had always loved that about her.

When their parents died and Uncle Charles had taken Regina and her sisters to live in his home, the quiet had been unbearable. Uncle Charles, being a bachelor, hadn't seemed to know how to talk to children, and the servants had avoided them. Regina supposed it was difficult to find anything to say to three young orphans, but Aunt Beatrice hadn't been at a loss. She'd filled the home with enough chatter to chase away the gloom, at least for significant parts of Regina's day until she no longer hurt as badly as she had in the beginning.

Regina and Joy lifted opposite ends of the tub and shambled to the spare bedchamber, navigating the long corridor and around the tight corner leading to the doorway. Mr. Vistoire was asleep, but his eyes fluttered open as they placed the tub on the wooden floor with a soft thump.

"What are you doing?" He sounded hoarse and he seemed to lack energy to raise his head. "You shouldn't be lifting tubs."

"And why not?" Regina punched her fists to her hips, more comfortable pretending her searing cheeks were a result of irritation rather than from imagining him stripped down to nothing. "I'm as able-bodied as Joy."

He frowned. "I hardly think an explanation is required. You are a lady."

"I will bring the water, miss." Joy spun toward the door, but not fast enough to hide her grin. The maid had vocalized a similar sentiment before agreeing to prepare a bath for Mr. Vistoire, but if Regina didn't help with the tub, who would?

He yawned and scrubbed a hand over his whiskers before pushing to a seated position. His fingers curled gently around the edge of the mattress as he slumped forward. The day he'd regained consciousness, he'd been unable to sit up for more than a couple of minutes without becoming queasy. Yesterday had been no better. But today, he'd sat up for an hour without becoming sick. It seemed he was on the mend.

"Have you experienced any nausea today?"

"No, and my headache is better at the moment."

She studied his ruggedly handsome face, wondering if they had ever been at the same assemblies. How she could have ever missed him, she didn't know. He was different from most of the gentlemen she encountered in the ballrooms. He didn't possess a doughy middle. In fact, he more closely resembled the Elgin Marbles at the British Museum than most flesh and blood men of her acquaintance.

"How did you break your nose?" she blurted.

"It was broken for me." He reached to touch the flat raised hump where his nose met his face. "Does it make me ugly?"

"Absolutely hideous. I can barely stand looking at you. Should I retrieve a mirror so you can see how unsightly you are?"

"Perhaps I shouldn't if it is *that* bad." His green eyes twinkled, revealing he understood she was having a little fun with him.

When she just stood there, he raised his eyebrows. They disappeared beneath the dark curls hanging down on his forehead. "Well, are you going to allow me to take a look at myself or not?

She held up a finger. "One moment."

Her smile stayed with her as she returned to her chambers for a handheld looking glass. Mr. Vistoire was far from ugly, but the fact she found him uncommonly handsome was irrelevant. He was leaving. She would never see him again. She was perfectly content with the arrangement.

After retrieving the mirror from her dressing table, she grabbed the sliver of her favorite soap from the chintz dish on the washstand and headed back to his room. He was waiting on the side of the bed, rubbing the back of his neck, but he dropped his hand to his side when he saw her.

"How much does it hurt?" she asked. "I could make a trip to the apothecary this afternoon and request a powder."

"No, thank you, mademoiselle. I've had worse pain. This will pass." When he lifted the mirror to see his reflection, he grimaced. "You were telling the truth. I look revolting."

"I beg your pardon? You do not."

"I look like something stuck to the bottom of someone's boot." He dropped his hand with the mirror to his lap.

"Let me have the mirror." She took it before he could respond and held it in front of him so he could see his reflection. "What, pray tell, do you find revolting?" Lord knew she needed help seeing his physical flaws, because in her opinion, he was too attractive by half.

One dark eyebrow lifted. "To begin with, I need a good shave." He plowed his fingers through his curls. "And I'm beginning to suspect Cupid thinks this mop of hair makes me a pooch, just like him. Only larger. That would explain his fascination with me."

Regina laughed; the last traces of tension in her spine melted away. "You don't look like an overgrown poodle."

"But I do need a haircut." With his head hanging forward again, he angled a smile at her that she couldn't help returning.

"A shave and a haircut. My, aren't you the dandy, Mr. Vistoire?"

"At one time, I fancied myself quite the swell."

"Are you flirting with me?"

"No, miss." One side of his mouth inched higher. "I am being friendly."

"Humph."

Joy returned with a bucket of steaming water. Regina jumped to help her dump it into the tub and took the empty bucket when they were finished. She hadn't intended to dawdle with Mr. Vistoire, but he could be distracting.

"Stay where you are," she called over her shoulder as she headed for the door. "The tub will get filled quicker with two of us working."

She and Joy made three trips each with buckets of warm water, but the tub was only a quarter full. When they traipsed downstairs a fourth time, Cook apparently couldn't hold her tongue any longer.

"Miss Darlington, what are you doing? If you wish to take a bath, Mrs. Cox and I can help Joy."

Regina feigned an airy laugh and swiped away the perspiration dampened her brow with the back of her hand. "No, no. This is part of my exercise. The bath is my reward for when I am done."

Cook frowned but said nothing more on the subject.

Regina and Joy resumed filling their buckets and slogged upstairs. The maid entered ahead of Regina, gasped, and slid to a stop. Regina nearly ran into her. Water sloshed from the bucket and drenched them both. Looking up, she located the cause of Joy's distress and the reason Regina's slippers were saturated. Mr. Vistoire was sitting in the tub. And he was bare from the waist up. In fact, he might have been bare all over, but Regina didn't dare look. She closed her eyes and prayed he wouldn't notice her erratic breathing.

"Mr. Vistoire." She cleared her throat and tried to sound stern. "I thought I was clear you should remain seated."

"I *am* seated," he replied with an air of nonchalance.

"I didn't mean in the tub. What if you'd had another dizzy spell and fallen again? You should have waited for assistance."

"Pfft! If you are able-bodied enough to carry pails of water upstairs, I'm strong enough to walk from the bed to the tub."

The sound of dripping water reverberated in her ears, and all she could think on was the naked man across the room. As tempting as it was to satisfy her curiosity and steal a peek, she wouldn't. That would make her vulgar, and ladies were never vulgar. She hadn't considered the unfairness of being held to a higher standard than gentlemen until this very moment.

"*Merci*, mademoiselles." His voice was too much like a caress and left her flustered. "Leave the buckets and take your rest. I can manage alone."

Regina plopped the bucket on the floor and more water splashed her slippers. "If you think we were planning to bathe you, you are as mad as a March hare, sir. You'd best be able to manage alone." She turned on her heel, opened her eyes, and stormed from the room, her slippers squishing with each step.

Of all the nerve, assuming she and Joy were going to wash him. Even though she had considered that he might require help, he was still a presumptuous cur.

Six

After soaking his sore muscles until the water had grown cold, Xavier climbed from the tub feeling refreshed. He scrubbed the droplets from his face and chest then wrapped the bath sheet around his waist. The dizziness had subsided, and his appetite was returning with a merciless vengeance. If his rumbling stomach were any indication, he could clean out the Darlingtons' pantry and still be on the search for food.

He wouldn't, of course. The Darlington sisters had shown him much kindness this past week, and he wouldn't repay them by being a poor guest. In fact, he'd outstayed his welcome. It was time to say farewell so the women could reclaim their home, and Miss Darlington's fears could be put to rest. He wouldn't tell anyone about his stay at Wedmore House. He'd given his word. Besides, he wouldn't be loitering in England long enough to speak with anyone. He'd decided during his bath that he would leave after dark tonight.

The clothes he'd been wearing when he'd arrived at Wedmore House were hanging in the wardrobe. They smelled freshly laundered, much to his appreciation. He would have nothing else to wear on the journey home. All of his belongings had remained at the boarding house when he'd been snatched outside of the gaming hell.

Mrs. Zachery might have tossed everything in the rubbish bin by now, or perhaps she no longer ran the house, but he needed to pay a visit to his former residence. Money and his letter of introduction to prove his identity were hidden beneath a loose floorboard in his old bedchamber. He would have to take his chances that he could gain entry into the boarding house, because stealing jewelry from the Darlingtons was no longer an option.

A feminine clearing of a throat caused him to turn toward the doorway. The Darlingtons' maid stood in the threshold with one hand over her eyes. A progressive blush invaded her cheeks. "I came to set out your clothes, sir."

"I found them. No need to bother."

"Yes, sir. I will inform Miss Darlington." She whipped around and practically dashed from the room.

Xavier smiled knowingly. It seemed he'd shocked the women earlier with his state of undress, which had been his aim. Not that he made a habit of such behavior. It had been a risk considering Miss Darlington believed he'd come to Wedmore House with the intention of seducing her, but he'd needed to convince her that he had enough water. She'd been so damned determined to fill the tub, and sitting by feeling useless while she exerted herself hadn't set well with him.

Xavier retrieved his drawers and trousers from the wardrobe and proceeded to dress. As he pulled the shirt over his head, a soft knock sounded at the door.

"Are you decent, Mr. Vistoire?"

This time it was Miss Darlington standing in the doorway with *her* hand over her eyes.

"*Oui.* Yes." Sometimes he reverted to his native tongue without thinking, which he'd come to learn the English did not appreciate. "Thank you for the bath. I feel much better."

She dropped her hand to her side. "Splendid." A pair of scissors dangled from the hand she hadn't used to cover her eyes. "Are you ready for that haircut, sir?"

"By *you*? What do you know about cutting a man's hair?"

She sniffed and crossed to the desk in the corner to pull out the chair. "I'll have you know I'm excellent with a blade."

"That is not reassuring."

Patting the chair rail, she offered an angelic smile. "Come sit. I will be gentle."

Despite his initial hesitation, he couldn't resist her summons. He'd grown to crave her touch, even though he could not allow it to show or she would raise her guard again.

He sat in the chair and tipped his head back to see her standing behind him. "Just a little off the top and sides, and I prefer to keep my ears intact."

To his surprise, she smiled and tugged his ear. "These old things? It is not as if you use them. You certainly didn't bother earlier when I told you to wait on the side of the bed."

"If I'm to receive a lecture, I withdraw my request. Please, take them off first."

"I should just to spite you." Her mischievous smirk and irreverent teasing endeared her to him even more.

She draped the bath sheet over his shoulders, and he sank against the seatback. He'd missed the companionship of women. Not just the physical connection, but also their gift for banter and conversation. He'd especially come to enjoy Miss Darlington's company over the past few days. She was quick-witted and challenged him in a way no other lady ever had. He admired her mettle.

She retrieved a comb from the desk drawer then moved back into position behind him. Xavier closed his eyes as she drew the comb through his curls. As promised, she was gentle, even when she encountered a snarl. Pleasing tingles cascaded down his back and arms.

"I could have cut my own hair." His protest lacked force.

"I cut my own hair once," she said as she took the first snip. "It was a disaster. Believe me, you are better off allowing me to perform the task on your behalf. You may shave yourself, though."

Xavier melted beneath her hands, savoring the scent of her soap on both of them. It was as if they'd shared the tub.

Sacre blue. Now he couldn't strike the vision of her naked and straddling him from his mind. And his imagination ran rampant. Warm bath water streaming over and between her small breasts, nipples as rosy pink as her lips, erect and begging to be licked. Passion smoldering in her amber and green eyes. Her elegant fingers skimming his chest, her nails grazing his skin.

God, he had to stop thinking of her in that way. He was getting hard and the extra room in his borrowed trousers wouldn't disguise it much longer. Shifting his position on the chair, he tried to think of something witty to say, but he found he was tongue-tied.

"We are almost finished," she murmured as she came to stand between his legs. Her concentration never wavered from her task, but all he could focus on was her nearness. He wanted to touch her so badly he ached. Blood pounded through his veins. She swayed closer, lifting to her toes to reach the top of his head. Her breasts were level with his face and the damned spicy sweet smell of her soap filled his lungs. He grasped the seat of the chair, his spine rigid, and battled against the temptation to embrace her.

Her gaze strayed to his face and she drew back. "What is it? Are you feeling ill?"

He shook his head, uncertain if he should explain or allow her to believe he wasn't feeling up to snuff.

She furrowed her brow. Her hands drifted down to her sides. "Your face is flushed. You are *not* well. Let's put you to bed." Turning, she placed the comb and scissors on the desk, and when she reached for him, he captured her hand. Her eyes flared as she locked gazes with him.

"Miss Darlington, I'm well. I swear it to you." He stroked his thumb across her knuckles. "This is difficult—being close to you. I find you very tempting, but I promised to behave as a gentleman, and I intend to keep my word."

"Oh." She eased her hand from his light grasp and backed toward the desk to perch on the edge. Her mouth opened and closed. He hadn't suspected she would ever be at a loss for words, but he appeared to have caught her by surprise. After a while, she regained composure. "May I ask a question, Mr. Vistoire?"

He inclined his head.

"You mentioned plans to travel to New Orleans. Do you have a home there?"

"I do." He settled against the seatback, more at ease now that she'd recovered her ability to speak.

She tipped her head to the side and regarded him with tiny creases marring her brow. "You don't sound like any American I have ever encountered."

"French is the predominant language. Besides, I am Creole."

"Creole." She drew out the word, rolling it around on her tongue. "What is Creole?"

"It means my ancestors settled New Orleans. My family has been there for a century." He held his head higher. "I am anxious to return. I've been away from home a long time."

"How much longer will you be in London?"

"I will book passage to New Orleans as soon as I leave Wedmore House. My sister needs me, and I have responsibilities for a ward, my young cousin."

"I see. I thought perhaps if we met outside Wedmore House, we could pretend this never happened. We might even strike up a friendship."

He didn't try to rein in a pleased grin. "Surely you aren't developing a tender spot for me. Are you, Miss Darlington?"

She wrinkled her nose and a corner of her lips twitched as she fought back a smile. "You really *are* as mad as a March hare. I'm quite certain I despise you."

He laughed, realizing she teased him. If it were possible to remain in England, he would be pleased for them to become better acquainted. He suspected they would get on very well if she could truly forgive him.

"I am sorry for the strain I placed on you and your family this week. I had a moment of weakness. I am deeply ashamed of my behavior."

She shrugged one shoulder. "People make mistakes. Thank you for keeping your word and behaving yourself."

Her gaze lingered on him as she twirled a loose strand of silky hair that had fallen from her coiffeur. Her unselfconscious boldness was intoxicating, and it was all he could do to keep from pulling her onto his lap and ravishing her.

"What will you do now that you've abandoned your wicked ways, Mr. Vistoire?"

"Oh, I'm not giving up my wicked ways," he said with a wink. "Just breaking into homes."

Her eyes shone brightly when she smiled, warming him from the inside out

"I'll send Joy in with a razor so you can shave."

Still smiling, she whisked from the room

Seven

Regina ran through the drills Uncle Charles had taught her, punching the wall mounted sandbag in patterns of three. *High, high, low. High, low, high. Low, low, high.* Hit after hit without pause. But no matter how many times she struck the bag, she couldn't erase the sensation of Mr. Vistoire's thumb having stroked across her skin.

Her heart banged against her ribs as much from the man as from her exercise. The memory of his smoldering eyes, raw with desire, refused to vacate her mind. She drew in a choppy breath and tried to deny her own excitement, but her body was more honest. Every inch of her was awake and tingling as if she had a sort of itch that she didn't know how to scratch.

She was also aware of how ridiculous her reaction was. Mr. Vistoire would find any woman foolish enough to enter his bedchamber tempting. He was a man, after all, and a self-proclaimed rake. He wouldn't be particular about his choice of bed partner. Yet, when she'd stood close to trim his hair, he had wanted *her*. Her stomach fluttered in acknowledgment of the truth.

Xavier Vistoire was dangerous to her future. A simple caress had given birth to a rather pesky question. Could she remain content never knowing the pleasure of being loved by a man?

She dropped her hands to her sides with a loud exhale. "Oh, what does it matter?"

Spinsters did not think on such matters, and even though she wasn't quite on the shelf, that was her aim. It was best not to indulge her curiosity. She would be smart to avoid him the rest of his stay.

Unfortunately, no one had tended to him since Evangeline delivered a supper tray to his chamber a couple of hours earlier, and Regina was the only one home. She'd managed to beg off attending the opera with her aunt and sisters, but she wouldn't be allowed to bow out of evening entertainments much longer. Aunt Beatrice had given her the sour-faced look when she'd asked to be excused that afternoon.

It was a well-known fact among Wedmore House residents that tight, puckered lips from Auntie signaled unpleasant things to come. While she was a cheerful companion most of the time, one didn't want to be on the receiving end of a lecture from Auntie. She spoke her mind freely, and even though she was never cruel, she often had a lot to say. She could hold court an hour at a time. If she ever learned about Mr. Vistoire, Regina and her sisters would be gray before they heard the end of it.

Yes, an intelligent young woman would stay away from a man who excited her imagination.

The house creaked as it settled, and she resumed her drills, wishing wisdom wasn't such a boring virtue. She pummeled the bag as fast as she could, striking in patterns of three and tossing in an elbow to break the monotony. When the men's shirt she'd donned grew damp and clung to her, she ceased her exercise, leaning one hand against the wall and panting.

"He doesn't appear to be talking." Mr. Vistoire's voice cut through the quiet. She jumped and swung toward the doorway. He was leaning against the doorjamb with his arms casually crossed and a wry grin on his cleanly shaven face. "Would you like me to take a go at him?"

"Pardon?"

He pushed off the doorjamb and nodded toward the sandbag. "I thought you were trying to extract information from the chap. Beatings seem to be the English's preferred method of loosening one's lips."

She couldn't refrain from returning his smile as he neared. Without his beard, his defined jaw was no longer hidden, and his nose—even in its imperfection—appeared regal. "And how do the Creole loosen one's lips?" she asked.

"The *right* way, Miss Darlington." He stopped in front of her, so close she could feel his body heat. Suddenly, she couldn't catch her breath for a different reason. Xavier Vistoire was a stunningly handsome man in a way her countrymen were not.

"What is the right way to extract secrets?"

He leaned close to her ear but seemed to take pains not to touch her. "With kisses," he whispered.

The wisp of his breath danced over her skin. She shivered.

"Oh." Her voice was thready. "I can imagine how that might be effective under certain circumstances."

His self-satisfied grin caused her knees to wobble. "It's a trick handed down from my French ancestors."

When he withdrew completely, she fought the impulse to grab his jacket and pull him close again. *Jacket?* She blinked and stepped back to run her gaze over his attire. "You are dressed as if you are leaving."

He shrugged, his smile seemingly tinged with regret. "It's time for me to go."

Earlier, she'd thought she wanted to hurry him on his way, but now the thought of him leaving caused her to feel slightly adrift.

"Perhaps you should recuperate a while longer. You were only able to leave your bed today." Yes, that was exactly what he needed. More rest. She took his arm to guide him back to his room, but he resisted.

He covered her hand, the heat of his skin against hers searing. "Miss Darlington, I am grateful to you and your sisters for your compassion and care, but it is best for everyone if I go. I'm sure you would like to resume your life."

Until the Season ended, she had no life of her own. Returning to the marriage mart was a waste of time, and dealing with loathsome men like Lord Geoffrey was making her miserable. She'd already chosen her path, and it did not involve marriage or leaving her kin.

"Resume my life," she muttered, bitterness seeping into her words.

"*Oui.* You should have more time for this." He gestured to the sandbag and then her trousers. "Uh, what is this, exactly?"

Her face flushed as she considered what he must think of her dressed in men's clothing and glistening from exertion. Until the tussle with Lord Geoffrey, she'd kept her unladylike pursuits private. But Mr. Vistoire wasn't glaring at her with disdain as Lord Geoffrey had done. He appeared genuinely interested.

"Wing Chun," she said. "My uncle learned it while traveling in the South Orient. He has practiced the ancient warrior arts since before I was born."

"Fascinating. And he allowed you to learn? That is rather unconventional."

Regina chuckled at his diplomatic response. "Yes, that does describe Uncle Charles. He taught me himself. For protection."

Mr. Vistoire's eyes narrowed. "Protection from whom? Did someone try to hurt you? The bastard best have swung from the gallows."

She shook her head, lowering it to hide evidence of the flush of pleasure on her cheeks. "No one wished to hurt me. I had an active imagination as a child. After our parents were killed, I was afraid the murderers would come for my sisters and me. Uncle Charles tried to reassure me, but I refused to believe we were safe, so he taught me what to do if anyone did mean to do me harm."

"Your uncle sounds like a wise man."

Her head shot up to determine if he was laughing at her, but he simply regarded her with his intense green gaze. She'd made the mistake of confiding in her uncle's godson once when they were children. Crispin had scoffed and called her ignorant.

The blackguards are across the Irish Sea. They cannot walk on water, and they haven't a pot to piss in. How are they going to pay for passage on a ship?

Uncle Charles must have overheard them talking, because he'd made Crispin do extra drills while she watched and corrected his mistakes. A hard pill to swallow for a boy on the cusp of manhood. Neither of them had held a grudge against the other, and they had been back on friendly terms the next day.

She smiled at Mr. Vistoire for reminding her to be grateful for her unique upbringing. "Uncle Charles is wise without letting on he is trying. When reassurance was ineffective, he gave me something better: control. I didn't need to rely on someone else to save me when I could save myself. My fears went away as soon as I knew what to do if those men ever did come for my sisters and me."

"Your uncle possesses the best type of wisdom, it seems." He smiled, too, and nodded toward the sandbag. "I've never heard of Wing Chun. It must be a well-kept secret."

She turned back toward the bag when he approached it. "You aren't going to kiss it, are you?" she teased.

He laughed before lightly punching it and glancing over his shoulder at her. "If you refuse to tell me more, perhaps I'll have to kiss the secrets out of *you*."

Her lips parted, but she couldn't find her voice. The only secret he was likely to discover was that she *wanted* him to kiss her. She blinked, breaking eye contact, and eased away a couple of steps.

"It is said Wing Chun was created by a woman, an abbess, who came upon a white crane fighting a snake. The goal is to deflect an attack and strike hard when your attacker can be caught by surprise, so you may escape."

Fittingly enough, the legend said the abbess Ng Mui trained a young woman to fight in the ways of Wing Chun in order to defeat a local warlord who was trying to force her into marriage. It seemed overbearing lords were not unique to modern London. Only a young lady's privilege to challenge the ne're-do-wells had gone by the wayside.

Mr. Vistoire held out his hand as if requesting to escort her to a ballroom dance floor. "I would love a demonstration, if you please."

She hesitated half a breath before placing her hand in his and allowing him to draw her toward the middle of the room. When they were a safe distance from the wall, he dropped her hand and squared his body in front of her. "Tell me what you want me to do."

Hold me. Kiss me. "Er..." She captured her bottom lip between her teeth and tried to focus on what she was supposed to be doing.

His mouth slanted up on one side. "It just occurred to me to ask. Am I the white crane or the snake?"

She snapped to attention. He wanted to see how her training worked in a real situation, not stand by as she fantasized about him. "You are the snake, sir. Try to strike me."

"*Strike* you? But you are a lady."

"Or try to grab me."

His sculpted jaw hardened. "I would never hurt a woman."

"I know, Mr. Vistoire, but not every man has honor. If you wish for a demonstration, you must pretend to be something you are not."

"You say this with the confidence of a woman who has encountered such men."

She shrugged. "Uncle Charles taught me to judge a man on what my instincts tell me and not by his station, appearance, or promises. This advice has served me well, and my encounters with such men have been rare."

"Even one time is too many. I'm afraid I must insist you enlist your uncle's godson to escort you about Town from now on."

"You are not in a position to insist on anything, sir." A warm tingling sensation expanded in her chest despite her protest. It was silly to want him to care for her when he would be on a ship embarking by high tide tomorrow, sailing toward a place she would never see.

Nevertheless, she savored the possibility that he might hold some affection for her. That he might remember her fondly through the coming years and wonder about her from time to time. It seemed only fair since she suspected she would be doing the same when it came to him. "Do you wish for a demonstration? If so, try to strike me."

He didn't offer any more arguments and assumed a fighting stance. Focusing on his torso, she watched for hints of movement before he reached for her. She swept his arm to her left, knocking him off balance, and drove her right hand toward his face, stopping short of gouging his eye with her thumb.

He flinched. "Faith! You are quick. Are you certain you aren't the snake?"

She laughed and released his arm. "You didn't commit, Mr. Vistoire. You are too gentlemanly to pose a threat, but I can protect myself when I must."

"Perhaps."

He poised himself to attack. She could tell from his stance that he'd had training in boxing. His body was positioned at a slight diagonal, his weight evenly distributed between both legs, and his dominant hand in back. He struck and she deflected his blow again. As they continued to spar, he grew bolder, throwing more than one punch at a time. She fanned her arms, each move flowing into the other. It was all very similar to a dance in her mind, although she was more graceful when practicing Wing Chun than she was dancing a waltz.

They were both breathing heavily when they eventually stopped. The curls around Mr. Vistoire's face were damp. "My confidence in your ability to protect yourself has increased," he said, "but I would still prefer you have an escort."

"I will consider your request."

He stepped toward her and brushed a strand of hair that had slipped from the knot on top of her head and moved it behind her ear. His thumb lingered on her cheek. "I am forever in your debt, mademoiselle. *Merci.*"

Cradling her face, he brushed his lips against her cheek then kissed her other one. She exhaled and turned toward his kiss just as he drew back. They stared at one another with lips parted. His breath stirred the hair at her temple, creating a delicious tickle that traveled down her back. His hand still cupped her face.

"You are not deflecting me." The husky sound of his voice competed with the drumming in her ears.

"I know," she whispered.

"You promised to protect yourself." His fingers slid to her nape, and he gently pulled her toward him. He flashed a rueful smile before pressing his lips to her forehead. She sank against him and his other arm circled her waist. He held her a long time, their jagged breaths intermingling.

"I am not a man to deny himself," he murmured. "Resisting you is taking all the strength I possess."

When he released her, she barely held in her cry of protest. "Stay safe, Miss Darlington. The world is a kinder place with you here."

As he walked away, she knew she'd been wrong about avoiding him. She wasn't any better off for having never experienced his kiss.

Eight

Xavier reluctantly crossed Wedmore House's threshold to be swallowed up by the murky night. Miss Darlington closed the door, and he stopped on the walk to listen for the turning of the lock. When the telltale clank sounded, he smiled. She wasn't abidingly stubborn at least.

He drew in a deep breath, filling his lungs with the dank London air, and tried to get his bearings in the fog. The hour was growing late for decent folk. Lingering with Miss Darlington might have cost Xavier a chance to catch his former landlady before she retired for bed. Nevertheless, he couldn't have slipped away without expressing his gratitude and saying good-bye to the kind young woman who'd cared for him this past week. Unfortunately, once he was in Miss Darlington's presence again, his drive to go had wavered.

He glanced back at the four-story town house with only one window aglow. Miss Darlington was likely curling up with a book and her rascally dog to await her family's return. The pull to rejoin her was a strong pulsing in his chest.

She fascinated him. Beautiful. Tenderhearted. Vulnerable in her innocence. And yet, she was no helpless maiden. Frankly, she'd impressed the hell out of him, matching him move for move when they'd sparred. She seemed to know what he was going to do even before he did.

Perhaps this would have made him uneasy in the past, to meet a woman who could read him so easily, but he derived a certain satisfaction from it now. She appeared to understand him. Perhaps she'd even recognized his true character in the end. Xavier was not a criminal or a reprobate. He was a desperate man grabbing for freedom.

Dragging his fingers through his hair, he issued a low growl of disgust with himself. This wasn't the time to have his head in the clouds. He needed to remain vigilant for signs of Farrin's men. Although he hadn't detected anyone lurking outside Wedmore House when he'd scouted the area earlier, he wouldn't rest comfortably until he was far from England.

A thick fog blanketed the neighborhood and rendered the street lamps nearly useless as he began the trek to his former residence. In the distance, the lamps' dim glow reminded him of fireflies he and Serafine once chased in the fields around *Le Bijou,* the aging house he and his sister called home.

He only had his memory of Mayfair to guide him, and with no clear landmarks, he couldn't be sure he was headed in the right direction. Trusting his instincts, he forged on and hoped he didn't plow into anything hidden in the fog.

His worries about becoming lost vanished when he passed Berkeley Square. He was halfway to his former bachelor quarters. As he reached a crossroad, a lone carriage turned onto the cobblestone lane. The dull clop of horse's hooves and a squeaky wheel hailed its approach. A prick of unease caused him to look over his shoulder. The mist formed halos around the lamps and hid the driver from view. The carriage crept down the lane as if in no hurry to reach its destination.

Or they are searching for someone.

Xavier's mouth grew dry as the carriage drew closer. His muscles tensed. At the last moment, he darted behind a hedge to crouch low. The carriage rolled past, the squeaking of the wheel grating to his nerves. He remained hidden until the sound faded and eventually disappeared. When he was certain the carriage presented no danger, he rose from the ground, smacked the dirt from his hands, and strode on.

At the corner where Hill met Waverton, he was afforded a clear view of Mrs. Zachery's modest town house. Light peeked through a crack in the curtains. She was awake. He exhaled, only now realizing he'd been holding his breath, and hurried his step. Even if he'd had to scale the trellis in the backyard and enter through a window, he would have found his way inside. Discovering the light turned up, however, would make his task easier.

He bounded up the stairs and banged on the door, noting that even after two years the paint was still peeling. As he lifted his fist to knock again, the door flew open.

A diminutive man wearing a blue satin banyan stood in the doorway, squinting up at him. His wispy, blond hair had been carefully brushed to sweep across his baldhead as if creating a bridge from one ear to the other. He seemed all that was proper, which was likely the reason his blunt greeting came as a surprise. "Who the hell are you?"

Xavier fell back a step. The town houses on the street butted against one another and looked similar, but he'd been certain he was at the correct place. "Is this the Zachery residence?" he asked. "I am seeking Mrs. Zachery."

"I am Mr. Zachery, her nephew." The man's dour expression didn't alter. "What is it you want?"

"If you would be so kind as to retrieve your aunt, so I might speak with her."

Mr. Zachery's blank stare was less than encouraging.

"Uh... I am a former tenant—of Mrs. Zachery," Xavier said. "I've come to collect my personal belongings, if you please."

Her nephew's shoulders sank and he sighed wearily. "I thought that sordid mess was finally behind me. Well, I suppose you will want to come inside and sift through everything."

Mr. Zachery proved to be more cooperative than his gruff manner had suggested. He moved aside and gestured for Xavier to enter. "Follow me."

He led Xavier down a narrow corridor past the stairwell. "Aunt Gert was up to quite a bit of mischief over the years. I only discovered her misdeeds after I inherited the house and found the crates. I shouldn't have been surprised when gentlemen began arriving at the door to demand their belongings." He stopped in front of a door built beneath the stairs.

Xavier offered his condolence on Mrs. Zachery's passing, but her nephew provided no indication he heard him. He tugged hard on the handle with both hands before the door gave way. From floor to ceiling, the small space was jammed with items.

Mr. Zachery shrugged. "She must have been stealing from her tenants for years, although no one has been able to prove she took anything of value. I will bring you a candle for light."

He turned on his heel and walked away.

Xavier rubbed away the tightness gathering at his temple. It could take all night to sift through everything in the closet. Fortunately, what Xavier came for was upstairs. Before Mr. Zachery returned, Xavier darted up the staircase and stalked toward his former rooms. The door was unlocked, so he let himself inside.

Men's clothing littered the floor, indicating a new tenant was letting the apartment, but he'd apparently stepped out for the evening. Xavier hurried to the loose board in the floor, kicked the current tenant's slippers aside, and bent to pry up the board. Blindly, he reached into the niche and grabbed the purse.

"You there," Mr. Zachery called from the stairs. "What are you doing? You shouldn't be up here. Where are you?"

Xavier shoved the purse into his pocket and felt around for the papers that proved his identity and worth. Everything of value was exactly where he'd left it. He'd replaced the board and was walking toward the door when Mr. Zachery appeared in the threshold with a candle.

"I suspect you are right about my belongings being under the stairs," Xavier said, "but I haven't the time to search."

The man scrambled out of his way as Xavier swept into the corridor and headed for the stairs.

"I told you where they would be," Mr. Zachery said.

"*Oui*, and I thank you." When Xavier reached the ground floor, he pulled six pounds from his purse—five to clear his debt to Mrs. Zachery, and one for her nephew's trouble. He dropped the bills on a small table by the front door and slipped outside to disappear into the fog.

Now that he could pay for a hack, he would hire one to carry him to the wharf. It was too far to walk, and the sooner he secured a room at one of the inns, the better. His luck had held out thus far, but he'd be a fool to believe the men who'd taken him prisoner had undergone a change of heart and wouldn't lock him away for good if they found him.

He determined his chances of finding transportation would be greater around the gentlemen's clubs and set off in their direction. He hadn't gone far, however, when he spotted a hackney coach stopped at the next intersection.

The driver might be waiting for another fare, but Xavier would offer double to carry him to the wharf if that were the case. Cutting across the road, he hailed the driver. "Carry me to the docks, and I will make it worth your time."

The driver touched the brim of his hat, inclining his head slightly. "Yes, sir."

Xavier climbed into the carriage, dropped on the bench, and froze. His heart hammered. Filtered lamplight glinted off the silver barrel of a flintlock pistol, and it was aimed at him. The click of the firearm being set to full cock reverberated in the small space.

"Mr. Vistoire, what a pleasant surprise."

Xavier cursed. It was Farrin.

The carriage lurched forward. The squeak of a wheel penetrated the interior. Xavier's hand curled into a fist against his thigh. He'd been followed. The blackguard had been toying with him since Berkeley Square.

"I was beginning to believe you and Benny had conspired against me. Perhaps you have, and I've intercepted you before any harm could be done."

Xavier forced himself to relax against the seatback. As long as he remained on alert, Farrin wouldn't lower his guard, and Xavier would have no chance to escape. "As you can see, I am alone. I've no idea where Benny has gotten off to."

The man lowered the firearm and leaned forward. One side of his face remained in shadow. "It is odd Benny never returned," the man said. "Perhaps my brother met with a foul end at your hands."

Xavier didn't deny the charge. If Farrin believed him capable of murder, perhaps he would reconsider the wisdom in holding him against his will. "Benny never mentioned having a brother. I see that he inherited the brains and beauty," Xavier drawled.

The man affected a laugh, holding his belly and drawing out the pretense by wiping fake tears from his cheeks. His jaw hardened, and his piercing gaze nailed Xavier. "You are hilarious."

Xavier ground his teeth. The man was an arse.

Farrin raised the pistol again, aiming at Xavier's chest. "Give me the bloody map."

"I don't have it. Maybe you should be searching for Benny."

"You can't expect me to believe Benny took the map. He does everything I tell him. The idiot cannot think for himself."

Xavier's spine stiffened. "He is quiet. That doesn't make him stupid." He'd heard his young cousin Rafe referred to as a simpleton too many times to allow the insult to pass.

"And here I believed Benny's love affair with you was one-sided. I think you do know where he is. You've been together this whole time." Farrin's voice dripped with derision. "Take me to the map."

"You must be a dreadful bore at parties with all this blathering on about dusty old maps."

Farrin growled low in his throat. "Take me to the map or I'll blow a hole in you."

"I don't have the map. Neither does Benny. And you are to blame." Xavier glowered. "You failed to mention Wedmore House has a dog."

"It is a small dog."

"And he *barks*. You were wrong about the servants, too. I barely escaped."

He was taking a risk with the tale, but if Farrin was lying about Benny's disappearance, he probably knew a woman had threatened them with gaol. Xavier wanted to keep Miss Darlington's involvement and his extended stay a secret to protect her and her family.

They sat in silence except for the incessant squeaking wheel and the rumble of the carriage bumping along the street.

"I should have sent someone with more experience," Farrin said at last. "Someone who knows how to deal with dogs and servants without becoming squeamish. Fortunately, there is still time."

A low roar built inside Xavier until it thundered in his ears. Miss Darlington and the women at Wedmore House would be no match for one of Farrin's men. "You can't send in another man."

"I can do whatever I please—with the dog, the occupants of Wedmore House, *you*."

"Allow me to try again." He prayed desperation didn't resonate in his voice. "I can retrieve the map."

"Garrick can retrieve it, and he won't fail."

"You sent me for a reason. We have no connection to one another. If I am captured or there are witnesses, the crime cannot be traced to you. You *need* me."

Farrin lowered the gun. Perhaps posing a danger to others grew tiring after awhile. "What did you retrieve from Mr. Zachery's house? Money? What is to keep you from going straight to the docks as soon as I allow you out of my sight?"

There was nothing to stop him. *Nothing except Miss Darlington.* Two years ago, he wouldn't have given a second thought to saving his own skin. But he'd had an abundance of time to reflect on his character during his captivity, and he'd found himself lacking. He'd vowed to stop living up to his father's expectations and become an honorable gentleman.

"I give you my word," Xavier said.

Farrin scoffed. "The word of a scoundrel."

Xavier drew himself up on the carriage bench. "The word of a *gentleman*. I will bring you the map, but you must allow me to find it my way. And I will need time."

Time would allow him to contact Lord Wedmore's godson, Margrave. The viscount could offer the ladies protection, and once Xavier knew they were safe, he could return to his family in New Orleans.

Farrin's glower appeared deadly. "Will your word as a gentleman stop you from running away? I fear not. Unless..." Farrin drummed his fingers against his thigh. "Unless your *sister* serves as collateral."

Gooseflesh rose along Xavier's arms. Farrin had no way of knowing about Serafine. Xavier had never spoken of his family, because he suspected his enemies would employ the knowledge to torture him.

Farrin's eyes glittered in the dim carriage, reminding Xavier of a wolf preparing to sink his teeth into his prey. "Haven't you heard your precious sister has made her home in London? Of course you haven't. What am I thinking? You've kept to yourself these past couple of years."

Xavier cursed Farrin for the liar he was, but the churning in the pit of his stomach suggested the blackguard was speaking the truth.

"Serafine." Farrin drew out the name and Xavier's blood chilled. "Your sister came to London looking for you and instead reunited with her American beau. Even an ocean cannot keep true lovers parted. I am certain your sister and Mr. Tucker missed you at their wedding, but when you retired from Society, you neglected to leave a forwarding address."

"Go to the devil!"

"I must say, it was a stroke of luck that dear Serafine found Mr. Tucker since she was already carrying his child. Bastards are a messy affair, are they not? By all reports, she birthed a healthy boy. We'll be at their door any moment, and we can see for ourselves."

Xavier's gaze narrowed on the pistol resting in Farrin's lap. "I will take you to the grave with me before you get anywhere near my sister."

"Calm yourself, Mr. Vistoire. You can see yourself to the door. My presence is needed elsewhere."

The carriage stopped and a few moments later, the door swung open. "You have a week to retrieve the map, Mr. Vistoire. Any longer and your sister can expect a caller."

Xavier's fists tightened. "I will do what you ask. Just leave Serafine alone."

"Splendid. We've reached an agreement. If you speak to Serafine, Wedmore's family, or to anyone about your task, know you are placing lives in danger—including your own. The interested party will not stop until the map is delivered to

him, and he values discretion above human lives." Farrin raised
the firearm and flicked the barrel toward the open door. "Get
the hell out of here before I change my mind about shooting
you."

"Stay away from my sister." He'd like to cross paths with
Farrin when he didn't have his pistol to protect him. The man
was a bloody coward.

As Xavier's feet hit the ground, he looked up at the modest
town house with its lights still aglow. Could it be true? Had his
sister come looking for him only to make a life for herself in
England?

God, he hoped it was true. At the back of his mind, he'd
always harbored the fear some tragedy might have befallen her
while he was locked away. Something he could have prevented
if he'd not allowed his pride to come between them. But
Serafine was here. She was well. And she had a family of her
own.

Suddenly, his throat was too tight and an ache radiated in
his chest. Serafine was just as proud as he, perhaps even more.
Forgiveness did not come easy to her, and no apology could
erase his bad deeds.

"Seven days, Mr. Vistoire," Farrin called from the carriage.
"You are wasting time."

Xavier tossed a glare over his shoulder, then took a deep
breath and approached the town house door. The carriage and
its squeaky wheel pulled away, leaving Xavier a few seconds to
collect himself before the door swung open.

An older woman answered the door. "May I help you, sir?"

"I would like to request an audience with Serafine."

The housekeeper looked down her nose. "Mrs. Tucker is
not in the habit of receiving callers this late, sir. Perhaps you
should consider returning at a decent hour dressed in
appropriate attire."

"Mrs. Oats, who is it?" Xavier's breath caught at the sound of his sister's voice. "Is everything all right?"

She swept into the foyer, as willowy and regal as he remembered.

"Serafine," he murmured.

His sister skidded to a stop, her elegant fingers catching her gasp. Her face paled.

"Sera, was someone at the door?" a man called from the top of the curved staircase—Serafine's husband. His accent was American without a hint of the lyrical accent of Xavier and Serafine's people. When his sister didn't answer, her husband came to investigate. His sensible brown slippers became visible before the rest of him. He leaned down to see halfway in his descent, his blond hair falling forward on his forehead. His gaze shot back and forth between Xavier and Serafine.

"Do you know this man?"

Serafine nodded. Apparently the shock of Xavier's sudden appearance had rendered her mute.

"Thank you, Mrs. Oats," Serafine's husband said as he reached the foyer and crossed to her side. "You may go."

The housekeeper dawdled as she went, perhaps hoping for answers to her mistress's strange visitor. When they were alone, her husband slipped his arm around her waist as if she needed help standing and offered Xavier a hesitant smile.

"Darling, are you all right?"

Serafine broke free of her trance. "He is my brother. Xavier, Sweet Mary! You're alive."

"Yes. Yes, I am." Xavier rushed forward to meet his sister and envelop her in a hug.

Serafine clung to him, laughing as tears rolled down her cheeks. His own eyes burned with long suppressed emotion. He didn't think she was ever going to release him, but when she did, he realized he should have held on longer. Sparks ignited in her eyes. He was about to receive the scolding of his life.

She threw her hands in the air. "*Where* have you been?"

Because he couldn't think of any excuse to account for his disappearance, he told her the truth—or the parts he could reveal without endangering her.

"The dimwitted British thought I was a spy."

Nine

Regina hid a yawn behind her fan and hoped the Countess of Norwick didn't notice and take offense. Alas, her hostess for the evening was a keen observer.

Lady Norwick's chocolate brown eyes sparkled with amusement. "Tired so soon, Miss Darlington?"

Regina dropped her gaze to the intricate block pattern set in the wood floor as heat washed over her face. If ballrooms incorporated a trap door like theatre stages, she would gladly disappear through it. "My apologies, Lady Norwick. I'm afraid my sleep has been poor lately."

After Mr. Vistoire's departure from Wedmore House two nights ago, she'd paced the length of her bedchamber, stopping to look out the window more times than she would ever admit. It wasn't like her to fret over a gentleman, especially one she barely knew and would never see again.

Still, she'd worried for him. London could be a dangerous place where footpads and murderers prowled for victims, and pedestrians stumbled into the river to drown. Neither fate was one she wished on Mr. Vistoire. Last night, she hadn't slept much better for thinking about him.

"Hmm," the countess murmured. "And here I thought fending off advances from that wretched Lord Geoffrey might account for your fatigue."

Regina's heart jumped into her throat. Every sidelong glance she'd received that evening took on new meaning.

"I thought the scoundrel might swoon when the footman announced your arrival," the countess added in a stage whisper.

Regina wet her lips. Perhaps she and her family should leave before the evening turned nasty. "What are the gossips saying?"

"Not a word." Lady Norwick's smile vanished; her nostrils flared slightly. "Lord Norwick and I do not abide gossips, and everyone is aware of our position. Unless one wants to be tossed from Norwick Place and excluded from future gatherings, one does not discuss others' affairs."

With all of Society clamoring for invitations to the Norwicks' unorthodox parties, the lady's threat likely caused many to tremble in fear, which afforded Regina some measure of relief.

"Thank you," she said with genuine gratitude.

"No thanks are necessary, Miss Darlington. I had my fill of gossips a few years ago, and swore they would never control my life again." Lady Norwick patted her arm comfortingly. "Only Lord Norwick and I are aware of your run-in, so please don't fret. Lord Geoffrey pulled my husband aside to request he keep you far away this evening, and the blackguard looked none too pleased when Norwick demanded an explanation. I cannot fathom Lord Geoffrey wants anyone else knowing what transpired. He will keep quiet."

The mischievous smile the countess was known for played upon her lips. "Did you truly have Lord Geoffrey groveling at your feet? I do hope he wasn't exaggerating."

"Is that what he said?"

Lady Norwick nodded.

"Well, I hate to disappoint you, but he was not groveling. Expanding my knowledge of vulgar language, yes, but no pleading was involved."

The countess tossed back her head and laughed with abandon. Her laughter was the richest, most genuine, infectious sound Regina had ever heard, and she couldn't hold in her own soft chuckle.

"Oh, I do like you, Regina Darlington. I think we could become fast friends."

Regina had no lady companions outside of her sisters and aunt. She'd always seen herself as too different from other ladies to fathom they would want her friendship, so she'd kept to herself. But the countess had something in common with Regina—Lady Norwick was different, too.

"Oh, for pity's sake, Bianca," a voice called from behind Regina. "That braying laugh of yours carries everywhere."

Lady Norwick offered a blinding smile for her detractor. "Fiona! How lovely to see you."

Regina spun around to find three fashionable ladies making their way through the crowd gathered around the ballroom floor chatting while the dancers enjoyed the set. Lady Norwick had designated a set for partnering with widows, matrons, and spinsters only, and the gentlemen were highly encouraged to comply. This was simply more evidence of Lady Norwick's uniqueness.

The countess took the older woman's hands in hers and placed kisses on each of her prominent cheeks. "Fiona, I wasn't certain you would feel up to socializing so soon after arriving home. Did you have a pleasant stay in Vienna?"

Fiona, Lady Banner, returned her sister-in-law's greeting with affectionate kisses on her cheeks as well, discrediting rumors the two ladies had been enemies at one time.

"Vienna was tolerable," Lady Banner said. "How is my darling niece? Has she missed her auntie?"

"Not a day has passed without little Fi asking after you. You must call tomorrow. We all missed you."

The countess welcomed the other two ladies with the same enthusiasm before all four began talking at once. The friends shared a gift for communication that didn't seem to require anyone to complete a full sentence to be understood. Regina held back, not venturing to join their conversation. She knew

the ladies by reputation only, and she didn't want to appear
forward by speaking out of turn.

Lady Norwick glanced in her direction and waved her
forward. "Fiona, Amelia, Serafine. Allow me to present Miss
Regina Darlington, Lord Wedmore's eldest niece."

The ladies regarded her with expectant smiles as the
countess completed the introductions. Regina curtsied to Lady
Banner then returned Amelia Hillary's and Serafine Tucker's
smiles with a shy one of her own.

"It is an honor to meet you," she said.

The ladies reassured her the pleasure was theirs then began
asking polite questions about her and her family. Their show of
interest made her feel oddly at ease when she typically did not
like to talk about herself. Invariably, when she had opened up
in the past, ladies would comment on her *unique* family, and
they had a way of making the word sound insulting.

Eventually Lady Norwick directed the conversation toward
a different topic. "Serafine, I thought your brother was
accompanying you this evening. I've been anxious to lay eyes on
him ever since your message arrived yesterday."

The willowy young woman with the dewy skin smiled. "He
is here, but he received an invitation to partner for the waltz."
Serafine Tucker had a pleasing airy sound to her voice, like a
gentle breeze.

"Brava for the lady in question," Lady Norwick said. "I
admire a woman who pursues what she wants. It sounds like
your brother could be in trouble, unless he doesn't mind being
led around by the nose."

Mrs. Tucker's striking green gaze briefly met Regina's before
the other woman looked away.

Lady Banner snorted. "Do you have a twin, Bianca?"

"What do you mean?"

"If I remember correctly, not long ago *you* were the lady pursuing what she wanted. Poor Tubs didn't know what hit him."

The countess laughed good-naturedly. "I'll have you know your brother is perfectly happy being at my beck and call."

"That he is," Lady Banner conceded with a satisfied nod.

Mrs. Tucker swept a hand toward the dance floor. "My brother is headed this way" —she nailed the countess with a pointed glance— "and his partner is simply charming."

Curious, Regina craned her neck for a glimpse of Mrs. Tucker's brother and his charming partner. Her eyes locked onto a plume of red and black feathers, much like the ones Aunt Beatrice had been wearing in her headdress when they'd left Wedmore House that evening.

Oh, dear.

Regina's mouth grew dry. Aunt Beatrice sometimes ignored the fact she was no longer a young lady. Most gentlemen overlooked her harmless flirtations, but the insufferable members of the *ton* made a joke of her when they thought Regina and her sisters wouldn't overhear. She felt slightly queasy as it occurred to her the countess might be having fun at hers and Aunt Beatrice's expenses.

Lady Norwick's face lit with a bright smile as she linked arms with Regina. "Isn't that your great-aunt, Miss Darlington?"

Regina braced herself for the snide remark she knew was forthcoming.

"Miss Allred is glowing," the countess said. "This is exactly what I'd hoped for this evening, a lovely time for *all* of our guests."

The lack of guile in Lady Norwick's manner chipped away Regina's defenses, and she allowed herself to take in the scene. All she could see of Aunt Beatrice's dance partner was a pair of broad shoulders, but she wasn't really looking at him anyway.

With blue eyes twinkling, Aunt Beatrice turned a slow circle under her partner's arm and giggled like a debutante.

Regina covered her heart and sighed. She already liked Mrs. Tucker's brother, for he was allowing Aunt Beatrice to re-experience the joy of her youth. Gratitude welled up inside of Regina.

"Auntie is having the time of her life," she said.

"*Oui.*" Serafine smiled fondly in the couple's direction. "Xavier is enjoying himself as well."

The name hadn't quite penetrated Regina's awareness when Aunt Beatrice and her partner turned the corner, allowing Regina her first glimpse of his handsome face.

"Oh, my," she uttered with a rush of breath.

Aunt Beatrice's partner was Mr. Vistoire. And he looked positively dashing. Black breeches hugged his slim hips as if they had been tailored for him, and the red and black damask waistcoat was simply exquisite topped with a black jacket.

Blood thrummed through her veins. How was he here? He'd told her that he was sailing to New Orleans without delay to reunite with his sister, and as long as Regina had been out in Society, Serafine Tucker had resided in London.

"How many siblings do you have, Mrs. Tucker? Do you have a sister in New Orleans?"

The woman's soft smile fell away. "I am surprised you remember where I'm from."

A prickly heat invaded Regina's body. "I've always had a good memory for details. You arrived in London with your American cousins and your cousin's husband, Captain Hillary."

"You *do* have an excellent memory." Mrs. Tucker's smile reappeared. "We have no more family in New Orleans. Xavier and I were our parents' only children. What about you, Miss Darlington? Is it just you and your two sisters?"

"Yes, three girls." Regina narrowed her eyes as she watched Mr. Vistoire guide Aunt Beatrice around the floor. What game was he playing?

"He is enthralling, is he not?" Lady Norwick murmured in her ear. "I can barely look away."

Regina reluctantly forced her gaze from Mr. Vistoire only to discover the countess wasn't watching him at all. She was regarding Regina with a slight curve to her ruby lips.

Regina cleared her throat. "I have never seen my aunt on the dance floor. It is a pleasant surprise."

"Yes, I can see the pleasantness and surprise written all over your face."

Regina warmed under the countess's scrutiny, and she flicked her fan to create a breeze as the last of the string quartet's notes faded on the air.

"Serafine, you must make introductions," Lady Norwick said. "Would you collect your brother?"

"Of course. I'll only be a moment." Mrs. Tucker slipped into the crowd.

Regina would have taken her leave as well, if not for Lady Norwick attached to her side.

"I have already had the pleasure of meeting Mr. Vistoire," Amelia Hillary said, "and I see my husband coming this way to claim the next dance. We will catch up later, dearest." The petite blond kissed the countess's cheek before waving to Regina and Lady Banner. "Good evening, ladies."

Lady Banner came up on Regina's other side as if she and the countess were colluding to keep her from running away. "It's a wonder Mr. Hillary allowed his wife from his sight as long as he did," Lady Banner said.

"Oh?" Regina's curiosity was piqued despite her wish to escape before Mrs. Tucker returned with Mr. Vistoire. "Is her husband the overbearing type?"

"Jake Hillary is the *smitten* type," the countess said. "I've never seen a man more in love with his wife, aside from my own."

Lady Banner pursed her lips. "I believe we've already established you have my brother wrapped around your finger, Bianca, and quite happy to be there. Does he deny you anything?"

"Never." The countess winked at Regina. "Jasper realized early on it was an exercise in futility to try to talk me out of something when I've already set my mind to it."

Regina didn't know why, but she felt like Lady Norwick might have set her mind to something involving Regina, and she wanted nothing to do with being the lady's plaything. "I really should see to my aunt. She has a tendency to over-exert herself at times."

The ladies released her with reassurances that she should do what was best for her family.

"Thank you," Regina said, bemused by how amendable they were. Perhaps she'd misjudged them. Before she could bid them a good evening, she spied Aunt Beatrice strolling in their direction on Mr. Vistoire's arm. Regina shifted her weight to her toes, poised to dash into the crowd before Aunt Beatrice found her. She refused to receive Mr. Vistoire politely while everyone observed.

He had taken her in completely. He'd invaded Wedmore House. And the worst of it was, she had forgiven the reprobate. She had believed his apology was sincere and trusted he was leaving London. Therefore, he would never have had the chance to utter a word about surprising her at home alone.

"There is my lovely niece." Aunt Beatrice's voice rang out in the ballroom. "She has not yet chosen a suitor, so you are in luck, sir."

Good Lord. Where was that trap door when Regina needed it?

Ten

Xavier wasn't one to question good fortune or allow an opportunity to slip through his grasp. Yet, he broke into a light sweat as Miss Beatrice Allred lead him across the ballroom to present him to her niece. Partnering with Miss Darlington's aunt for the waltz had not been by design, but that didn't stop the annoying twinges of a guilty conscience from bedeviling him. It seemed he wasn't above using her aunt to further his cause.

He had hoped to cross paths with Regina Darlington this evening. Only five days remained until he was supposed to deliver the map. When he'd stepped outside of his sister's house this morning to revel in his reclaimed freedom, he'd realized his cell had simply expanded. Two of the men who'd interrogated Xavier during his incarceration had been waiting at the corner. Neither spoke or made threatening gestures, but the warning was clear. As long as Farrin and the man financing him were alive, Xavier's family was in danger, and so were the ladies of Wedmore House.

But he had a plan.

To gain access to Lord Wedmore's town house, he would court Miss Darlington. To protect her, he must convince her to marry him. Unfortunately, he'd falsely confessed to being a rake set on seducing her. The odds of winning her hand were not in his favor.

"Where did that girl disappear to? I know she was just there." Aunt Beatrice, as she insisted he call her, dug her fingers into his forearm as if she was worried he might try to escape and tugged him in another direction. She was as marriage-minded as any mother trying to arrange a match for her daughter, and she was determined to catch a husband for her niece. "I expect you will fall head over heels for her in no time."

He chuckled, despite the nearly cannonball-sized knot settling in his gut. He'd already fallen for Miss Darlington. And cracked his skull in the process. The true challenge would be making her fall for *him*.

Aunt Beatrice drew to a sharp halt. Her face scrunched as she looked up at him. Her nose twitched every time she blinked. "You are a delightful dancer, Mr. Vistoire, but do the ladies find you handsome?"

"Now, Aunt Beatrice. How am I to answer honestly without appearing vain?"

She hooted with scandalized laughter and squeezed his arm. "Charming *and* clever. There she is. Wait here while I retrieve her."

The lady released her grip on him and disappeared into the crowd. She waved at a young woman who didn't seem to know her. The lady's forehead puckered in confusion as Aunt Beatrice elbowed a path through the bodies standing in her way and called out to her.

Xavier shook his head in amused disbelief. While he waited for Aunt Beatrice to discover her mistake, he allowed himself the pleasure of watching the real Miss Darlington gracefully weave toward a set of French doors on the far side of the room. Her gown shimmered under a waterfall of diffuse light from a massive brass chandelier. The rosy hue lingered somewhere between pink and crimson and lent her cheeks a healthy glow while the silk hugged the gentle curve of her bosom.

When she reached the open doors, she paused and locked eyes with him. He couldn't tear his gaze from her. His breath churned thickly in his lungs. "*Enchanteresse*," he murmured.

Her pink tongue darted over her plump bottom lip, leaving her mouth shiny and as tempting as sin. Slowly, she turned away and slipped outside.

Xavier tensed. Where the devil was she going? The gardens at night were no place for a lady, with or without an escort. He started toward the doors to talk some sense into her and see her safely back inside, but another man reached the exit before him and shot into the dark in quick pursuit.

Damnation.

Xavier shoved through the maze of bodies, earning several disparaging words, but he didn't allow their censorship to slow him. Miss Darlington's pursuer outweighed her by several stones. She'd not be able to defend herself for long against him if he caught her.

When Xavier stepped outside, a humid breeze washed over him. Pierced tin lanterns lined the stone railing around the empty terrace, casting splattered dots of light across the surface. He sprinted down the stairs and halfway into the gardens before he stopped to listen for signs of where Miss Darlington had gone.

The hypnotic trill of crickets was broken by a sharp crack of a stick deeper in the garden. Xavier hurried toward the sound, moving as quietly along the gravel path as possible. A white dome nestled among the trees in a corner of the garden shone like a beacon in the darkness. As he continued along the gently curving path, the entire structure and its occupants came into view.

He could make out Miss Darlington in her light colored gown and the darker shadow of the man. They were facing one another as if in conversation, but Xavier was too far away to hear their exchange. The man lunged and she squealed in surprise. His huge arms circled her waist, dragging her against him.

A guttural growl rose in Xavier's throat, but before he could charge the portico, small hands closed around his wrist. The shock of someone jumping from the bushes brought him to a full stop and saved him from creating an embarrassing scene. The woman beneath the portico laughed and threw her arms around the man's neck to draw him to her for a kiss.

"Mr. Vistoire," a voice hissed. "Come."

It took a moment for him to realize it was Miss Darlington tugging his arm. He stopped resisting and followed her into the heavy vegetation. "What are you—?"

She shushed him. "Come."

He glowered in return. Did she think he was her pooch to order about? "No, you come with me," he whispered and changed their course just to prove he had a mind of his own.

She allowed him to lead the way while still holding onto his wrist. When they were a safe distance from the portico, she asked, "Do you know where you are going?"

"Not really."

She planted her feet. He stopped and turned toward her. His eyes had adjusted to the darkness enough to see her pretty face. She notched her chin. "If you don't know where you're going, why are you leading?"

Her defiant stance fanned his smoldering temper to flames. "The better question is why are you sneaking around the gardens alone? Have you no sense?"

He was truly beginning to believe that was the case. First, she'd kept him secreted away at Wedmore House instead of summoning a runner, and now she was risking body and reputation for what? If he'd interrupted her own tryst, he might be unable to refrain from taking her over his knee.

"I'm not alone," she said in a reasonable tone that did nothing to dispel his temper. "I wanted to speak with you in private."

"And how did you know I would follow you?"

She gestured toward him with a flourish of her hand.

He gritted his teeth. She did believe he was no better than a pooch content to run after her. The worst of it was he *had* chased after her, and he would do it again. Not because he needed to charm his way back into Wedmore House, but because he couldn't stand the thought of another man laying hands on her.

"You are fortunate it was me following you and not some rake meaning to do you harm."

She scoffed. "That is hypocritical considering you are as rakish as any man I know."

"What have I done to earn such a reputation? Aside from becoming foxed and wandering into Wedmore House, I mean."

"You did not *wander*, sir. You broke the lock on the backdoor."

"Yes, well. Other than those unfortunate actions... Did I not behave like a gentleman while you played nursemaid to me? I admitted I made a mistake. I wasn't myself that evening. And you are deflecting, Miss Darlington. What if you had been set upon by a true scoundrel?"

"I'm capable of defending myself, and I didn't lure you outside to lecture me. Please, come with me." Taking his hand, she urged him deeper into the garden, away from the house and other guests. Curiosity overrode his pride, and he didn't resist.

Neither of them spoke as they weaved through several mulberry bushes, passed a small pond covered in lily pads, and walked beneath a rose-laden trellis. When they reached what Miss Darlington apparently felt was a comfortable distance from the house, she dropped his hand and spun on her heel. Her fists landed on her hips.

"Imagine my surprise at finding you here. Aren't you supposed to be on a ship, sir?"

She was no more surprised than he was.

"Change of plans," he said.

"Change of plans?" She bristled. "You promised no one would learn about the incident at Wedmore House. You swore your servant wouldn't say a word, because you were leaving immediately. You said your sister was in New Orleans and needed you. Serafine Tucker moved to London my first Season."

Merde. Why must she recall every detail of what he'd said? He had enough trouble without adding a too-clever woman to the mix. "I had only arrived in London that evening, and I'd had no contact with my sister for a long time. I didn't know she was in England until the night I left Wedmore House. An old friend told me."

Old friend. The lie was bitter on his tongue. With friends like Farrin, he'd rather become a hermit.

"How am I to believe anything you say when I've already caught you in a lie?" she asked. "I maintain you are just another scoundrel dogging my heels this summer. Perhaps you believe without Uncle Charles around to discourage you that I am helpless. I assure you, I am not, as one lord who shall remain nameless learned when he tried to force himself on me."

The fire inside him blazed hotter, and a rolling whoosh filled his head. He would kill the man. "Give me the blackguard's name. I will rip him limb from limb. I'll challenge every bloody rogue who has been bothering you until they've all been put in the ground. I want names. *Now.*"

"Goodness," she said on a wisp of breath and held a hand to her head. "I have no idea what you just said, but it sounded serious."

He blinked. Her unexpected response caused him to forget his righteous anger for a moment. "Pardon?"

She bit her bottom lip. "I never learned to speak French fluently."

He hadn't realized he'd stopped speaking English.

"I'm afraid I spent more time avoiding my lessons than it would have taken me to complete them," she said. "I was too young to recognize the value, and my governess was not insistent."

"I see."

"I learned a few words, but not enough to read or speak your language with any proficiency. I know *petit bâtard*."

Little bastard. "You learned *profanity*. From your governess."

"Of course not! I learned it from the milkman. He shouts at Cupid every time the *petit bâtard* rushes the door."

Xavier lifted a brow. Was she trying to distract him? If so, her tactic wasn't working. "I want the scoundrels' names."

"Whatever for? Do you fancy you will challenge them?" She shook her head and released a humorless laugh. "The gossips would love such fodder. It would keep them busy for days speculating on the nature of our association."

"If you truly believed I would take advantage of you or worried about rumors, you wouldn't have brought me to the gardens."

"I would if I wanted to confront you without an audience. Besides, no one knows we are here."

He shook his head and allowed a sinuous smile to ease across his face. She stiffened as he took a step forward.

"I can defend myself, sir."

"Even against seduction?" He slowly closed the distance between them.

The sharp intake of her breath and her hand on his chest gave him pause. A good fright might set her straight so she wouldn't act rashly again, but he didn't want her to fear him. He held still, waiting for the slightest pressure from her to demand his retreat.

Her fingers curled to lightly grip his jacket. She lifted her gaze and licked her lips. His heart slammed beneath her palm.

The warmth of her touch spread to his blood. It ran fast and hot through his veins, rushing to his cock.

Merde. Who was seducing whom? The temptation to touch her, to feel her lush mouth beneath his, strummed inside him. His body trembled with fading restraint. He stroked his thumb along the curve of her cheek and her lips parted. She desired his kiss as much as he hungered for hers, but surrendering would not prove he was different from the men who wanted to conquer her.

Nevertheless, her allure was powerful. He placed a kiss at her temple, lingering and savoring her sweet scent. "I think we are fortunate I don't want to seduce you, Miss Darlington."

She frowned when he drew back to look into her eyes. "Why not?"

Her affronted tone made him smile. "Because I want to court you."

"I don't welcome your courtship, Mr. Vistoire."

"Perhaps not." He slid his thumb over her protruding lower lip and a puff of warm breath fluttered over his skin. "But I think we both know you want to be in my bed as much as I want you there, and I will only take you as my wife."

The strength of his conviction shook him. Yes, he wanted to protect her and marriage was the most effective means, but he wanted much more from her. He hadn't realized what had been missing in his life until they had sparred that night at Wedmore House. He needed someone who understood him— someone who recognized when he was on the verge of taking the wrong path and challenged him to make the correct choice. And he was determined to be a better man, because he didn't deserve Regina otherwise.

"I don't want to marry you," she whispered as her eyes closed. She lifted her face as if seeking his kiss.

God, he wanted what she was offering in the worst way, but he would fail her if he surrendered to the temptation.

He released her and stumbled back a step. "If you don't want to be caught in the parson's noose, then you'd best return to the house before someone discovers us and forces your hand. I'd prefer to do this properly, but I suppose I would have you either way."

She dropped her hands to her sides and scowled. "I'll not welcome you at Wedmore House, so do not waste your time calling." Spinning on her heel, she stormed back toward the house.

"If you are half as welcoming as you were a moment ago, I'll have no cause for complaint."

"*Petit bâtard*," she tossed over her shoulder before disappearing from sight.

Xavier chuckled under his breath. Regina Darlington had fire in her. He could understand why the rakes were drawn to her like moths to a flame, but he'd be damned if they got within ten feet of her again.

Eleven

Regina rubbed the grittiness from her eyes the next morning as she descended the oak stairs at Wedmore House. She'd suffered another sleepless night, thanks to Xavier Vistoire and his preposterous claim that he wanted to marry her. Did he fancy himself in love after only a week?

"Ha," she scoffed, but an infinitesimal trill originated beneath her breastbone. She hugged herself to contain the exhilaration building inside her. Decisions shouldn't be based on the whims of one's body. She never ate a whole apple pie when her sweet tooth demanded satisfaction, and she wouldn't marry a blasted scoundrel just because her blood ran hotter when he was near. Besides, he'd probably want to take her back to America, and that would never do.

"Enough of Mr. Vistoire," she muttered and forced her thoughts to more pressing concerns. She had a household to run. Wedmore House was without a butler, which meant she had no one to turn away Mr. Vistoire if he called this afternoon. Much to her displeasure, she must face him again, for no matter how mortifying a future encounter might be, she wouldn't ask her sisters for help. Evangeline and Sophia would demand an explanation, and she'd rather cut out her tongue than admit to leading Mr. Vistoire into Lady Norwick's gardens only to accuse *him* of trying to seduce her.

She'd behaved like a lunatic last night, and Mr. Vistoire had responded with threats to make her his wife. She shook her head in bewilderment. He was battier than she if he showed up today.

Upon reaching the ground floor, she headed toward the library in search of her sister. Evangeline was helping her draft an advertisement for the vacant butler position this morning, and Regina hoped to drop it by the printer's shop in time for the advertisement to be included in tomorrow's newssheet. She found Evangeline exactly where she was most mornings—bent over papers fanned across the colossal mahogany table in the center of the library.

"What are you studying?" Regina asked.

Her sister's head shot up with a soft gasp. Her auburn hair was fashioned into a knot on top of her head, but several riotous ringlet curls had escaped to frame her face. "Nothing." She raked the papers into a pile with both hands, her gaze darting guiltily to the stack in front of her. "I mean, the same notes I've been studying. Nothing new."

Regina sauntered toward her. "Uncle Charles's notes on his Egyptian excavation?"

"Of course." Evangeline folded her hands on top of the stack as if trying to block Regina's view.

Before Sophia and Evangeline were born and Regina was still in nappies, Uncle Charles spent a year in Egypt racing against Napoleon's band of antiquarians to uncover Egyptian artifacts to claim for the British Museum. In the end, Uncle Charles didn't have much to show for the time he'd spent searching for tombs to raid, but he'd returned with a treasure trove of stories.

"You've read his pages a thousand times."

"I have," Evangeline said with a challenging tilt of her head, "and I remain fascinated by his records. They contain valuable information about the fine details of orchestrating a dig. If I want to go on my own expeditions some day, I must be prepared."

Even as young as four, Evangeline had perched on the edge of her seat with wide-eyed wonder, listening to Mama read from Uncle Charles's letters about his many adventures. Evangeline would come into her majority at the end of the summer and gain access to her inheritance just as Regina had a year and a half ago. Evangeline was already forming plans to travel with Uncle Charles, although Regina wasn't certain Aunt Beatrice would approve.

"You could recite his paper word for word. How could you be any more prepared?" Regina claimed the chair across from Evangeline and folded her hands on the table in front of her, mirroring her sister. "Do you remember how annoyed Papa would become when Mama spoke of Uncle Charles's bravery?"

Evangeline puffed out her chest and sputtered in a perfect imitation of their father. "Damned foolish, I'd say. It is a wonder your brother wasn't captured and killed. Papa never liked Uncle Charles, did he?"

Regina shrugged. "I think he disliked sharing Mama's admiration. Papa couldn't have been too conflicted about Uncle Charles, since he named him our guardian."

Evangeline grinned. "Perhaps because he disliked his own brother more."

Regina conceded the point. It didn't matter why their father had chosen Uncle Charles. He'd arranged for her and her sisters to have a home, and it was a happy one.

She glanced at the stack in front of Evangeline; her sister snatched up the papers and hugged them to her chest.

"Keep your secrets. If they make you happy, then I am happy."

Evangeline's mouth puckered. "You're just trying to make me feel guilty."

"I am not."

"You *are*. You trick me into telling you everything by making me feel bad for having secrets. You've been that way since we were girls."

Regina laughed at her sister's accusation. Perhaps it was partly true, but only because it was the easiest way to rattle Evangeline and uncover whatever mischief she was up to. Regina barely needed to say a word for her sister to tattle on herself.

"Oh, very well," Evangeline said with a huff. "I'm not studying his notes on Egypt again. I found these in Uncle Charles's top desk drawer."

"I thought he kept it locked."

Her sister's cheeks bloomed with color. "He does, but the letter opener was simply lying there, and I couldn't help myself."

"Evangeline!"

"I know. I've done a horrible thing."

Regina laughed. "Uncle Charles is more likely to be impressed by your nefarious activities than angry with you for picking the lock."

"Perhaps. I suppose if he didn't want me to use the skill, he wouldn't have taught me it."

"I doubt he ever thought you would use it against him." Regina leaned forward onto her elbows, curious about what her sister found. "What is it?"

"Something more exciting than mummies." Evangeline's blue eyes sparkled. "He is searching for an ancient band of mercenaries rumored to have lived at least 800 years ago. Crusaders first encountered the group in Dyrrchion, but there are tales from Rome to Antioch of violent altercations with the Black Death."

"The Black Death. Like the plague?" Regina wrinkled her nose. "Why on earth would any group choose such a horrid name?"

"It was given to them. According to Uncle Charles's research, the warriors were like ghosts slipping into a camp unseen and unheard then leaving death and devastation in their wake. But there was one account of a warrior entering a camp in the middle of the day to assassinate a rival tribe's chief. Needless to say, the warrior met his end as soon as he committed the deed."

Regina shivered in revulsion. "I will never understand your passion for warfare."

"I am not interested in war per se, but I cannot deny some ancient methods of warding off attacks were ingenious. For instance, did you know sand was often used to defend medieval castles? Not only could it stop invaders from climbing the walls, it made the enemy's armor itchy."

"That is rather brilliant," Regina admitted. "And less gruesome than your usual stories, which I don't care to hear, so let's change the subject."

"You asked what I was studying."

"My mistake." Regina was interested in one part, however. "Why would Uncle Charles search for a group of warrior assassins? Doesn't he realize he is no match?"

Evangeline flopped against the seatback and laughed. "The Black Death is extinct, silly, if they were ever real. Uncle Charles's notes say the group is likely a myth. He is looking for proof of their existence."

"Oh!" Regina brightened. "That is a relief. For a moment, I feared perhaps he hadn't returned yet, because he'd found them."

"I'm sure he is caught up in his work." Evangeline hopped up to retrieve a sheet of foolscap, inkpot, and a quill from a writing desk in the corner. "I have already composed the advertisement in my head. Let's get it on the page."

Regina offered suggestions for a different word here and there, but overall, Evangeline didn't need her input. Once her sister sanded the page and folded it, she passed it to Regina.

"Would you like me to accompany you?" Evangeline asked.

Regina shook her head. "Go back to your studies. I will have Joy walk with me."

It wasn't ideal to drag their maid away from her duties, but Regina couldn't go out alone. The *Morning Times* office was too far away for Aunt Beatrice to walk, and yet, it wasn't far enough to justify calling for the barouche.

Regina retrieved Joy from upstairs then collected her bonnet and gloves from the narrow table by the door. As she and the maid reached the front walkway, someone called out, "Good morning, Miss Darlington."

She jerked her head up and discovered Mr. Vistoire strolling in their direction with a walking stick in one hand and a blond-haired little boy who was no older than two, if that, snug in the crook of his arm. A young woman dressed in gray fustian trailed close behind.

The brass handle of Mr. Vistoire's walking stick glinted in the sunlight, and a sharp click accompanied each strike against the ground. Impractical white trousers skimmed his long legs and complemented the dark blue tailcoat he wore. Every inch of him from his beaver hat to polished black boots revealed his genteel upbringing.

"Mr. Vistoire." She eyed him warily as he approached. When he stopped in front of her and flashed his handsome smile, she turned her gaze on the boy. He shared Mr. Vistoire's rare green eyes, but the bow shape of his sweet little mouth and the serious slant of his dark blond brows marked him as Serafine Tucker's son—Mr. Vistoire's nephew. And he was just as adorable as Mr. Vistoire was handsome.

She crossed her arms to stifle the friendly feelings welling up inside her. "Good morning," she mumbled. She'd feared he would follow through with his threat to call on her, but she'd hoped for more time to fortify herself.

The little boy wrapped his arms around Mr. Vistoire's neck and laid his head on his shoulder. He popped his thumb in his mouth.

Blast. How was she supposed to remain aloof in the face of such a darling display of familial affection? The man was diabolical.

As if he could read her thoughts, he nuzzled his nephew's hair and grinned. "You don't seem surprised to see me."

"Why should I be, sir? You announced your intentions last night." And then his secret weapon was deployed. The little one gave her a shy smile that melted her heart. "Most suitors bring flowers, Mr. Vistoire. Perhaps you are wiser than most. I do hope you introduce me to this charming young lad."

"This is my sister's boy, Simon. He remarked on the lovely morning over breakfast and thought we should go for a walk. As you can see, his nanny and I are the ones doing the walking. Simon's legs grew too tired to carry him before we were out of sight of the house."

She couldn't help smiling at the boy, and Mr. Vistoire's exaggerated accounting of how they'd come to be outside Wedmore House. She highly doubted a child Simon's age was capable of verbalizing his wants so succinctly. "You are a smart boy, Simon. If I could manage it, I would have Mr. Vistoire carry me, too."

Mr. Vistoire's eyebrows shot up. "Perhaps if you asked nicely..."

"I meant if I were a child." Heat swept over her.

He shrugged as if it made no difference to him that she was grown. "I was under the impression it was impolite to pay calls this early."

She savored the sweet taste of victory. He'd passed her the perfect excuse to turn him away. "It is customary to call in the afternoon. Perhaps another day, Mr. Vistoire."

"I suppose it is fortunate it wasn't my intention to call on you this morning. Simon and I are on our way to feed the geese at the park." He directed his attention toward Simon's nanny. "Are you still in possession of the bread, Miss Lillywhite?"

"Yes, sir." The raven-haired young woman held up a white wicker basket as if inviting Regina to inspect it.

"Then we should be on our way. Good day, Miss Darlington." He tipped his hat to her.

"Good day," Simon echoed in his darling little voice, mashing the words together so they sounded like one.

Regina gaped after the small party as they continued their journey without a backward glance for her.

Joy sidled up to her to watch them march away. "I'm sure you could join them if you wanted."

"I most certainly will not." She swallowed to ease the unexpected ache in her throat. "Not without an invitation."

"I don't think the gentleman would complain," Joy said. "I saw the way he looked at you when he was a guest at Wedmore House."

"He wasn't a *guest*. He—" She glanced around the street to make sure no one had overheard then lowered her voice even though the street was deserted this early. "I only made his acquaintance last night. Please don't ever say otherwise."

Joy cast down her eyes. "Of course, miss. I was not thinking."

Regina sighed. She hadn't meant to sound scolding. "If it makes you feel better, he has a similar effect on me. I become a blithering idiot every time we meet. In truth, I'm relieved he didn't come to see me."

"I am sure you are, miss."

It was a lie. She knew it. Joy knew it. But they entered into a silent agreement to pretend otherwise and set off to complete Regina's errand.

Twelve

Xavier's step was a little livelier when he returned to Wedmore House that afternoon. The shocked expression on Miss Darlington's face when he'd told her that he wasn't there to see her still made laughter build up in his chest. Lady Luck had been with him this morning when Miss Darlington appeared on the walkway just as he was passing. He'd hoped she might catch a glimpse of him when he'd chosen to take that particular route to Hyde Park. An actual encounter was even better.

She wanted him, but she would never admit it unless her desire for him was greater than her damnable pride. In the short time that he'd known Regina Darlington, he'd discovered a couple of truths about her. She liked to remain in control, which would be difficult for her to accomplish if he refused to play by her rules.

He'd taken a gamble this morning by pretending he had no interest in seeing her when in reality, she'd stolen his breath. Every time he saw her, she grew more beautiful. He hoped his pretense had unbalanced her and left her less resistant to receiving him.

Secondly, she was a nurturer. The soft glow of her eyes when she'd looked at Simon only confirmed his opinion. A nurturer would not appreciate a bouquet that would perish in a few days, which was the reason he hadn't come with flowers. Instead, he had brought a plant.

Arriving at the double-hung black doors of Wedmore House, he shifted the potted orchid to his other arm and reached for the doorknocker only to snatch his hand back.

"*Sacre bleu!*" He blinked, studying the unusual design. For a second, he'd believed he was about to be struck by a serpent, but it was merely a harmless iron reproduction. He grabbed the snake's tail and knocked.

Several moments passed without an answer. He was reaching for the knocker again when the door drifted open, and Miss Darlington peeked through the crack.

"Mr. Vistoire, what are you doing here?"

He narrowed his eyes. "You are still without a butler. You promised to speak with Lord Margrave."

"I have the matter well in hand, not that it is any of your concern." She kept her body hidden behind the door. Her tongue nervously darted over her lips as her fingers tightened on the edge of the door.

"What are you doing in *there*?" He craned his neck to see what or whom she was hiding. If one of those blackguards she'd mentioned last night had shoved his way inside, Xavier would toss him out on his bum. "Who is in there with you?"

"No one. I wasn't expecting visitors." She frowned. "Including you. I thought you decided against calling today."

"I never said I had changed my mind, Miss Darlington. I was simply waiting for an acceptable time." He lifted to his toes to peer over her head and into the foyer, unconvinced everything was in order like she said.

She opened the door wider and pushed her hand against his shoulder. Her amber green eyes sparked with ire. "Stop spying on me. What do you want?"

Finding the hall behind her empty, he dropped his guard. Tension drained from his body, and an indulgent smile spread across his lips. "You," he drawled.

"*Me*? What about me?" She stepped back and flung the door open. "You might as well come inside. Lingering on the stoop all day is going to set tongues wagging."

A shrill bark echoed off the domed ceiling and the rapid click of nails against the marble floor sounded in the room.

"Oh, no!" Miss Darlington grabbed Xavier by the front of his waistcoat and ineffectively tugged. "Hurry! He's coming."

Her panicked tone spurred him into action. He slipped inside Wedmore House, and she slammed the door just as Cupid launched himself at them. The dog crashed into Xavier's shins and fell on his side with a yelp, but he was back on his feet in no time. Hopping on his hind legs, Cupid clawed at Xavier's new trousers. The little dog's pink tongue flopped from the side of his mouth and saliva dripped onto Xavier's boots.

"Cupid, no!" Miss Darlington grabbed for the poodle, but he skittered out of her reach. "Blast!"

She straightened and her hands landed on her hips. "Mind your manners, you little beast."

Cupid barked several times as if defending his actions before returning to jump up on Xavier and drown his boots in drool. A rancid odor assaulted Xavier's sensibilities. He covered his mouth and nose to block the smell. "Good Lord! What is that stench?"

"I'm not sure. Cupid either rolled in the neighbor's freshly fertilized flower beds or found something dead." Miss Darlington wrinkled her nose. "Perhaps both. I was preparing to give him a b-a-t-h before you arrived."

"Give him *two* baths. He smells disgusting."

The dog ceased trying to climb Xavier's legs. His ears flattened, and a deep-throated growl came from the bundle of black curls.

"Splendid. Now I'll never get him in the b-a-t-h."

"Why are you spelling bath?"

Cupid snarled and snapped. Xavier leapt back in surprise, bumping into the door at his back.

"Because Cupid knows that word and hates what it *means*. He's a devil to catch if he knows what is in store for him." She lunged for the dog and collapsed on her hands and knees when he shot out of her grasp. Cupid tore down the narrow corridor leading to the back of the house. The housekeeper was exiting a room as he zipped past, and she screeched.

"So sorry, Mrs. Cox," Miss Darlington called.

The woman pursed her lips, but said nothing as she moved on with her bucket and mop.

Miss Darlington sighed. "It is no use. We'll have to tolerate the smell until Aunt Beatrice returns."

"How long will that be?"

She sat on her haunches. "She and Sophia are attending Lady Chattington's garden party. I suppose it depends on how much Sophia is enjoying herself."

If the layout of the house matched the drawing he'd received, the library was located toward the back of the house. He knew how he was going to search for the map.

"That is entirely too long." He offered his hand, juggling the plant to keep it from being crushed between them as he pulled her to her feet. Once she'd gained her balance, he held out his gift. "For you. Perhaps you could find a safe place for it while I give chase."

She accepted the potted orchid with a smirk. "Good luck. I'll be in the drawing room when you have discovered it is a hopeless cause."

"Nothing is hopeless, my dear."

After two years of captivity, he was a free man. Hope had gotten him this far, and he didn't intend to abandon it now.

He deposited his hat and gloves on the table in the foyer and strolled along the corridor, whistling for the dog in order to hide the fact he was actually snooping around Wedmore House. Multicolored woven carpets laid end to end muffled his footsteps as he moved deeper into the house. Sunlight spilled through the massive leaded window at the end of the passage, making navigation easy.

The first doorway he reached opened to another passageway. He'd likely find Lord Wedmore's study if he followed it. If there was time, he could search the earl's private space next, but he would start with the library.

"Cupid," he called absently while taking in as many details about the house as possible. Although he hoped for more opportunities to search for the map during the daytime, he needed to be prepared in case he had no other option besides breaking in again.

As he neared an open door at the end of the corridor, an oddly familiar and pleasing musty smell infused the air. Inside, floor to ceiling shelves lined the walls, and each shelf was crammed with leather bound books. A vacant table dominated the center of the room, and a bow window with stained glass panels projected trapezoids in shades of green and blue onto the hardwood floor. Charles Wedmore's personal library was one of the most impressive Xavier had ever seen. The earl must have collected thousands of books.

"*Merde*," he muttered. That meant there were thousands of places to hide a map. Where should he even begin? The small writing desk by the bow window seemed the most obvious place to search, and therefore, the most unlikely place to hide something one didn't want found. Still, it was a start.

He walked toward it, knowing he didn't have time to waste.

"Are you looking for Cupid?"

Xavier startled and spun toward the sound. Evangeline Darlington was tucked into a corner, high up on a ladder with a book in her hand. His good fortune had run out.

He offered a friendly smile. "*Oui*. Your sister said he is in need of a b-a-t-h."

"Very badly in need of one. Let me shelve this, then I can help you search." She stretched across the shelf, standing on her toes and grasping the ladder with one hand as she slid the book into an empty spot.

"Did he come in here?" Xavier winced as she scrambled down the ladder and nearly fell. She caught herself and made it to the ground unharmed.

"I didn't see him, but I know how to lure him from wherever he's hiding." She pulled a couple of books from a shelf and withdrew a small tin that had been hidden behind them. "Biscuits," she announced then shook the container.

Cupid heard the rattle and darted out from under the desk to claim a treat. She scooped him into her arms before feeding him a biscuit. Scratching his head, she made a face. "The stink has gotten worse, if that's even possible." She thrust the poodle into his arms. "Hold tightly to him, or he will break free. He is famous for his daring escapes."

Xavier smiled. "Another thing we have in common," he said under his breath. He wouldn't be searching the library today. God only knew how he'd ever find an excuse to search Lord Wedmore's study or chambers above stairs. He nodded toward the books. "Your uncle keeps an impressive library. I've had no access to a good library for some time, and I miss reading."

"You are welcome to return and select a book whenever you like. Uncle Charles wouldn't mind."

Perhaps his luck hadn't abandoned him after all. "*Merci*. I accept your kind invitation and will return soon. For now, however, your sister needs my assistance."

Tucking the dog under his arm, he bade her good-bye and headed back to the drawing room. Miss Darlington glanced up from her place on the settee. Her jaw dropped. "How did you catch him?"

"A man must keep some secrets. Where are you planning to do the deed?"

"I set up a small tub on the veranda." She pushed up from the settee and came to hold her arms out for Cupid. "I'll take him. Thank you."

"I have him." Xavier hugged the dog and nearly gagged from the stench, but he refused to relinquish his captive. "Show me the way, and I will stay to assist."

"Absolutely not. I don't require your help."

He lifted the little dog as evidence to the contrary, and Cupid's wet tongue swiped across his cheek. "Either show me to the veranda, or I will find it myself."

She crossed her arms, her chin lifting an inch.

"Very well." Turning on his heel, he stalked from the drawing room.

"Wait." The patter of her slippers told him she trailed behind.

He didn't stop. Her refusal suited his mission, although it vexed him greatly. Taking the other corridor he'd found earlier would allow him to explore the house further.

"Mr. Vistoire, would you please slow your step?"

He gave no indication he heard her and entered the passageway. The first door he encountered was closed, but the second stood ajar and revealed a small sitting room with another bow window draped in luxurious green brocade with gold fringe. He was guessing Lord Wedmore's study rested behind the closed door.

"Mr. Vistoire, *please.*" Miss Darlington's desperate plea caused him to draw up short. She closed the distance between them and rested her hand on his forearm. Her touch sent a jolt racing up his arm. "You will ruin your clothes if you insist on helping me."

Oui. That was likely to be the outcome, but the harder she tried to push him away, the more determined he was to stay by her side.

He leaned closer to whisper into her ear. "I'm happy to remove as many articles as necessary to alleviate your worry, darling."

The soft intake of her breath made him smile. "Perhaps only your coat and cravat."

Thirteen

Regina concentrated on lathering Cupid's fur as best as she could, all the while mindful of Mr. Vistoire's bare forearms. His muslin shirt had become translucent and plastered to his chest after the dog nearly escaped from the washtub.

"Not much longer, sweetheart," she crooned to the dog as another tremor shook his small body.

"He couldn't be cold, could he?" Mr. Vistoire's hairline was damp from exertion, causing his dark brown hair to curl at the ends.

"No, he is melodramatic."

Cupid was being especially uncooperative with his bath, and she was grateful Mr. Vistoire had insisted on helping her. "Ah, he has a future on stage. That explains why he's behaving like a diva."

She sent a sidelong glance toward him where he knelt beside her and rinsed her hands in the water. "Have you known many divas?"

"A couple, as well as several actresses."

Cupid made another attempt to bolt from the tub, but Mr. Vistoire's strong hands clamped around his sides to thwart the dog's plans. Lean, golden brown muscles bulged in Mr. Vistoire's forearms, and water droplets clung to the dusting of dark hair. Her gaze followed the map of veins traveling up his arms, disappearing beneath his rolled up shirtsleeves. The sensuous display of masculinity held her as still as the dog.

"Are you ready to rinse?" he asked, spurring her into action.

"Tip his head up." She grabbed the small pail and carefully poured clean water over Cupid, avoiding his eyes. Once the suds were washed away, she pushed to her feet to retrieve a bath sheet that was draped over the bench. She held out her arms to take Cupid. Mr. Vistoire surrendered the dripping dog, and she swaddled him in the bath sheet, cuddling him like an infant.

Mr. Vistoire rubbed the dog's head with an end of the bath sheet, standing close enough for his scent to tease her. Hints of bergamot and cocoa, and something spicy she couldn't identify.

"Why didn't you join your aunt and sister at Lady Chattington's garden party?" he asked. "You obviously were not waiting around for me to call."

She sat on the bench and hugged the little dog to soothe him, and perhaps herself. Her legs were shaking as much as Cupid was. "I see no reason to attend social gatherings unless Sophia needs a companion."

"Why not?" He joined her on the bench, foiling her attempt to put distance between them.

"Because I am not looking for a husband."

"Hmm..." He reached to scratch Cupid's chin, his thigh pressing against hers. "Have you always wanted to remain unmarried?"

She shrugged. "Not always."

"What changed your mind?"

"I'm not sure, but I have made my decision. Aunt Beatrice never married, and she is happy with her circumstances. I will be as well."

"You don't want to have children?" He nodded toward Cupid, who she still held like he was a babe. "You are a natural caretaker."

A pang throbbed in the center of her chest, but it was gone in an instant. "I will take care of my family. Aunt Beatrice requires some assistance now, and eventually Uncle Charles will need someone to manage his household and see that he his cared for."

Mr. Vistoire's head almost touched hers as he stretched to scratch behind Cupid's ears. The dog closed his eyes and blissfully panted. "And what about after your great-aunt and your uncle are gone? Will you live alone?"

Alone? Her stomach clenched, and she forced her thoughts away from Aunt Beatrice and Uncle Charles growing old and leaving her some day.

"I will help Sophia. She will make a match and have children. My sister will welcome me if I need a new home some day." She hoped Sophia's future husband would as well. "What about you? You must be thirty."

"Nine and twenty, but I lost two years, so theoretically, I'm younger than my age."

"How does anyone lose two years? That makes no sense."

He cocked an eyebrow. "Doesn't it? Perhaps your own nonsensical reasoning is influencing my thinking."

"*My* reasoning is perfectly rational."

"If you say it is..."

"I do, and I think you are still suffering the effects of bumping your head." She swiveled toward him on the bench. "Why have you never married, Mr. Vistoire? Even before adjusting your age due to misplacing a couple of years, you were old enough to have a wife."

"True enough." He retreated to his half of the bench to rest his hands on his thighs. "I didn't have the funds to support a wife. My father disinherited me and left everything to my sister."

"Oh, dear. I am sorry. I didn't mean to pry."

He waved away her concern. "You should know as much as possible about the man courting you. I don't mind."

"You aren't courting me."

"I am, but we will agree to disagree on that point."

She smiled even though she knew it would only encourage him. "No, we won't. Why would your father disown you, if you don't mind my asking?"

"I wasn't the son he wanted. I did not approach life with the appropriate amount of somberness, and I relied on my charm rather than hard work. That was his opinion of me."

She glanced at his ruined white trousers and smiled. "Well, you are charming, Mr. Vistoire, but the stains on your knees do not suggest laziness. In fact, it is rather uncouth in London for a gentleman to even give the appearance of having engaged in labor. I am grateful for your help, however."

He grinned. "I suppose I should have been born an English nobleman. Perhaps in my next life."

"Yes, you really must make better plans in the future." Her smile faded as she considered what he'd shared. "If you were hoping to increase your wealth through marriage, I'm afraid you will be disappointed. My income is modest, but I must admit to enjoying having it at my disposal. I do not need a husband to make decisions on my behalf."

"And I'm not in need of a wealthy wife. After our father's estate was settled, Serafine insisted on restoring what had been promised to me. The property, house, and its contents belong to me, but I couldn't allow her to give away everything."

"You provided her with a dowry."

"We divided our father's riches evenly. It is her fortune to use as she pleases."

Regina inhaled sharply in surprise. "To live independently?"

"If she'd wanted to make that life for herself, I wouldn't have stood in her way, but she wanted Isaac Tucker. Now she has Simon too, and she wants more children some day."

Regina really wished that blasted twinge in her heart would go away.

"In the spirit of being completely honest," he said, "I wasted most of my inheritance before I left New Orleans. I won back the majority of it at the gaming tables. In addition, my accounts earned interest over the last couple of years and increased substantially. I am solvent, and I plan to stay that way, so I've given up gambling. Nevertheless, I wouldn't want you to fret over handing control of your inheritance to a man with my history. I wouldn't ask you to surrender it if you agreed to become my wife."

"Oh." She didn't quite know how to respond to his candid revelation. The few gentlemen who had tried to court her had spent their time boasting of their accomplishments. Never once had any gentleman mentioned his shortcomings. "Thank you for your honesty."

"I know it is important, especially since the circumstances of our initial meeting were less than ideal." He reached a hand toward Cupid, and the dog licked his fingers, but Xavier's gaze was locked to her mouth. His scrutiny made her insides jittery and she swallowed hard. "Is he dry enough?" His voice had turned husky.

"Your shirt is soaked. Uncle Charles will have one you may borrow." She hopped from the bench. "I'll retrieve it."

"I know the way." He bounded to his feet, snatched his discarded attire, and followed her toward the house. "Why don't you see that Cupid is settled, and I will change in your uncle's chambers? If you don't think he would mind."

They stopped just inside the town house's rear door, and she allowed herself one more sweeping gaze of his torso. Uncle Charles wouldn't be thrilled with the prospect of a stranger in his bedchamber, but she couldn't send Mr. Vistoire on his way with his shirt molded to every hard plane of his chest. She could even see a smattering of dark hair through the thin material. The neighbors would wonder what they had been up to, and if she'd learned one truth about the *ton*, it was that they had wicked imaginations.

A prickly heat invaded her body as her own imagination took an inappropriate detour. "Very well, but please be quick. Aunt Beatrice and Sophia could return earlier than expected, and I don't want my aunt to find you above stairs."

"I promise to do my best." She caught the flash of a grin a heartbeat before he swooped down to place a peck on her cheek. She turned toward his kiss, but he withdrew and was brushing past her before she could get her bearings.

Cupid scrambled to be released, so she placed him on the floor and went to find Cook in the kitchen.

"Please prepare a pot of tea and a plate of biscuits," she said. "I will be entertaining Mr. Vistoire in the drawing room."

Cook's eyes flew open wide when she caught sight of Regina.

Regina brushed a hand over the large dark splotch on her gown as if she could erase it. "I should change gowns first."

"Yes, miss. I will put the kettle over the fire."

"Thank you."

She made one more trip to the library to enlist Evangeline to join them for tea, then hurried to her chamber to change before Mr. Vistoire was dressed and began to look for her below stairs. She chose an apron front gown in peach for the ease and rushed from her chambers only to discover Uncle Charles's door was still closed. Moving closer, she listened for sounds coming from within and heard the squeak of a drawer followed by a quick slam. What in the world was Mr. Vistoire doing in there?

She rapped on the door. "Were you able to find something to fit? Do you need assistance?"

"*Oui.* One moment, *s'il vous plaît.*"

Muffled sounds continued to emanate from behind the door. He was taking much longer than she'd anticipated. She knocked again.

"Mr. Vistoire, please come out. Aunt Beatrice and—"

The door swung inward suddenly, and he was there in the threshold. Much too close and every bit as handsome dressed in a shirt that was too big for him. She peered into the chamber. "Did you find everything you needed?"

He frowned slightly and held up his damp shirt. "I'm unsure what to do with my soiled one. Carrying it across town would look conspicuous."

"Oh! I will take it and make sure it is laundered. Joy will deliver it after laundry day." He passed the wet garment to her, then waited in the corridor until she'd returned from placing it in her chambers.

Evangeline met them downstairs. Regina had just poured tea into the Limoges cups when Aunt Beatrice and Sophia returned home. Aunt Beatrice made a fuss over Mr. Vistoire's visit, declaring it a pleasant surprise indeed and sent Sophia for two more teacups and saucers, so they could join the small party.

Regina sat back to observe Mr. Vistoire with her family. He *was* charming—she couldn't deny it—but he was also genuinely kind to her sisters and aunt. By the end of his call, she had begun to feel more at ease in his presence.

She and Aunt Beatrice saw him to the door. With his hat in hand, he addressed Regina's aunt. "Miss Allred, I would be honored if you and your nieces would join my family and me for a picnic lunch in the park tomorrow."

Aunt Beatrice beamed. "How lovely. We accept."

Regina rolled her eyes, but she wasn't truly put out with him for using Aunt Beatrice to circumvent her. She had enjoyed his company today. If he'd extended the invitation to her, she might have accepted, although her position on marriage had not budged—not much, anyway. His mention of children had caused her to sway a bit, but it had been a momentary lapse.

"Good afternoon, sir."

"Good day, Miss Darlington." He gallantly took her hand to place a kiss on her lace glove. "Until tomorrow."

Fourteen

Xavier returned to his sister's town house to change clothes after the pleasant and somewhat productive afternoon spent in Miss Darlington's company.

Pleasant because she hadn't slammed the door in his face. Somewhat productive since he'd been able to steer their conversation toward marriage without her trying to drown him in the washtub.

They shared an undeniable attraction, and even though she couldn't see it yet, their temperaments were well suited. He didn't want a wife molded into a proper miss. He wanted one who delighted him with her uncensored views and independent pursuits. Regina was a type of lady he hadn't known existed.

Given enough time, he expected he could prove himself trustworthy and break through her resistance to marriage. Unfortunately, time was not a luxury he had. Perhaps he should tell her the true reason he'd broken into Wedmore House—despite the threats made to her and her family—and pray she would see the wisdom in coming under his protection.

He would have to tell her eventually if he hoped to have the type of marriage he desired, but he worried she would use his confession to support her unfavorable opinion of him and toss him from Wedmore House. He couldn't risk losing the small gains made today when time was running out. On the other hand, he could lose her forever if he made the wrong decision.

There was much to mull over before the picnic. He'd fabricated the outing on the spot and hoped his sister would agree to it without giving him too much grief. He would introduce the topic over dinner, but he wished to pay an early visit to Covent Gardens to ask about an actress he'd befriended two years ago.

He didn't know if Claudine Bellerose had remained in London after his disappearance—for her sake, he hoped she hadn't—but if she'd stayed, she might have overheard something that could lead him to the person responsible for his incarceration.

Serafine spotted him as he reached the ground floor and passed the drawing room. "Are you leaving again?"

Xavier stopped short then returned to stand at the threshold. His sister was perched on the edge of an upholstered chair, her back as rigid as if her spine had been replaced with a lightening rod. A leather bound book rested on her lap. Her husband Isaac's blond head remained bent over his desk where he was carefully marking lines on a large sheet of paper.

Over breakfast, Serafine had explained how Isaac's family disowned him when he married her, so he had discovered a way to earn his keep and support his wife and child without his father's fortune. He had become a draftsman in secret, adopting an alias to keep his identity hidden. Isaac Tucker posed as the go-between for the reclusive and highly acclaimed Mr. Dixon and the gentlemen who wished to hire him. Since Isaac had no part in handling money, he maintained a respectable standing in Society for Serafine and Simon's welfare. The more Xavier learned of his brother-in-law, the more he respected the man.

"I have an errand to tend," Xavier said. "I will be back before dinner."

"An errand?" Her thin brows rose on her forehead. "You were out all afternoon. Why didn't you see to your business earlier?"

Years ago, the suspicion in her tone would have instigated a row between them. Now her inquiry caused a bittersweet smile to cross his face. Two years with no contact altered his view of her interest in his affairs. She was worried. He came into the drawing room to sit for a moment to show his values had changed. He was no longer the reprobate who chose sinful pleasures over his family. He would never be that man again.

Isaac glanced up from his drawing. "Would you like a private moment together?"

Serafine shook her head. "You should be aware that I keep nothing from Isaac," she said to Xavier.

"Nor would I ask you to." Xavier flashed his most disarming smile. "I did not attend to my business earlier, because I was otherwise engaged. Last night I met a young woman. Miss Darlington."

His sister's eyes expanded. "Oh?"

"Do you recall I partnered with an older woman for the waltz? Miss Darlington is her niece."

"Yes, I know of both ladies." Her back lost some of its stiffness and her lips turned up slightly at the corners. "I didn't see you speaking with her. In fact, I lost sight of you for a while."

"I lingered in the refreshment room for a time. We must have missed one another." He cleared his throat and reassured himself that lying to protect a lady's reputation was less damning than one told for personal gain. "Miss Darlington and I find we have much in common, and she was agreeable to me calling on her this afternoon."

A full smile lit Serafine's face. "How lovely. Will you call on her again?"

"Mmm," he muttered vaguely while he debated when to tell his sister about committing her to an outing without having consulted her. If he dallied much longer, the actresses would be ready to go on stage, and he would have to wait to ask after Claudine. But his sister appeared so hopeful that he might be settling down, and he wanted to please her. "I'm afraid I overstepped my bounds and invited Miss Darlington and her family to join us for a picnic tomorrow. I should have spoken to you first, but—"

Serafine held up a hand to stop him. "I don't mind. We haven't picnicked together since before Mother died. I will look forward to it."

"As will I," Isaac said, "and Simon loves the park, as I am sure you discovered this morning."

Xavier was surprised by how quickly the boy had taken to him. Serafine believed talking about Xavier since Simon was a babe had played a role. Sixteen months seem too young for the boy to grasp a word of what Xavier's sister had likely said about him, but Serafine was happy they got on well. And so was Xavier.

"Then it is settled," Xavier said, smacking his hands against his thighs before pushing to his feet. "As I mentioned earlier, I have an errand to run, so if you will excuse me..."

"Of course." Serafine lifted her book to continue reading. "Be certain to choose something nice for Miss Darlington."

A gift was a splendid suggestion. *Make it two errands.* He bade his sister and her husband good-bye then secured a hack to carry him to the theatre.

As he'd walked home from Wedmore House earlier, he'd reflected on his stay in London before his abduction. He had spent a good deal of time being entertained by actresses, both from the stage and in their dressing rooms.

Claudine hadn't been one of his offstage entertainers. She'd been a quiet sort who mostly kept to her dressing room, and the gents who frequented the theatre had known to leave her be. Claudine Bellerose had belonged to a duke.

Xavier kept his distance as well in the beginning. She seemed to have made a comfortable life for herself, and he hadn't wanted to cause any trouble. He had appreciated her talent, however, and became as captivated during her performances as everyone else in the audience.

The Duke of Stanhurst had been careful never to leave evidence of his mistreatment of his mistress in places where others could see, but Xavier began to notice the dwindling light in the actress's beautiful blue eyes. Perhaps he'd recognized her defeated spirits, because he'd experienced his own moments of hopelessness over the years when his father's hatred of him had reared its head. Xavier had been unable to ignore her suffering.

One evening, he'd approached Claudine in the Grand Saloon at the Theatre Royal to offer his congratulations on her splendid performance. The duke stood guard not far away, but he was otherwise occupied. Stanhurst was known for his jealousy and rarely allowed Claudine to venture from his side, but his duchess had accompanied him that evening. Xavier had raised Claudine's delicate hand as if to place a courteous kiss on her glove and instead whispered his offer of help in the native language they shared.

Several days later, she had approached him backstage and asked if he could help her reach Vienna where a fellow actress she knew would offer her lodging. He and Claudine were to sail as far as France together, then she planned to travel on to Vienna, and he was to sail home to New Orleans.

The morning after he'd been taken, she would have been waiting with her trunks for him to collect her, nervous and eager about what her life would be like in Vienna. In his heart, Xavier hoped the actress had escaped her lover without his help. Nevertheless, if she had stayed in London, he would like to speak with her. He needed someone who might be able to help him make sense of the last two years of his life.

The hack rolled to a stop outside the Theatre Royal by way of Russell Street, ending his musings on the past. He paid the driver and approached the stage door used by the players and crew. The main doors would not open to theatre patrons for a couple of hours, but the actors, actresses, and stage crew had much to do before a performance.

A stage door keeper with biceps the size of hams and a puffy red scar extending from the corner of his mouth to his temple glanced up as Xavier approached.

"Good evening," Xavier said and passed him two shillings.

The man accepted the offering with a satisfied grin before stepping aside to allow Xavier access to the theatre. Stage door keepers were hired to chase away undesirables and encouraged to look in the other direction when gentlemen arrived at the door.

Xavier stopped inside the shadowy bowels of the theatre to get his bearings. The stagnant air reeked of perspiration and mildew, just as he remembered. In the trap room beneath the stage, two stagehands were arguing over a misplaced feather prop and paid him no notice, so he headed for the stairs leading to the dressing rooms a floor above.

Laughter spilled down the dark stairwell and greeted him at the landing. In the corridor, a woman dressed in only her shift was flittering from room to room calling, "Who has the pot of lip rouge? I need it *now*."

"Go away," another woman called from one of the dressing rooms. "Wait your turn."

"It's not for me. Madame Parma is asking for it."

The blond pixie disappeared for a few moments then shot back into the corridor with the lip rouge clutched in her hand. She eyed him curiously as she sped in his direction. He expected her to sweep past to complete her task, but she stopped in front of him.

"I remember you." She drew out the last word and aimed a flirtatious smile at him. "If you haven't come for anyone specific, I have a few moments to spare."

He nodded toward the hand holding the lip rouge. "Isn't Madame Parma expecting you?"

"She won't keep me long. She likes her *privacy*," she said with an exaggerated accent that he suspected was meant to sound mockingly sophisticated.

A few of the other actresses wandered into the corridor.

"I see," he said. "Well, thank you for the offer, but I've come to inquire about Claudine Bellerose? Is she still an actress with the theatre?"

The diminutive girl lifted her turned up nose. "I have never heard of her, but I am sure she is a talentless, old hag."

"Zoe, you know very well who Claudine is," one of the older women grumbled. She spoke with a thick Austrian accent. "Stop being petty and take him to Madame Parma. She will know Claudine's address, sir."

Xavier thanked the woman then followed the blond below stairs to Madame Parma's larger dressing room closer to the stage. Zoe took a deep breath, released it slowly, and knocked on the door. "Madame Parma, I've brought the lip rouge you requested." Her words dripped with sweetness now.

"Enter," an imperious voice said from the other side of the door.

Zoe raised her finger to her lips, signaling him to stay quiet. "Let me talk to her first," she whispered. "She doesn't like being interrupted before a performance."

He gave a sharp nod. She slipped inside the room and closed the door. A muffled conversation ensued for several moments, and he was beginning to grow impatient with the wait when the door flew open.

Zoe smiled sweetly. "She will see you now."

The door swung open fully, and he was met with the sight of Madame Parma perched on a gold velvet fainting couch. Her deep auburn hair was piled high on her head, and emerald earbobs swayed with her slightest movement. "You've interrupted my meditation, Mr. Vistoire."

She remembered him.

"My apologies, Madame. It is a matter of importance. Otherwise, I would not have come."

One pointed glare from the leading lady sent the pixie scrambling for the corridor. The door closed with a soft snick, and they were alone.

She reclined on the fainting couch, causing the white satin wrapper she wore to slide from her shoulder to reveal the plump swell of her bare breast. "Would you care to join me?"

"*Merci,* but I do not practice meditation." Xavier knew the real meaning of her invitation, but his days of dallying with actresses were finished. "I will be brief, so you may return to your preparations for the evening. I am searching for Claudine Bellerose. The women above stairs were under the impression you might know of her whereabouts."

Madame Parma pulled the wrapper tight around her and laid her head against the couch. "You cannot blame me for trying. My days at center stage are dwindling, and every actress is in the market for a benefactor. I've grown intolerant of hunger these last few years."

Xavier smiled in appreciation of her flair for drama.

"I am afraid Claudine gave up the stage some time ago," she said. "She has become a ladybird kept in a gilded cage."

"Does that cage have an address?"

"It does, Mr. Vistoire. I will not share it with you, however."

"And why is that, Madame Parma?"

All traces of congeniality faded, and the actress's icy gaze narrowed on him. "Because you *betrayed* her. She was waiting for you, but you never arrived. When Stanhurst discovered her trunks, he knew she was lea—" Her voice cracked. She took a deep breath to compose herself. "She was leaving him, and he became furious. If you had seen what he'd done to her..."

A sour taste rose at the back of his throat. "Perhaps I can still help her. Please, tell me where she is."

"What is to keep you from breaking your word again?"

He came to the side of the fainting couch to appeal to the actress. "I didn't leave without her. I was set upon the night before we were to sail, and Claudine might have information that would lead to the person responsible."

"Claudine is not a criminal, sir, nor does she associate with them. I fail to see how she could be of any assistance."

Xavier sighed. "I know she wasn't involved, but perhaps she heard something. Maybe she questioned others about my disappearance. There is a chance she knows something without realizing its relevance. I would like to speak with her. Whether you believe me, I'm sincere in my wish to help her break free of Stanhurst. She doesn't deserve to be mistreated. Please, tell me where to find her."

Madame Parma shook her head. "If the duke catches her trying to leave again, he might kill her this time, and I cannot be responsible. She is my friend. If you want to save her, forget you ever knew her and keep your distance."

Perhaps she was correct about his presence placing Claudine in more danger, but he couldn't walk away without her at least knowing the truth. "Could you give her a message? Tell her I'm sorry. I didn't abandon her willingly."

"I can grant you that, Mr. Vistoire. I will make a point of calling on her soon and delivering your message."

"*Merci.*" He started for the door.

"Do you love her? Is that the reason you refused my offer?"

He glanced back over his shoulder. "Claudine and I shared a friendship. She is a good woman who deserves a better life."

"But you are not in love with her."

"No."

"Then perhaps you made your decision in haste." Madame Parma slid the wrapper from her shoulders, baring herself to him. The satin puddled around her waist. "I rarely extend an invitation more than once, Mr. Vistoire."

She was practiced at seduction and temptation. Most likely, she never needed to ask twice.

"There is someone else," he admitted and stalked from the dressing room without hesitation. The only woman he wanted was Regina—his tenderhearted, strong, willful goddess.

It was dark when he exited the building, then everything went black when his hat was knocked to the ground and a sack was shoved over his head. Two men grabbed his biceps and hooked their arms around his thighs. He was airborne for a brief moment before he landed on a hard surface.

"Where is my bloody map?"

Merde. "You again." Xavier pulled off the sack and glowered at Farrin from his position on the carriage floor. One of the blackguard's men shoved his way inside and dropped on the bench beside his boss. The carriage lurched away from the curb.

"Was this necessary?" Xavier shook the sack in his fist.

Farrin smirked. "I thought you'd enjoy the theatrics."

"You ruin my enjoyment of everything. What the devil do you want now?" He pushed off the floor and sat on the carriage bench opposite.

"You've been strolling through the park, attending balls, visiting the theatre. What you have not been doing is retrieving my map. You have four days, Mr. Vistoire."

Xavier glowered at Farrin and the brute sitting next to him. "I am well aware the sand is slipping through the hour glass. I hope you don't intend to interrupt my plans every day to remind me."

"What exactly are your plans?

"And stop having me followed," Xavier said, ignoring his inquiry. "One of the Darlington sisters is likely to notice your men lurking about and think he is with me. I could lose access to Wedmore House and the map."

Farrin's eyebrows shot up on his forehead. "You clever devil. You think you can seduce your way into the earl's home. Which lady has her eye on you?"

"Who is responsible for my incarceration?"

Farrin's eyes hardened. "Some questions are better never being explored. If you were seeking clues at the theatre, you were wasting your time. Count your blessings you are still alive and pray that you stay that way."

"Likewise," Xavier said through clenched teeth. "I need more time to search for the map. I was able to access Lord Wedmore's chambers today, and I've been invited to borrow a book from his library any time I wish."

Farrin's expression remained impassive for several moments. Eventually, he gave a sharp nod. "You have a week from today, but no longer. If I don't have the map by then, you are no longer any use to me and I will send in my own man."

Xavier would have liked more time, but he'd been afforded room to breathe. "Splendid. Now have your driver stop and let me out. I'm expected for dinner."

Farrin nodded toward his man who lunged across the carriage and grabbed Xavier around the neck, trying to choke him. Xavier landed a punch to the side of the brute's head, but it didn't slow him. He jerked Xavier from the bench and opened the carriage door.

"Wait," Farrin called. He reached into Xavier's jacket and withdrew his purse. "Now."

His henchman shoved Xavier from the moving carriage. He rolled on impact with the cobbled street and scrambled to his feet as another carriage barreled toward him. He dove for the walkway and felt the rush of wind from the Berlin as it flew by without the driver even trying to slow his team.

Gradually, he picked himself up from the deserted walkway and looked down at the hole in the knee of his trousers. *Blast and damn!* The tailor had charged Xavier a fortune to attire him quickly so he could rejoin Society, and he would require a new wardrobe by the week's end if he continued at this rate. And he'd lost his hat!

He dusted off his trousers and glanced at his surroundings, trying to determine where he was and how to make his way back to his sister's home. Farrin had left him in a neighborhood with modest homes and no lights burning in the windows. He set off for home, limping for a bit until the initial pain of impact began to fade.

Xavier felt like he wandered the streets forever before he finally recognized a landmark. It took another half hour to make his way home without the money to hire a hack.

He was going to find that bloody map, and when he did, he would use it as leverage to learn who was responsible for stealing two years of his life. Then he would track down whoever had hired Farrin to retrieve the map and was placing his and Regina's families in danger. In the end, he would see all of the men dead.

When he walked in the house, Serafine met him at the door. "Where have you been? You missed dinner, and I've sent Isaac to look for you." Her face flushed and her eyes took on a feverish glow as she ran her gaze over him. "Would you look at yourself? Please tell me you are not gambling again."

He sighed, knowing his appearance wasn't helping to convince his sister that he had mended his ways. "I wasn't at a gaming hell. I was at the theatre. Footpads attacked me as I was leaving Covent Garden and took my money." He opened his jacket and pointed to his empty pocket. "I had to return on foot and I became lost for a while. I'm sorry I missed dinner."

She bit her bottom lip and her green eyes misted. "I want to believe you. I want your change to be real."

He captured his sister's hands between his. "It is real, Sera. I am a different man. Even more than you want to believe in me,

I want to be worthy of your faith." He placed a kiss on her cheek. "Allow me to prove myself, please."

She took a deep breath and released it slowly. "Of course. I am sorry I assumed the worst. Perhaps I am the one who hasn't changed."

"Well, you've always been nearly perfect. I don't believe it is necessary for you to change."

His sister smiled and hugged him. "I am glad you are back."

"Me too."

Fifteen

It was the perfect day for a picnic, and Regina couldn't imagine any two families getting on better than hers and Mr. Vistoire's. One might think Aunt Beatrice and Serafine Tucker had been friends forever given the ease with which they had fallen into conversation with one another in the carriage. Regina's aunt was not always the easiest person for others to tolerate with her propensity for blunt speech, but Mr. Vistoire's sister seemed to value a direct approach, as she demonstrated the moment she and Regina were left alone.

Mr. Vistoire was escorting Aunt Beatrice and Evangeline on a stroll through Hyde Park, while Sophia had joined Simon and his father at the water's edge to throw breadcrumbs to the geese.

"I've been watching Xavier with you today. I think you are good for him."

Regina blinked in surprise.

Serafine regarded her with intense green eyes that seemed capable of delving into the most private places of Regina's psyche, and she was uncertain she liked anyone nosing around there. She turned her attention toward the trio on the bank of the Serpentine.

"I'm not sure I take your meaning."

Simon reached a chubby hand to take his father's offering of a small chunk of bread, but it slipped through his fingers and landed on the grass. As Simon squatted to pick it up, a goose honked at him. The boy screamed and his father scooped him in his arms so he could watch the geese feeding from a safer vantage point.

"Xavier has never courted a lady," Serafine said. "It is a testament to his regard for you."

"I see."

The fact he had never courted a lady at his age seemed to confirm he was a rogue just like she'd thought, but he wasn't behaving like any of the scoundrels that had been bothering her this Season.

For one, in her moment of weakness when her curiosity had overruled common sense and she'd wanted him to kiss her in the garden, he hadn't accepted her unspoken invitation. Instead, he had proclaimed a desire to court her and arrived on her doorstep with a gift the next day.

In addition, Mr. Vistoire was kind to her family, and he was especially agreeable when it came to Aunt Beatrice. At this very moment, he was allowing Auntie to parade him through the park as if he were a prized stallion. He seemed to take genuine pleasure in her aunt and sisters, and that made him more dangerous than any of the other men set on conquering her. The way to Regina's heart would always be through her family, and she suspected Mr. Vistoire was privy to this information.

Involving *his* family, however, perplexed her. She saw no advantage to introducing her to his sister unless his intentions truly were honorable, and that did not match his story about becoming intoxicated and accepting the challenge to seduce her.

"Do you fancy my brother?" Serafine asked. "I don't want to see him disappointed."

If Regina were not accustomed to her aunt and Evangeline speaking without restraint, she might be offended by his sister's direct manner. "I understand. I don't like to see my sisters disappointed either," she said, avoiding the question. "I would rather be the injured party than watch either of them suffer."

Serafine smiled and didn't press her for an answer. "I will worry about him if he is alone in New Orleans."

Regina didn't have a ready response, so she welcomed the sight of her sister returning with Mr. Tucker and Simon.

Mr. Vistoire's nephew released his papa's hand as the party neared the blanket and ran toward his mother. His small legs worked with as much grace as he could manage, the uncoordinated motion reminding Regina of a tottering windmill.

He stopped at the edge of the blanket, extended a hand toward Serafine, and crooked his plump fingers to summon her. "Raw?"

"No more rocks," his mother said and extended her arms. "May I have a hug?"

He grinned and threw himself against her chest. She hugged and kissed him, then tried to settle him on her lap, but it wasn't long before he wiggled free. This time he appealed to Regina. "Raw?"

"Now, Simon." Serafine's attempt at scolding her son fell short with laughter in her voice. "Allow Regina to rest."

"I don't mind." Regina stood, grateful for a chance to move. She'd never been one to rest during the day. In fact, she would have joined Aunt Beatrice, Evangeline, and Mr. Vistoire on their stroll, but they left while she'd been entertaining Simon the first time. The boy loved the water.

She took Simon's hand and led him back toward the water's edge for another game of ducks and drakes—which amounted to him flinging small rocks toward the water. Some made their destination and others fell short on the grass.

Simon squealed in excitement as they strolled toward the lake. A persistent warm breeze rippled the Serpentine's surface and shivered the leaves on the trees, creating a shushing noise.

As they reached the water, he grinned and sighed with pleasure. Her heart melted.

She searched the shore for small stones, and when she'd gathered several, she handed one to him. He drew his arm over his head and flung the rock approximately a foot.

"More!"

She passed him another, delighting in the knowledge he derived joy from such a simple act. He'd almost depleted his supply when Mr. Vistoire sidled up to her. He was alone. Regina glanced back toward the blanket to where Evangeline and Aunt Beatrice had joined the other picnickers.

"Did you have a nice stroll through the park?" she asked.

"It was enjoyable, thank you. Has Simon kept you at the water's edge all this time?"

"He allowed me a short reprieve." Simon thrust out his hand for another rock. "We will need more. I believe he could be at this all afternoon," she said to Mr. Vistoire.

"Or you could tell him it's time to return to the picnic."

She scrunched her nose at him. "Have you seen how adorable he is? One imploring look from those big green eyes, and I'm putty in his hands."

"Is that so? At last, I've discovered your weakness." He winked, and it dawned on her that he and his nephew shared the same gorgeous green eyes.

She ducked her head as warmth stole into her cheeks. "I'll gather more rocks."

"More raw?" The boy's sweet voice was just as dangerous as his soulful eyes. He might run her ragged all afternoon, and she would be powerless to refuse him.

"I am looking," she said.

"I have one." Mr. Vistoire pulled a stone from his pocket, and his nephew snatched it from his palm. "Thank you for entertaining Simon this afternoon."

She bent forward to pick up a rock and glanced in his direction. "Thank you for entertaining Aunt Beatrice. I know she can be trying at times."

"Trying in what way? It was a pleasure escorting your aunt and sister around the park."

Regina returned with her bounty. Mr. Vistoire took the stones from her to form a pile at Simon's feet.

"I've overheard complaints that she talks too much," Regina said. "I believe Lady Lovelace is responsible for the moniker Babbling Beatrice."

"Lady Lovelace sounds like a shrew. I consider myself fortunate never to have made her acquaintance."

Regina smiled at his candidness. "Well, don't count your blessings too soon. The widow is quick to set her cap for every new bachelor joining Society. I'm certain it is just a matter of time."

"That is a problem easily solved."

"How so?"

He swayed toward her, their shoulders brushing, and he twined his fingers with hers. "You could changed my status from bachelor to husband," he said softly in her ear, his warm breath creating a pleasing tingle across her skin.

Regina's heart lodged in her throat. Her glaze flicked toward him and he smiled. "It's only a suggestion, but if you care about protecting me from Lady Lovelace and those of her ilk..."

Regina released the breath she'd been holding and chuckled. "I'm certain you can manage ladies like Celeste Lovelace without my assistance."

"I know, but you could protect me with those fancy Wang Fu moves you do." He released her hand to playfully spar with her.

Laughing, she blocked his exaggerated, sluggish moves. "It's Wing Chun, and I only employ my skills to discourage annoying men."

"Ouch!" He covered his heart and staggered as if she'd plunged a dagger into his chest. "You've mortally wounded me, Miss Darlington."

She rolled her eyes. "I wasn't referring to you."

He abandoned the pretense and gifted her with his handsome smile. "Are you saying you *don't* find me annoying?"

"Only a little."

His smile grew. "You like me, don't you, Regina Darlington? Admit it."

"I do not."

"Yes, you do." He reached for her hand, drawing her closer. "Regina likes Xavier," he said in a teasing singsong.

They were standing much too close for the park, so close she could feel his body heat and detect the faintest shadow of whiskers on his jaw.

"I don't like you," she murmured, her eyes drifting to half-mast, revealing her lie. "Only a little."

His thumb drew an arc on her inner wrist, against her bare skin. "If we were alone, I might kiss you."

"If we were alone, I might allow you."

A loud splash caused them to jump apart.

"Simon!" Mr. Vistoire's panicked voice sent her heart on a tear, but they both seemed to spot him at the same time.

"Oh, thank heavens," she said.

The boy was busy wrestling a large rock from the dirt close to the water's edge, and when he pried it loose, he wobbled a couple of steps and dropped it in the lake. Water shot up and drenched his shoes. He slapped his hands together to dust off the dirt.

"That's enough rocks." Mr. Vistoire swept the boy off his feet to toss him in the air and catch him under the arms.

Simon squealed with laughter and demanded more. Mr. Vistoire complied several times, stopping to throw his nephew and catch him as they made their way back toward Simon's parents. He wrestled with the boy a few more minutes before surrendering him to Serafine.

His mother wrapped him in her arms then frowned at his wet shoes. "Did you walk in the lake?"

He puffed out his chest. "Throw raw."

Serafine threatened to send Simon and her brother to bed with no dinner, but Regina could tell from the twinkle in her eyes she wasn't angry. When the picnic ended, Mr. Vistoire insisted on escorting Regina and her family to Wedmore House. Aunt Beatrice and her sisters dispersed the moment they arrived home, leaving Regina alone with her gentleman caller, as Aunt Beatrice had been referring to him all day.

She and Mr. Vistoire stood in the foyer facing one another. His flirting at the picnic seemed more in line with what she expected from a libertine, and as much as it galled her to admit, she'd enjoyed it. Perhaps if she invited him to kiss her now, he wouldn't be quite the gentleman he was attempting to portray.

She cleared her throat and raised her eyebrows.

"Yes, Miss Darlington? How may I be of service?"

"We are *alone*, Mr. Vistoire."

A sinful smile spread across his lips. "You want that kiss, no?"

"Yes." She tipped up her face, challenging him to show his true character.

He placed his hands on her waist to draw her to him. His touch was gentle and not at all demanding. He kept distance between their bodies. Their only contact was his hands curled around her waist, but it was enough to shower her with tingles everywhere. He didn't try to kiss her, which made her crave him even more.

"Mr. Vistoire?"

"Xavier," he whispered and leaned his forehead against hers. "Call me Xavier."

His scent filled her with longing, but she had no experience with men other than deflecting unwanted advances. She wanted this—*him.*

"Is something wrong? Aren't you going to kiss me?"

His smile was like a caress. "No, darling. I am not."

"I beg your pardon?"

"I said I am not going to kiss you."

She pulled away and her hands landed on her hips. "Why not? You said you would kiss me if we were alone."

"I said I might, and I have decided it would be improper since you have not yet agreed to marry me."

She issued a small cry of outrage. "What is your game, Mr. Vistoire? I know you cannot truly be interested in marriage."

"You are wrong. I am only interested in marriage."

There was a small tic at his jaw. She pointed at it. "You are *lying.* I could see it in your face. You don't want to walk away without kissing me, so what is stopping you?"

"Hope."

His response stole her momentum. "Hope? I don't understand."

"At one time, I was a drunk, a wastrel, and a philanderer just as you think. I will never look back, Regina, because when I am with you, I see the happy future we could have together." His green gaze held her captive. "My hope is you will come to see it too, but that won't happen if I prove myself unworthy of you."

A lump had formed in her throat, and she swallowed around it. Too many thoughts raced through her mind to grasp on to one. She needed time to sort through his revelation—to make sense of everything—but if she didn't make some overture in return, he might decide courting her was pointless. She wasn't ready to see him walk away.

She cleared her throat. "Lady Ellis is hosting a ball tomorrow evening. I think you should come. The countess has taken a liking to Sophia. I'm sure my sister could procure an invitation for you. Perhaps we could start again and forget what we believe we know about one another."

His smile caused her heart to batter her ribs. "I would like that very much. Would you allow me to claim the supper dance?"

"I suppose I could save the supper dance for you. I did say I like you a little."

"That is progress." He winked. "Enjoy your evening, Miss Darlington. I look forward to meeting you for the first time again at Lady Ellis's ball tomorrow."

"I hope you make a better impression this time," she teased.

"As do I."

Sixteen

Late the next afternoon Regina and Sophia sought out Evangeline in the library. As usual, their sister had Uncle Charles's papers spread across the table, but her attention was squarely on a thin, leather bound notebook open in front of her.

"What have you found now?" Regina asked.

"It is one of Uncle Charles's expedition logs." Evangeline held up a small piece of ripped foolscap. "I found this tucked inside."

Regina came up behind her to read over her sister's shoulder and recognized Uncle Charles's messy handwriting. "It looks like gibberish to me."

Evangeline glanced up as Sophia slid into a chair on the opposite side of the table. "I have been staring at it for the last half hour, and I cannot make sense of it."

"Let me see." Sophia stretched her hand across the table, and Evangeline passed the note to her. A crease appeared between Sophia's brows as she broke up the continuous string of letters and tried to sound out the note. "WUU AZMLQ YIP FACUPPGN... I give up." She tossed it on the table. "Is it a strange form of Latin?"

Evangeline shook her head. "I can decipher Latin. This is something different."

Regina grabbed the note to study it, but soon abandoned the task and returned it to Evangeline. "Languages were never my forte. I will leave the translating to you."

"I'm uncertain it is worth my time. For all we know, Uncle Charles was deep in his cups when he wrote it."

It was a rare occasion when their uncle overindulged, but it was not beyond the realm of possibilities.

Regina sat in the chair next to Evangeline. "We should discuss our strategy for keeping Aunt Beatrice out of mischief at the Ellis's ball tonight. Sophia's dance card will likely fill up quickly, so I propose you and I divide the evening. I will watch her until the supper dance, and you can relieve me."

"I could take a turn with Auntie," Sophia piped up.

Her sister's thoughtful offer elicited a fullness in Regina's chest as if her heart were expanding to twice its size. "Most of your days are spent helping Aunt Beatrice on shopping excursions and at garden parties. Your evenings should be free to husband hunt."

"I enjoy our outings," Sophia said. "Besides, I would be unable to leave the house if Aunt Beatrice was unwilling to venture out every day."

Regina smiled. "We all enjoy her company. I didn't mean to imply—"

A tremendous boom shook the ceiling, and the chandelier crystals clinked together. Regina and her sisters gasped. Their heads shot up to gape at the ceiling.

"Auntie!" Regina bolted from the chair to race for the stairs. Her sisters were close on her heels.

Joy had taken the servant staircase and met them in the corridor. Cupid, who had been napping in the kitchen earlier, accompanied her. Deep lines crisscrossed the maid's forehead. "I never heard the bell, miss. I'm sorry."

"Neither did we," Regina said to reassure her as they reached her aunt's bedchamber door. She barged in without knocking and found Aunt Beatrice flat on her back beside the wardrobe and groaning. A chair was tipped on its side.

"Dear Lord." Regina hurried to her aunt, barking orders to the maid and her sisters. "Joy, go for Dr. Portier. You two, help me get her into bed."

"Yes, miss." Joy dashed from the chamber while Evangeline and Sophia came forward to assist.

Regina knelt beside her aunt. "What happened?"

Aunt Beatrice blinked up at her. "Isn't it obvious I fell?"

"Yes, but *how* did you fall?"

Sophia knelt too, and cradled their aunt's head in her lap. Aunt Beatrice winced. "Be careful. I hit my head."

"You poor dear," Sophia cooed. "Where does it hurt?"

She gingerly walked her fingers along Aunt Beatrice's scalp then paused to glance up. "She already has a goose egg on the back of her head."

Evangeline righted the chair and looked in the wardrobe. "Were you trying to reach something on the top shelf?"

"I wanted my jewelry box." Aunt Beatrice tried to move and winced.

"You could have rung for Joy or asked one of us." Evangeline stretched on her toes and pulled the small box from the shelf. "Haven't we warned you about climbing on the chair to reach items?"

Aunt Beatrice scowled. "I am perfectly capable of getting what I want without anyone's assistance. I am not an invalid."

Sophia smoothed their aunt's gray hair from her face and bent forward so they were eye-to-eye. "You're on the floor, Auntie. It is time to surrender."

"Never."

Sophia grinned and placed a kiss on their aunt's forehead. "You are impossibly stubborn. I think we know from whom Regina inherited the trait."

"Is it any wonder she is my favorite?"

Sophia laughed. "Now Auntie, you said earlier today I am your favorite."

"No, that cannot be," Evangeline said as she closed the wardrobe doors. "*I* am Aunt Beatrice's favorite. She told me so yesterday on our walk with Mr. Vistoire."

"You are all my favorites, but you were not supposed to tell each other I had singled you out."

"Can you move everything?" Regina asked.

Aunt Beatrice tested both arms and legs. "Yes, but I'm stiff as always."

"I think you'll be more comfortable in bed." Regina motioned Evangeline to grab Aunt Beatrice's legs. "I'll support her back. Sophia, you hold her shoulders."

Surprisingly, Aunt Beatrice didn't insist on walking, which reinforced Regina's fears that she was suffering more than she wanted to admit.

"On the count of three. One. Two. Three."

Aunt Beatrice hissed when they lifted her from the floor, but she offered no complaint. Her slight frame was easy to bear, although maneuvering her proved challenging. Regina and her sisters managed to shuffle the short distance to the bed and place their aunt on the mattress without incident.

When Dr. Portier arrived, their aunt reached her hand toward Regina. "Will you stay with me, dearest?"

"Of course."

Aunt Beatrice shooed Regina's sisters from the room with instructions to send a message to Lady Seabrook requesting a favor. "If she will act as chaperone, there is no need for any of you to miss tonight's ball."

"The ball is the least of our concerns," Regina said.

"I must insist you go without me. Mr. Vistoire is expecting you."

"Let's allow the doctor to examine you." She nodded to Sophia to do as Aunt Beatrice requested, although she had no intention of leaving Wedmore House with her aunt laid up in bed.

A couple of hours later, the doctor was gone and Aunt Beatrice was sleeping soundly after a dose of laudanum. Regina joined Evangeline in Aunt Beatrice's sitting room below stairs and collapsed on the velvet sofa with a weary sigh.

Her sister closed her book. "Lord and Lady Seabrook came for Sophia. How is Aunt Beatrice?"

"Resting," Regina said. "Dr. Portier gave her laudanum for the pain. He said at her age, it is a wonder she didn't break a bone."

"She made a lot of racket for a small woman," Evangeline said. "Is the doctor certain about her having no broken bones?"

"He said she bruised her ribs. She must have hit the chair when she came down. As Sophia noted, she has a large knot on the back of her head, but we are not to worry." Regina wished she felt as confident in Dr. Portier as he did in his diagnosis. Doctors made mistakes the same as everyone, but she had no choice except to trust his word. "I will look in on her often and send for the doctor again if her condition worsens."

"I'm certain Auntie will be all right. Sleep is likely the best medicine. Perhaps we shouldn't look in on her until morning unless she rings for assistance."

Regina tossed a dubious look in Evangeline's direction.

Her sister chuckled. "Point taken."

At least the creaky floorboards would alert them if she crawled from bed. For the moment, the floor above them was silent, so Regina allowed herself to sink into the plush sofa cushions and relax. "Why didn't you go to the Ellis's ball with Sophia? Lady Seabrook's offer to chaperone was extended to any of us who wished to go."

"It should come as no surprise I chose to remain at home." Evangeline held up the book she'd been reading. "Besides, between Lord and Lady Seabrook, their daughters, and Sophia taking the seats, I would have been forced to ride on the box with the driver. There is still time for you to dress and meet Sophia at the ball. I allowed Joy to go visit her sister, but I could help with your gown."

Regina waved off her sister's offer.

"Mr. Vistoire is expecting you," Evangeline reminded her.

"It cannot be helped. My duty is to Aunt Beatrice. If Mr. Vistoire does not understand, I see no reason to further our association."

The uneasiness that had been pestering her since her conversation with him yesterday returned, making her stomach churn.

"It's not any more your responsibility to care for Aunt Beatrice than it is mine," Evangeline said. "I will look after her while you are at the ball."

"No, it is best for me to stay. I shouldn't have promised to meet Mr. Vistoire. It was unwise to encourage him."

"I thought you decided you liked him."

Last night she had joined Evangeline in her bedchamber to share her conundrum. They had stayed up much too late talking, as sisters often did when they were the best of friends.

"I do. *Maybe*. Are you warm?" Regina hopped from the sofa, paced to the window, and threw the sash up. She breathed in the cooler air in a bid to clear her mind. "Liking a gentleman does not mean one should marry him, however."

Evangeline gasped. "Gi, you never said he'd offered marriage."

Regina twirled to face her sister with a denial on the tip of her tongue, but it died away when she saw Evangeline's glowing smile. Regina's sister had admitted to liking Mr. Vistoire as well now that she'd spent time with him.

Regina sighed. "I did not mention it, because I will not marry him."

"I don't understand." Evangeline left her seat to come stand at her side. Her sister's eyebrows were drawn together in concern. "I realize it is too soon to know if you love him, but why are you certain you won't marry him?"

Regina's bottom lip trembled. She pressed her lips tightly together as tears threatened to fill her eyes.

Evangeline touched her shoulder. "What is wrong?"

She inhaled deeply and tried to make sense of the onslaught of sadness. "I don't know," she admitted eventually. "When I think I could fall in love with him..."

The blasted tears fell on her cheeks. She brushed the wetness away with her fist and forced a smile. "It is simply the excitement of the afternoon. I am still shaken from Aunt Beatrice's fall. When I saw her lying there, I thought—"

Evangeline grabbed Regina's hands. "You thought Aunt Beatrice was seriously injured."

"I thought perhaps we'd lost her."

"Oh, Gigi." Her sister smiled sadly. "Auntie is fine. Her eyesight is failing, and she's not as steady on her feet as she once was. Accidents are bound to happen when she refuses to listen to sound advice, but she will recover. Come sit with me."

Evangeline led her back to the sofa and sat beside her, still holding hands. Her grip was firm and kept Regina tethered to her. "What does Aunt Beatrice have to do with Mr. Vistoire?"

Regina sniffled, the tickling of her nose warning of more tears to come. She was struggling to sort through the riot of emotions inside. Explaining to her sister seemed impossible.

"Aunt Beatrice is older. I realize she will not live forever, but I cannot stand the thought of saying good-bye to her. Or Uncle Charles or Sophia or you. I have so much to lose already. Does it make sense to love a man when I will lose him eventually too?"

"Regina." Evangeline released her hand to hold her own head. Regina could almost see the thoughts swirling in her sister's mind. "How long have you thought this way?"

She shrugged a shoulder. Perhaps this fear had always lurked in the background, but it had never taken form until now. When she said it aloud, it sounded ridiculous, but she couldn't deny the turmoil inside of her eased when she discarded any thoughts of marriage.

Evangeline dropped her hands to her lap and smiled sadly. "Loving someone is a risk to the heart, but is falling in love truly a choice?"

"Probably not after one reaches a certain point, but I am not there yet. Wouldn't it be better for me to end my association with Mr. Vistoire now while I still have the wherewithal to choose?"

"I have never been able to follow your logic," Evangeline said with a sigh. "As I see it, you have two alternatives: love and risk heartbreak, or keep every man at arm's length and secure a loveless existence."

"True." Regina nodded slowly, mulling over the situation.

"For pity's sake," Evangeline blurted and grabbed Regina by the shoulders. "How is a life without love even a consideration for you? Don't you want what our parents had?"

Their father and mother had been uncommonly smitten with each other well beyond their newlywed days. Every memory Regina kept of their parents together, they were touching, engrossed in conversation, or laughing and teasing one another. Of course she wanted what they had. But she wanted it forever, not fleetingly like her parents, and she didn't believe something so beautiful could last.

Regina clenched her fists. "Who are you to lecture me? You are guilty of the same crime. Before long, you will be traveling the world with Uncle Charles and immersed in your digs and research. Why is it acceptable for you to be a spinster but not me?"

"I never said I wouldn't marry. If I am fortunate enough to find a man who loves me and I love him, I will not hesitate to become his wife."

As usual, Evangeline obliterated Regina's argument before they had gotten a good row going. "You never said."

"You never asked," Evangeline retorted.

No, she hadn't. Regina had simply assumed her sister wouldn't want a husband to possibly interfere with her travels.

"Who will care for Aunt Beatrice and Uncle Charles if I leave Wedmore House?" Regina asked. "After today, there is no doubt she will need a caretaker before long."

"We could take our turns caring for Aunt Beatrice. Just like we do now."

"Not if I'm living in New Orleans."

Evangeline's eyebrows shot up on her forehead. "Would Mr. Vistoire take you away? His family is in England, and I thought he had no other relatives in America."

"He has a house and land. That is reason enough to return."

"Well, we will not allow it. He must first agree to stay in England before you will accept his proposal. Tell him I said so."

Regina laughed at the determined set to Evangeline's jaw. "Perhaps I should save the conversation for when he actually proposes."

"I will leave the timing up to you, but no promise means no wedding. I will not be swayed."

"Duly noted." Regina tossed her arms around her sister's neck and squeezed. "I love you, dearest sister."

Evangeline returned her hug. "And I love you, even though I want to shake you until your teeth rattle sometimes."

"Oh, now you are just being sappy."

Seventeen

"I am going to hell," Xavier muttered as he stood in the back garden outside Wedmore House with a crowbar he'd taken from the mews. Aside from the occasional croak of a frog or the echo of horses' hooves from the front street, the neighborhood was quiet. The town houses were like slumbering giants nestled among one another, appearing deserted this time of night.

Anyone of consequence in Mayfair was attending a party while their servants were snug in their beds—at least until the family returned home. He'd watched from the corner as Regina and her family left for the ball half an hour earlier. It had taken him that long to decide if he was going to search for the map while they were gone.

He was still debating.

After Farrin had complimented him on seducing his way into Wedmore House, Xavier felt queasy anytime he thought of searching for the map when he called on Regina. His intentions with her were honest, but this business with the map tainted everything. He just wanted the task behind him, so he could concentrate on discovering who was responsible for placing the ones he cared about in danger.

His grip tightened on the crowbar as he approached the servants' entrance. Before breaking another lock, he tried the handle and cursed when it opened without resistance. Not only had Regina disregarded his counsel on employing a manservant, she hadn't barred the doors.

He leaned the crowbar against the house and slipped inside, closing the door behind him. Skimming his hand along the wall to find his way in the dark, he located the servants' staircase.

Since Regina had interrupted him before he'd thoroughly searched Lord Wedmore's private chambers, he would continue his search upstairs before visiting the earl's study and library. If the ladies returned home before he was finished, a first floor escape would be easier. He just hoped the lady's maid was visiting her sister again.

Recalling his fall on these very stairs, he took more care with his footing than usual then hurried along the corridor toward Wedmore's chambers. Whimpering and the scrape of nails came from behind a closed door. Cupid must have gotten stuck in one of the bedchambers when the ladies left for the evening. He briefly considered setting him free then thought better of it. The dog would only cause a delay with his persistent begging for attention.

The uncovered windows in the master's chamber allowed enough light for him to make out the shadows of the massive Tudor bed and wardrobe. He crossed to the mantle to retrieve the tinderbox and candle he'd noticed the other day and worked to light the wick. Once the flame flickered to life and burned steady, Xavier carried the candle to the desk. He jerked open the top drawer only to discover an ebony hair comb and various cufflinks that appeared to have no match. Drawer after drawer held nothing of interest, not even a stack of foolscap.

Snatching the books stacked on the desk, he grabbed the top one by its cover, flipped it upside down, and shook. No stray sheets fluttered from the pages. None of the books proved to be hiding a map.

He pivoted on his heel, surveying the room. Searching the wardrobe again might uncover something he'd missed the other day, but he couldn't afford to waste time. His gaze landed on the bed and his eyebrow inched up. Maybe Lord Wedmore preferred to keep the map close. He stalked toward the bed to check beneath the mattress. Cupid's high-pitched bark shattered the quiet. The floorboards groaned as someone briskly moved along the corridor, headed in his direction.

Damn.

Had Farrin sent another man after he'd agreed to wait? Xavier shouldn't be surprised since the blackguard was a criminal.

He blew out the candle, sprang toward the chamber door for a better defensive position, and bumped his thigh on Lord Wedmore's side table. Something heavy banged against the floor.

The footsteps stopped outside the chamber door.

Xavier froze, not daring to make a sound as he waited for the enemy to decide if he'd heard something more than the dog barking. Every sound was amplified—the jagged whooshing of his breath, the pulsing beat of his heart in his ears, and Cupid's nails scraping wood in the room next door.

When the handle jiggled, he leapt behind the door, prepared to attack. The door wafted open, but no one entered. Xavier held his breath, his muscles taut. He felt more than saw the man step into the room. There was a subtle shift in the air. It was warmer, electrified.

Xavier pounced, trapping the intruder's arms against his sides. A gasp tore from the man. He was a wiry fellow—small framed like a lad—but he bucked and clawed with the ferocity of a wild cat. His head slammed into Xavier's chin. Pins of light burst in the darkness, and Xavier's grip slipped. In the distance, Cupid's barking grew frantic.

The captive twisted in Xavier's hold, and he clamped his arms tighter around the lad's waist. A foot slammed into Xavier's knee. He shouted in surprise as fiery pain radiated into his thigh and shin. They stumbled, Xavier fighting to stay on his feet. He lost the battle. They careened forward to slam against the edge of the mattress.

Xavier landed on top with his arms trapped between his opponent and the bed. His face was buried in silky hair that smelled faintly of oranges, and the soft mounds of a well-formed derriere shimmied beneath him as his captive tried to break free.

Merde! He'd captured a *woman*.

Light flickered at the doorway followed by the ominous click of a gun cocking. "Step away from my niece, so I don't accidentally shoot her instead."

Candlelight illuminated the gold spun hair of the woman beneath him. "Regina?"

Her breath caught and she ceased her struggles. He eased his arms from around her waist, lifted his hands into the air, and cautiously turned to face Aunt Beatrice and her small pistol. Evangeline stood slightly behind her aunt with a candlestick raised to cast light into the room. Her eyes were round and her mouth agape.

What the devil were they doing here? He'd seen them leave for the ball. They were supposed to be at the ball.

"Madame, this situation is not as it seems. There has been a misunderstanding. An accident."

Regina moved behind him to sit on the edge of the bed. He couldn't bear to look at her after what he'd done.

Her aunt pursed her mouth into a tight circle and drew her wrapper tighter around her body. "I do not know what matter of conduct is practiced in America, Mr. Vistoire, but in England, we do not mistake assault for an accident. Evangeline, have Deacon retrieve a Runner."

Regina's sister seemed oblivious to her aunt's command and remained rooted to the floor.

Aunt Beatrice waved the barrel of the firearm at him. "Move aside so there is no risk of shooting my niece if the pistol should fire by itself."

Her steely glare suggested it would be no accident if she shot him. Xavier swallowed hard. He wouldn't allow Regina to be harmed. "All right, I am moving." With his hands raised, he shuffled to the side.

"Wait!" Regina bolted from the bed to place herself between him and her aunt's pistol.

"Regina," he said with a growl.

Aunt Beatrice averted her aim, pointing the barrel toward the floor. Xavier grabbed Regina by the shoulders and wrestled her behind him. Why couldn't she just be agreeable for once? "Stay put."

Regina's aunt frowned in their direction. "What is going on here? Regina, was this man trying to assault you or not?"

"He was not. He...he was..."

Aunt Beatrice's eyes narrowed. "I see what was occurring now."

"It's not what you think, Auntie." Desperation clung to Regina's words and drove him to protect her.

"We are betrothed," he blurted.

Regina gasped.

Aunt Beatrice and Evangeline must have been as shocked as she, because no one spoke for a long time. Eventually, Regina's aunt found her voice.

"Is this true, dearest? Because if it is not, I will see him taken to gaol."

"It's true."

"You really are *betrothed*?" Aunt Beatrice's mouth hinted at a smile. "Mind you, I do not approve of such activities before the vows are spoken, but I was young once."

"No, we weren't—"

Regina lightly punched him in the back. He grunted in surprise. She came forward, dropping her head and posing as a contrite young miss when she'd done nothing wrong. He ground his teeth in frustration. He didn't want her family believing lies about her.

"Forgive us, Auntie," she said. "I only wanted to show Mr. Vistoire the wooden dummy Uncle Charles had built for me. It seemed only fair that my betrothed should be informed of my unusual interests."

Aunt Beatrice nodded. The firearm dangled in her limp hand at her side. "A wise choice. And what is Mr. Vistoire's opinion of your Wing Chun?"

"He *approves*." Regina injected a good deal of enthusiasm into her lie. Not that he objected outright to her unladylike exercises, but they'd never had the conversation. "He wants to have a dummy built as a wedding gift. One I may take wherever we set up house. That is the reason I brought him above stairs, and then we—uh—we lost our heads."

Evangeline's auburn brow arched, but she kept quiet.

"Well, that is a different kettle of fish." Aunt Beatrice disengaged the trigger and passed the pistol to Evangeline. "I understand the reason you brought your young man upstairs, but why are you in your uncle's chambers?"

Xavier hated that the burden of explaining his presence fell on Regina. He placed his hand on the small of her back. "I misplaced my watch. I thought I might have left it in Lord Wedmore's room when I changed into a dry shirt the other day."

Regina stiffened.

Splendid. He'd just dug them into a deeper hole.

"I *see*." Regina's aunt drew out the last word and crossed her arms. Her glower was piercing. He'd likely be gasping out his last breath if her silent wish were granted. "I think it is best not to delay the nuptials under the circumstances. I'll not have any gossips questioning my niece's reputation when a babe comes early."

Regina groaned and buried her face in her hands. He drew her close, wanting to shield her from this mortifying situation. "There will be no issue arriving early, ma'am."

The woman sniffed. "I would rather not leave it to chance, sir. Tomorrow I will summon Lord Margrave. He has connections that will enable you to receive a special license." She jabbed a finger in his direction. "Arrive on our doorstep at nine o'clock tomorrow morning, or you will rue the day. Lord Margrave has many connections. Some you would prefer never to meet so do not test me."

Xavier strained to maintain a polite smile. "I will be here."

"Very good." She held out her hand to Regina. "Help me back to bed. Your sister will see Mr. Vistoire to the door."

Regina rushed forward to offer her arm to her aunt. Aunt Beatrice grimaced and leaned against her as she limped from the room. Once they exited, Evangeline waved for him to follow her.

They didn't speak as she led him down the main staircase, but she kept slanting odd looks in his direction. When they reached the front door, he couldn't stand not knowing the meaning behind her stolen glances. He planted his feet, refusing to be tossed out or judged by a slip of a woman.

"Is there something you would like to say, Miss Evangeline?"

She shrugged. "I am simply trying to understand why my sister lied for you."

"What makes you believe she was lying? We formed a secret agreement yesterday after the picnic. It was only a matter of time before we planned to speak with your aunt."

Evangeline shook her head as if she couldn't fathom his gall. "I know all about what occurred after the picnic, and I was with Regina tonight when we heard you moving around upstairs. We thought it was Aunt Beatrice, and Regina went to look in on her." She glared. "If you hurt my sister, Lord Margrave's connections should be the least of your concerns."

For the love of St. Peter, the English were keen on threats. And he'd had enough. Squaring his jaw, he leaned toward her slightly to speak in a quiet voice. "I am trying to keep all of you *safe*."

Evangeline's eyes expanded. "What is your meaning?"

He'd said enough already. "I will speak with my betrothed tomorrow. Good night, mademoiselle." He sketched a bow then strode from Wedmore House with his head foggy on how he'd created such a mess.

Eighteen

Regina winced when she spotted Evangeline at the bottom of the staircase. Her sister's arms were crossed, and the rapid slap of her slipper against the marble floor announced her impatience. She was waiting for answers.

"Aunt Beatrice is tucked into bed," Regina said as she descended the stairs in an attempt to delay the inevitable. "She insisted on a nip of brandy first. In this case, a nip was the same as the two fingers Uncle Charles pours for himself. I don't expect Auntie will be up and about anymore tonight."

Evangeline pounced the second Regina's toes touched the ground floor. "You lied for him."

"What would you have had me do? Aunt Beatrice was going to summon Bow Street."

"Of course she was. Auntie thinks he compromised you. I think we are lucky she didn't shoot him."

"Yes, well. I'm certain you understand the reason I misrepresented the truth."

Evangeline maintained her implacable stance. "Misrepresented the truth. Lied. It is one in the same."

With a groan, Regina pushed past her sister to return to the sitting room, where they had been reading before she went upstairs to investigate the noise.

"We are not finished." Evangeline dogged her heels all the way to the sitting room. "I don't give a fig about the moral implications. My point is you acted to protect him, and now you are betrothed. Are you all right?"

"I don't know." Regina pinched the bridge of her nose and exhaled. "And I wasn't protecting *him*. I was thinking of

Sophia." Her claim might be more convincing if she hadn't thrown herself between him and Aunt Beatrice's pistol. She hadn't made a rational choice, but she didn't know how to explain the stab of panic in her chest when she'd seen the gun's barrel aimed at him. She didn't fully understand it herself.

Regina plopped onto the sofa and held her head with both hands. "If a Runner had been summoned, what is to say he would have left before Lord and Lady Seabrook carried Sophia home from the ball? Our sister would have been embarrassed, and *I* would have been mortified. We picnicked with Xavier yesterday. How long would it take before the gossips began to speculate on the real reason he was found in Wedmore House?"

Evangeline sat on the sofa beside her and rubbed Regina's back like their mother had done to soothe them when they were ill or overwrought. "I understand," her sister said in a quiet voice, "but you shouldn't have to marry to protect our reputation. Love is the only sound reason."

Regina lifted her head and sent a half smile in her sister's direction. She'd had no idea Evangeline was such a romantic. Her sister had always seemed too practical and focused on intellectual pursuits to entertain romantic ideals.

"I cannot say with certainty that a desire to protect our family name is fully responsible for my actions. When I saw Aunt Beatrice aiming at him..." A wave of nausea swept through her. "What if the firearm had discharged? His family loves him the same as you, Sophia, Aunt Beatrice, and I love each other. Little Simon—" Her throat squeezed off her words.

Regina had been eight and Evangeline almost seven when their parents were killed. At the age of four, Sophia barely remembered them. Simon would be too young to hold on to any memories of his uncle. Regina couldn't be part of stealing an important piece of the boy's past and future.

"Nothing happened, Gigi. Mr. Vistoire is safe, and he'll be back at our door before you know it. What are you going to do about him?"

"I wish I knew." Perhaps there was nothing she could do except marry him. Her unsophisticated heart raced at the thought even though she had enough sense to realize tying herself to him would be a mistake. She would never trust him after tonight.

"What do you suppose he is after?" Regina asked. "He thought we were at the ball, so his explanation for the first time he broke into Wedmore House is clearly a lie."

"But he is not lying about caring for you. You should have seen his face when you shielded him with your body. He was scared witless."

Regina shook her head; the backs of her eyes burned. With Aunt Beatrice's fall and now this, she was spent. "He had a pistol trained on him. Of course he was frightened."

"Not until that moment. His feelings for you are not a lie." Evangeline nibbled her bottom lip, and Regina could almost see her turning over the evening's events in her head. "It is a peculiar situation to be sure—his breaking into the house again. Before he left this evening, he said something odd. He said he is trying to *protect* us."

Regina blinked. "Protect us how?"

"He wouldn't tell me. He said he would speak with you tomorrow."

The front door hinges squeaked, and Sophia's voice carried into the sitting room. "Please thank your mother again for allowing me to accompany you this evening."

"We were pleased to have you, Sophia." Apparently, her best friend had walked her to the door. "Will your aunt be well enough to attend Lady Wexbert's at-home tomorrow?"

"I'm uncertain. She could be laid up for several days."

"Then you must join us. Mama will insist."

Regina allowed herself a brief smile. Seeing Sophia's desire for a normal life being fulfilled lightened Regina's burden for a moment. The front door closed and the lock tumbled. A bit later, her youngest sister swept into the room.

"Good. You waited to retire for bed." Her cheeks were rosy and she sounded slightly breathless. "I kept watch for Mr. Vistoire all evening, but he never made an appearance."

Evangeline shifted on the sofa. "How was Lady Ellis's ball?"

"Oh, you know what it is like. I barely sat the whole night." Sophia flounced to a chair adjacent to the sofa and plopped onto it. "My feet are aching terribly." She propped her ankle over her knee, removed her satin slipper, and kneaded the sole of her foot.

"Did you enjoy yourself, achy feet aside?" Regina asked.

"Very much." Sophia's smile revealed the dimple in her cheek. She was the most beautiful of the Darlington Angels, as Society had dubbed them. Her full dance card did not come as a surprise. "Lord Ingram partnered with me for two dances, and he hinted that he wishes to call on our uncle when he returns. Did we receive any word from Uncle Charles today?"

Typically, Sophia raced to collect the post when the carrier arrived, but Aunt Beatrice's accident had caused quite a commotion that afternoon.

"I'm afraid not, dearest."

"Oh." The twinkle in her eyes dimmed and her shoulders drooped slightly. Regina's sister needed Uncle Charles's permission to marry since she had not reached her majority— unlike Regina, who might become a bride in a matter of hours if Crispin could procure a special license.

She cleared her throat, hesitant to share her news. "There has been a development this evening."

Sophia's head shot up. "Is Aunt Beatrice all right?"

"She is asleep and well."

"Well enough to brandish a pistol and threaten a man," Evangeline said.

Regina aimed a look at her that promised an unpleasant outcome if she continued this conversation.

Evangeline shrugged one shoulder. "I see no reason to misrepresent the truth."

Regina supposed she wouldn't. Her sister had never mastered the art of the white lie to protect one's feelings. Regina could hardly expect her to hold her tongue now.

"I wanted to be gentle," she said. "Not withhold the truth."

Sophia rested her hands in her lap, so proper and refined these days. "There is no need to be gentle. Whatever you reveal will not send me running to my chambers in tears."

Perhaps a couple of years ago her sister would have reacted in such a manner, but at nineteen, she was more mature than many young ladies her age. Regina wasn't worried about her behavior. She didn't want her sister to be hurt by the fact Regina could marry, and she had to wait.

Regina took a cleansing breath before continuing. "Xavier didn't attend Lady Ellis's ball, because he was at Wedmore House."

Noting Evangeline's raised brows, Regina opted to tell Sophia all that had transpired before Evangeline delivered the details with her characteristic lack of delicacy. At the end of Regina's tale, Evangeline recounted her own encounter with Mr. Vistoire when she saw him to the door.

Sophia tipped her head to the side, studying Regina. "Will you follow through with the wedding?"

"I don't see that I have a choice."

"You always have a choice, Gigi," Sophia said. "Aunt Beatrice will understand if you cry off. Can you marry someone you don't trust?"

Regina settled on complete honesty. "No."

"Then you must speak with him alone. Unless he tells you the truth, and you are satisfied with his answer, you cannot marry him."

Evangeline nodded. "Sophia is correct. He needs to be honest with you."

"And if he refuses?"

"You will persuade him," Sophia said.

A smile eased across Regina's face as an idea began to take hold in her mind. "Yes, yes I will."

She would offer him exactly what he claimed to want and force him to admit he hadn't come to Wedmore House to seduce her. He was looking for something, and she wouldn't stop until he confessed what he wanted.

Nineteen

The next morning, Xavier arrived at Wedmore House a half-hour earlier than Regina's aunt had commanded. The threat of Viscount Margrave's unsavory associates had little to do with his arrival time. The men would have to stand in a line behind Farrin's thugs for a turn to rough him up. Xavier's main concern was for Regina's state of mind.

Everything had happened too quickly last night, and he needed to speak with her alone before Lord Margrave arrived and the situation escalated. Xavier regretted his rash action last night. His claim that they were betrothed would tie her to him for the rest of their lives. His aim all along had been to marry her, but he hadn't wanted to force her hand or use deceit. Nevertheless, he'd seen an opportunity and taken it, which made him feel like he was as rotten inside as Farrin.

He feared Regina would despise him forever, but a glimmer of hope fought to stay alight as he grabbed the serpent doorknocker at Wedmore House and knocked.

Sophia answered. Her usual expressive face remained impassive as she greeted him. "Good morning, Mr. Vistoire. Follow me, please."

He frowned when she turned her back to him to lead him into the house. He discarded his hat and gloves on the entry table and followed her. She didn't speak as they crossed the foyer en route to the arched doorway marking the start of the corridor. The swish of her slippers against the floor seemed exceptionally loud in the somber quiet. He had a tickle at the back of his throat that he tried to ease by swallowing, but when his cough broke free, it sounded like the bang of a gavel.

Sophia paused in front of the closed door he'd seen the day he helped bathe Cupid. If he was correct, Lord Wedmore's study stood on the other side. His chance to possibly poke around and memorize the layout had arrived, and he didn't give a damn.

His escort knocked, and Regina's muffled command to enter filtered to the corridor. Sophia pushed open the door and stood aside so he could walk inside. His gaze locked on Regina sitting behind the desk. A small pistol lay on the surface. Wildly, he swung his head, searching the cluttered room for Viscount Margrave or Regina's aunt.

"We are alone." Regina slid the pistol across the battered desktop toward her and dropped it in a drawer. She smiled. "I took Aunt Beatrice's firearm while she was sleeping. Rest assured, our meeting will not be interrupted by a pistol-wielding spinster."

She was trying to lighten the mood, but the reminder of last night made his gut clench. "You could have been killed. What were you thinking by shielding me with your body?"

Sophia gasped and Regina's friendly demeanor evaporated. "I wasn't almost killed, Sophia. Mr. Vistoire is exaggerating. Please, allow us some privacy like we discussed."

"Auntie is not getting her pistol back," her sister said with a sharp nod.

Sophia didn't wait for a response before pulling the door closed. Regina didn't invite him to sit, so he stood, waiting for her to speak. She didn't. She tugged open a side drawer, retrieved a book, and began reading. When she turned the page, irritation flared inside him, but he held his tongue. If she was looking for a quarrel to justify ending their sudden betrothal, he wouldn't oblige her. He didn't want to argue or their relationship to end with bad blood. He didn't want it to end at all. If they could at least remain friends, he would be content.

Eventually, his feet began to burn from standing at attention for so long, and the items in the room called out to him. Lord Wedmore's study was like a small museum. Clay pots sat on the windowsill. Wood carved animals graced the shelves. A bowl of tarnished coins rested on a table along with a dented helmet that could have belonged to a gladiator at one time. A tapestry hung alongside a rusty set of shackles screwed into the stone wall.

"Would you like to look around?"

Regina's voice startled him.

"No." He cleared his throat. "No, thank you."

"Are you sure? Uncle Charles wouldn't mind. He is proud of his finds."

"Does he deal in antiquities?"

"His hobby is antiquities. He donates his finds to the British Museum or keeps them, but I've never known him to part with an item for profit."

Suddenly, he understood Farrin's desire to get his hands on the map. It was likely ancient and valuable, and not for sale. It could be on display in this very room.

Regina closed her book and stood. "But I don't want to bore you with Uncle Charles's trinkets. You came here for me. Let's get on with it, shall we?"

"I don't take your meaning."

"Oh, I think you do." Her calculated smile as she rounded the desk and trailed her fingers over the battered surface caused his mouth to go dry. She was up to something.

"Evangeline and Sophia will keep Aunt Beatrice occupied, and I've not yet sent a message to Lord Margrave. You needn't worry we will be interrupted."

She leaned against the desk and arched her back, thrusting her breasts toward him. A pretty pink blush rose in her cheeks, but she boldly held his gaze.

"Sweet Mary Mother of God," he said, his words running into each other as if they were one long one. "Are you trying to seduce me?"

"Of course not. You are here to seduce *me*, Mr. Vistoire. And I am ready to surrender."

He frowned. "I don't want your surrender."

"You don't?" She blinked as if she didn't understand, but Regina possessed a shrewd mind. He didn't believe her bewildered act for a moment.

With a small hop, she sat on the edge of the desk. Slowly, she drew the hem of her skirts up her legs, revealing defined, shapely ankles and affording him a tantalizing peek of her stockings-clad calves.

His heart rammed against his ribs. She held him spellbound. He remembered how glorious her body was beneath the layers of muslin, and his fingers itched to touch her, to explore her silky skin at leisure.

When the ruffle of her petticoat slipped over her knees and uncovered an inch of bare thigh above her stockings, the rushing whoosh of his breath filled his ears. He held his arms stiffly at his sides and willed himself to resist.

"Is something wrong, Xavier? Don't you want to t-touch me?" The slight quiver to her voice was the only sign of nerves she'd shown, and it snapped him from his trance.

"I do. I want you desperately." He stalked toward her, stopping with barely a sliver of space between them. Her breath caught with a small hitch, and she gazed up at him with wide eyes. "I hear the sensual smokiness of your voice as I lie in bed at night. Your scent and the sensation of your fingers in my hair are etched into my memory. I *crave* you, Regina."

A smoldering fire flickered in her amber green eyes. The tip of her tongue swept over her lips, wetting them.

He swallowed a groan and yanked her skirts to cover her legs. Distrustful of his resolve, he placed several steps between them.

She huffed. "What are you doing?"

He crossed his arms and leaned his shoulder against the only spot on the wall that wasn't covered with artifacts. "Once will never be enough for me. That is what you are offering, is it not? One moment of pleasure to prove I am the scoundrel you believe me to be."

"You are wrong. I wanted evidence to the contrary, and you provided it. Your appearance at Wedmore House was not the result of accepting a challenge."

He cursed under his breath.

She marched to where he stood and squared off with him, crossing her arms to mirror him. "You have lied to me from the start. I want to offer you another chance to tell me the truth."

He drew back in surprise and dropped his arms at his sides. "Why would you give me another chance?"

"My aunt expects us to marry, and I cannot pledge fidelity to a man I don't know or trust. If you are honest, I won't cry off. I will become your wife, and when you return to New Orleans, we will part ways."

He winced. This conversation wasn't likely to go well. "Will you sit with me?"

Her eyebrows slowly rose on her forehead when he held his hand out to her.

"Please, I have a lot to explain. It would be more comfortable to sit."

She warily placed her hand in his and accompanied him to a settee wedged between the table that held the bowl of old coins and gladiator helmet, and a tall woodcarving of an angry elephant.

Once Regina had settled her skirts, Xavier sat. It was time to tell her everything. She deserved that much from him, especially when she wouldn't be happy at the conclusion of their conversation.

"I didn't come to Wedmore House to steal your virtue. I was sent to find a map, although my true aim was to take a piece of jewelry to pay for my passage home."

A crease appeared between her brows, and he rushed on with his story, telling her everything that had happened to him in the past two years. Being nabbed leaving the Den of Iniquity. The interrogations and accusations that followed.

"You were accused of being a spy?" She laughed. "That is ridiculous. You couldn't sneak into Wedmore House without being thwarted by a small dog."

"Eh... Yes, well..." Heat crept into his face. "Farrin drew the same conclusion eventually. That I wasn't a spy. Not that I was inept."

She shrugged as if to say *maybe*. "After the Home Office took you into custody and determined you were innocent of the charges, why didn't they release you?"

"I don't believe Farrin is with the Home Office. I haven't been able to determine much about his group except he appears to be the leader. He is also for hire, which brings us to the map. He said he was hired to retrieve it. I intend to use the map as leverage to learn who wants it and who is responsible for my incarceration."

"And he is using you to get it." Her eyes narrowed to slits. "Did he order you to form an attachment with me so you could access the map?"

"God, no! He threatened to send in another man, and I couldn't allow it. I've had experience with Farrin's henchmen. They are more like beasts than humans."

She sniffed indignantly. "I am capable of defending myself and my family."

"Not against these men. They do not fight fair." He swiveled toward her on the settee, praying she could recognize his sincerity. "I didn't lie about returning home when I left Wedmore House. Farrin and his men found me before I could make my way to the docks. I didn't know Serafine had moved to London and married. Farrin threatened my sister and her family. He has no qualms about hurting you or your family either."

"But now that I know there is danger—"

"You underestimate the blackguard, and I won't allow any harm to come to any of you. You cannot fight these men and defeat them."

Her shoulders sank on a sigh. "Perhaps you are correct. Sophia and Evangeline know some Wing Chun, but not enough. And Aunt Beatrice is too vulnerable. It seems our best defense will be to find what he wants and get it out of Wedmore House. What type of map are we looking for?"

"Farrin wouldn't say, and I chose not to debate the reason that knowledge would be helpful. The man is easily provoked, so I didn't press the issue. Could it be something in your uncle's collection of antiquities?"

"Evangeline is better acquainted with Uncle Charles's finds, but an old map would require special care."

"Does your uncle keep all of his treasures at Wedmore House? Could he have hidden some away and drawn a map to recall the location?"

"It seems like a stretch. Uncle Charles wouldn't need a map unless he buried his finds, and that goes against the grain with antiquarians. My sister might have some ideas. There would be no need to proceed with the wedding once we turned over the map."

His gut clenched. He didn't want to let her go. When he was with Regina, his heart was lighter and heavy with fullness at the same time. She made him long for things he never had before, like setting down roots and creating a family with her.

She skimmed her hand up the back of her neck, squeezing different spots along the way. "We should find Evangeline and Sophia and begin looking."

He scooted closer and took over rubbing away the tight knots he discovered just below her hairline. "I'm sorry for surprising you last night," he said. "Did I hurt you?"

"No. Sometimes my neck bothers me for no reason."

By his observation, she had *many* reasons. Figuratively, she tried to carry too much on her shoulders, and the amount of responsibilities she assumed weighed a lot. She closed her eyes and leaned toward him to rest her head on his shoulder, allowing him better access.

Her nearness ignited a fire in his lower belly, and he couldn't resist the temptation to embrace her. His arm slid around her waist, and he continued to softly knead her neck.

"I don't expect your forgiveness, Regina, but I will beg for it. For lying to you. For misleading your aunt about our relationship. For every mistake that I've made or will make in the future. If you never believe anything I say again, please trust that my admiration for you is true."

He continued to work the tightness from her muscles, and she released a moaning sigh. "Perhaps soon we can put the past behind us and become friends," she said.

Placing a kiss against her hair, he breathed in the spicy citrus scent of her soap. He savored this moment of peace, knowing what he was about to say would likely mean losing the privilege of holding her like this. "There is something more I should tell you."

She eased back to eye him warily.

"I won't allow you to cry off," he said.

She sat up straighter. "I beg your pardon?" She bit off each word.

"I can guarantee your safety as your husband."

"No." She shook her head and tried to bolt from the settee, but he snagged her around the waist and made her sit again. "Consider this fair warning, Xavier. If you don't release me, you will regret it."

If she wanted to break free, she could have done it already. He wasn't holding her in place, and she had the skills to incapacitate him for a moment.

"Listen to reason," he said. "Farrin might have said he wants the map, but there could be more. I can't protect you if we are not together, and I care too much for you to see you harmed."

She scoffed. "I don't need a man's protection. I can save myself, thank you very much."

"We will agree to disagree. And as your husband, if I determine it is safest for you and your family to come to New Orleans with me, I will hear no arguments."

She lifted her chin in challenge. "How do you think you will stop me from crying off, Mr. Vistoire?"

He buried his fingers in her hair and tousled it.

She protested, jerking away. "Have you lost your senses?"

He reached for her again, and she smacked his hand.

"Stop that! How do you like having your hair mussed?" She dove forward and drove her hands through his curls. He simply smiled and let her do her best. She plopped back on her side of the settee and scowled. "Why are you smiling?"

He untied a decorative bow on the bodice of her gown. It accomplished nothing, besides making her appearance untidy and riling her temper even more.

"You scoundrel!" With her mouth set in a hard line, she grabbed his cravat and wrestled the knot free. When she was done, it hung loose around his neck. "There," she said with a satisfied nod. "I've bested you."

He raised an eyebrow. "Is that so, Miss Darlington?" He snatched the end of the sash around her waist and pulled.

Sparks shot from her eyes. "You incorrigible beast." She attacked the top fastenings of his waistcoat and drew back. Apparently thinking she could do better, she unfastened the rest and pushed the waistcoat and jacket off his shoulders.

She sat back, her hands still gripping his clothes. Her amber green eyes were nearly black, and they were both breathing hard. A wild hunger welled inside of him.

"Regina."

He didn't know who moved first, but their mouths collided.

Twenty

Regina twined her arms around Xavier's neck and sagged against his hard chest. He groaned deep in his throat, hugging her tightly, his arms like iron bands. Every part of her front molded to him—his hard muscles different from her own body.

His mouth possessed hers, his tongue sliding between her lips when she sighed. He tasted of mint and his kiss was deliciously hot. When he withdrew, she tentatively flicked her tongue into his mouth, testing the boundaries. He angled his head to allow her better access and splayed his hands on her back.

Before she was even close to feeling satisfied, he pulled away. She barely refrained from pulling him back.

"Regina," he murmured. Her name sounded more glamorous when he spoke it. "I didn't intend to compromise you in reality. I only wanted to make it appear that way."

His confession should have infuriated her, but she ached to kiss him again. She slid her hand to his chest and detected the violent throbbing of his heart. "Then make the trouble I've gotten myself into worth it."

Xavier murmured something in French—something similar to a prayer.

He caught the back of her head and covered her mouth with his. His fingers slid into her hair, and a pin pinged against the table. He tugged her hair, not enough to hurt but her scalp tingled, and he held her an inch away. When she tried to kiss him, he gave a gentle jerk to her hair to keep her in place. Her breath quickened. They sat there, embracing, exchanging a breath. Several rapid pulses between her legs caused her to whimper softly. He was in control of her body, her pleasure. For as long as she could remember, she'd fought to keep control in every situation. But now, in this moment, she chose faith over fear.

He flashed a wicked smile. "What should I do with you, goddess? You have learned my secrets. Perhaps now it is time for me to discover yours."

Her heart pounded as if she'd been practicing her exercises, and she couldn't catch her breath. She had no secrets to uncover, but she didn't mind him trying. "I heard the French method is very effective for loosening one's lips."

He laughed and released her hair, brushing the back of his fingers across her cheek before touching his lips tenderly to hers.

"Are you sure you wish for me to use the most powerful means available to me?"

"Yes," she whispered.

His fingertips skimmed her waist as he leaned to place his mouth to her ear. "I think you like trouble." His breath singed her skin.

She smiled. If she'd known trouble was this exciting, she might have gotten into it more often.

He slid his hands along the curves of her sides until he reached her breasts to cup them. "Tell me where you like to be touched."

His thumbs pressed against her nipples through her corset and drew slow circles. She sucked in a breath, shocked by the unfamiliar powerful currents traveling to her core.

"I don't know." She had touched herself a couple of times, but she would be mortified to speak of it.

He grasped the tie to her apron front gown and yanked. He had it loose in seconds and peeled away the fabric to bare her undergarments. "Tell me where you like to be touched, or I will be forced to become more persuasive."

Bending his head, he kissed the plumped flesh rising from her corset.

She closed her eyes and sighed. "I don't know."

He eased her back against the settee cushion and she sank into it, grateful for the support since her bones seemed to be dissolving with each stroke of his fingers across her nipples. His mouth found her neck, and he licked a tantalizingly slow path to the sensitive place behind her ear. She moaned as a wave of pleasure engulfed her.

"This is your final warning, Miss Darlington. Tell me the secrets to pleasuring you or prepare to accept the consequences."

His teasing tone made her smile.

"Never," she said.

"You are a challenge, *ma chérie*."

Flutters filled her stomach as he removed his waistcoat and jacket and knelt on the carpet before her. He grasped the hem of her skirts with a mischievous twinkle in his eyes. "I like trouble, but I love a challenge even more."

He slid his hands beneath her skirts, inching them up her thighs until he found the ties to her drawers. Regina's heart beat with a driving rhythm. The ache between her legs intensified. He helped her shimmy her drawers over her hips and drew them down her legs then tossed them over his shoulder.

Caressing just above her knee, he locked gazes with her.

"*Magnifique*," he murmured as his fingers moved to her inner thigh and glided up her leg in the most excruciatingly unhurried and teasing manner. "Your skin is as soft as the most luxurious silk."

Her face warmed at his extravagant praise. As he lifted her skirts higher and her legs were bared, she squirmed with anticipation. His fingers grazed her curls and she gasped. "*There.*"

A satisfied smile eased across his handsome face. "Here, lover?" He stroked her again.

"Yes."

He rewarded her honesty with another exquisite caress. She melted into the settee, closing her eyes on a sigh and surrendering to the sensual feel of his skin on hers. Grasping her hips, he pulled her to the edge of the settee and spread her thighs. Her eyes flew open. Her thoughts of protest vanished into oblivion with the first sweep of his tongue over her flesh. A moan slipped past her lips. Each lick carried her deeper into a world she'd never known existed, and never wanted to leave.

Xavier cradled her bottom as he continued to make love to her with his mouth, circling an especially pleasurable spot at the apex of her labia and driving her toward something she wanted with great desperation. Something she couldn't name or had ever experienced.

Every muscle quivered with expectation. Her fingers curled into fists. Her breathing ceased, and for a split second, she teetered on the peak. Then she was crying out as wave after satisfying wave rushed over her, and through her, until she was spent. She collapsed against the settee, her legs trembling. Xavier's hand splayed across her bare bottom, holding her as she recovered. He placed a lingering kiss on the fleshiest part of her thigh, watching her with nearly black eyes.

When her breathing began to even out, he released her, allowing her skirts to drop. He stood and kissed her softly before retrieving her drawers to help set her back to rights.

She brushed a loving hand over his dark hair as he knelt at her feet once more. "I could grow accustomed to having you on your knees," she teased.

He glanced up with a roguish grin. "Maybe next time you will kneel for me."

A fiery blush swept over her at the suggestion, but she mumbled, "Maybe."

"I should have done this the first time I was on my knees." He cupped her hand between his and all traces of teasing fled. Her eyes widened when she realized he intended to propose like a true suitor. He looked up with such earnestness, her heart skipped. "Miss Darlington, would you do me the honor of becoming my wife?"

To others, his proposal might sound silly at this point, but she appreciated the chance to have a say. "Yes, I will marry you."

Scratching sounded at the door, and Cupid's sharp bark echoed in the corridor.

"Aunt Beatrice must be awake," she said. Xavier pulled her to her feet, and she smoothed her hands over her wrinkled skirts. "I should slip upstairs to see to my hair before Auntie is dressed and comes down for breakfast. Sophia is to send for Lord Margrave as soon as we vacate the study."

Xavier captured her wrist before she could move toward the door and pulled her back to him for a kiss. "Regina, I don't want to quarrel with you, but I meant what I said about New Orleans. If that is the safest place for you and your family, I will insist upon everyone coming with me. Even Cupid."

Regina caressed his cheek, touched by his concern for her and her loved ones. She knew he meant well, but a long voyage would be a hardship for Aunt Beatrice. Sophia was on the verge of a betrothal, and Evangeline had plans to join Uncle Charles on his next expedition. Besides, they didn't know how to reach their uncle to inform him of any travel plans, and there was no one to see to the running of Wedmore House or the family manor home.

"I don't know if my aunt and sisters would agree to leave England, and I cannot desert them. Please don't ask me to choose."

"I fail to see that there is a choice to make. Your family has been threatened. I am offering my protection."

Her stomach pitched. There truly was no choice when it came to her family's safety, but at least she knew what dangers they faced here. "This is our home. We won't be driven out by anyone, but I need your help to defend it. Will you stand beside me? *Please*."

His sigh could almost be mistaken for a growl. "What choice do *I* have? If you stay, I stay."

He released her wrist, and she turned for the door, circling her hand over the burgeoning warmth in her chest. After the intimacy they had shared, there was no going back. She would marry him. Her conscience insisted it was her duty now, but she couldn't deny that he'd awakened longings she kept buried deep inside.

Suddenly, the life they could have together unfolded before her. Reading the morning newssheet to each other over breakfast. Playfully teasing one another and their children as they strolled through the meadow in the country. Everything her beloved parents had done to create a happy home for her and her sisters, she and Xavier could do, but more.

She would teach him Wing Chun, and they could spar together. Perhaps he'd show interest in Uncle Charles's studies and engage him in academic discussions over brandy. He would dance with Aunt Beatrice at every assembly if she wished it. Xavier would be Regina's companion, her love. And her newfound vulnerability scared her to death.

Twenty-one

"Wait," Xavier called to Regina as she opened the study door to admit the exuberant black poodle. Cupid dashed around her skirts then leapt at him. He scooped the dog in his arms and followed her into the corridor. "Regina, I asked you to wait."

She whirled toward him with a slight pucker to her forehead. "I really should hurry to my chambers before Aunt Beatrice asks for me."

He scratched the dog's chin to quiet his whining. "When you said you cannot leave your family, did you mean now while there is danger or never?"

She captured her bottom lip between her teeth, hesitating for several moments. "I was honest with you from the beginning. I vowed to never marry, because I intended to stay with Aunt Beatrice and Uncle Charles. Now I will have a husband—one that lives far away—but Aunt Beatrice's needs haven't changed. With Evangeline off on her expeditions and Sophia creating a home of her own, there will be no one left to watch over her. I thought you understood."

A heaviness settled in his chest. He'd been so focused on escaping England he hadn't thought about what was left for him in New Orleans. An empty old house and bad memories were the only things awaiting him. Everyone he loved had made a life in England. Even his ward was here, and he wouldn't take his cousin Rafe from his sister.

He cleared his throat. "Perhaps we should just focus on finding the map for now."

Cupid's ears darted up and he cocked his head to the side. A faint whistle sounded from deeper in the house. The dog whimpered, twisting his body to break free of Xavier's arms. He set Cupid on the stone floor before he took a tumble. His nails scraped the stone as he tried to gain traction, then he darted toward the foyer.

"It is Aunt Beatrice," Regina said with a groan.

Before she could escape, he entangled his fingers with hers and drew her to his side. "Promise you will be careful until Farrin and his employer have been dealt with. No venturing out without a proper escort. Joy would be of no assistance if Farrin's men accost you, and I want a manservant hired before the end of the week. I cannot be here all the time."

She smiled and his heart tripped. "In this instance, I will do as you wish, but don't grow accustomed to blind obedience. I might be challenging at times."

"I wouldn't have you any other way." He placed a kiss at her temple then released her to make a quick stop by her bedchamber before they met with her aunt and Lord Margrave.

Sophia found him waiting in the foyer. "Would you like to join Auntie? Regina said she would be along shortly, and I've sent for Margrave."

"Yes, thank you." Xavier expected he was in for a lecture, and he would prefer to get it over with before Regina came below stairs. She had suffered enough embarrassment because of his actions.

Aunt Beatrice greeted him with a wide smile. "Why Mr. Vistoire, what a pleasant surprise. What brings you to Wedmore House this morning?"

Xavier blinked and looked to Sophia for direction. She smiled pleasantly at her aunt. "Mr. Vistoire came to see Regina. They are betrothed. Isn't that wonderful news? Lord Margrave is assisting with obtaining a special license." She whispered behind her hand to Xavier. "The laudanum is causing her to be a little forgetful this morning."

Aunt Beatrice's mouth pinched. "I am not forgetful. I recall last night's situation. I simply chose to greet my future nephew with a civil tongue and give him a chance to ask permission for Regina's hand, as he should have done in the beginning."

"Yes, ma'am," Sophia said. "I'm sorry."

Aunt Beatrice lifted her spoon and wagged it toward the chair across the table before dipping into her porridge. "Have a seat, young man. There are words I wish to have with you. Leave us, Sophia."

"Yes, Auntie." She ducked her head and hurried from the breakfast room without glancing back.

Regina's aunt raised her brows, staring him down as if she were royalty. "I said sit, Mr. Vistoire."

"Yes, ma'am."

As soon as Xavier's backside touched the seat cushion, Aunt Beatrice launched into a diatribe on unbecoming behavior and the dangerous allures of lust. And because he was very recently guilty of every charge she heaped on him, he did his best to sit up straight while also appearing contrite.

"And further more, sir..."

After awhile, his spine lost some of its rigidity. Even his father's lectures hadn't gone on this long.

Eventually, Aunt Beatrice ended her set down with a loud sigh. "There. I have dispatched with my duties." She paused with her spoon halfway to her mouth. "Would you care for some porridge?"

"No, thank you. Please, don't allow my presence to interfere with your breakfast. I could wait in the drawing room until Lord Margrave arrives."

"Your company is most welcome, Mr. Vistoire. Tell me, what are your plans after the wedding?"

"I believe Miss Darlington would prefer to stay close to home, at least for a time. With your permission, we would like to stay at Wedmore House."

Aunt Beatrice directed her gaze toward the ceiling and shook her head. "Poor Regina worries too much about her sisters and me. I suppose it is best for a while, but I do hope you and she will plan a honeymoon trip. It would benefit her to venture from Wedmore House and discover the world is not as frightening as she believes."

"Oh?"

Regina hardly seemed the sort to hide from the world. Only half an hour earlier, she'd been ready to take on Farrin and his men.

"She was an impressionable age when her parents were killed while traveling abroad," Regina's aunt said. "The circumstances were tragic but uncommon. A riot. It was a stroke of bad luck, really."

"Miss Darlington mentioned her parents' deaths, but she didn't say how it happened. Now I better understand why she feared the men would come for her and her sisters. It sounded as if she outgrew such worries."

Aunt Beatrice's smile was grim. "Does anyone truly heal from childhood wounds, sir? Perhaps we forget about them with the passage of time, but our view of life has been altered and influences our decisions."

Xavier sank against the seatback and considered her words. Hadn't his own decisions been driven by hurt? His father had rejected him from a young age. He'd called Xavier worthless and predicted he would become a gadabout. And Xavier had. He'd become the best libertine in all of New Orleans—a reprobate gambler, a drunk, and a rake—because proving his father right about his character was less degrading than begging for approval he would never receive.

"There is wisdom in what you say." He drummed his fingers against his thigh as he mulled over his own life more. "I see how my childhood led me toward a certain path, but I made the choice to follow it. Ultimately, I am responsible for my mistakes."

Her broad smile lit the breakfast room. "Yes, and your choices have brought you to Regina. I expect you are wiser now and will take more care with your decisions in the future, because they no longer affect only you. We will pretend last night never happened." She winked and spooned a bit of porridge into her mouth.

"For what it is worth, I'm ashamed of my behavior. I never meant to disrespect your niece, you, or her uncle."

She discarded her spoon and stretched across the table, extending her hand. He placed his in hers and she squeezed. "All I ask is that you love her, if not fully now, some day soon. She deserves to be cherished."

A small lump formed in his throat. "You have my word, Aunt Beatrice. I already cherish her."

Twenty-two

Regina barley held her temper in check when Crispin, Lord Margrave, looked up from the marriage contract once again to peer at Xavier sitting in the chair opposite him at Uncle Charles's desk. Her uncle's godson leaned his elbows on the scratched wood surface and narrowed his intense hazel gaze on Xavier. Crispin's blank expression and the inordinate amount of time he stared without blinking was quite unnerving, but she'd become accustomed to his tricks over the years.

She rose from the settee where Sophia was scratching Cupid's belly and approached the desk. The four of them and the poodle had been ensconced in Uncle Charles's study for nearly an hour. It was high time the contract was signed, so she and Xavier could make their way to the Doctor's Commons to apply for a marriage license.

Regina knocked on the desk to gain Crispin's attention, but he didn't break eye contact with Xavier. "This is no time for a staring challenge," she said, "and we are no longer children. You've read the contract Evangeline drafted several times. Is it sufficient for our needs?"

Crispin didn't so much as twitch in response.

"Ludwig! You are infuriating."

"Hear, hear," Sophia interjected. "You should see how he tries to intimidate my suitors at the assemblies."

Regina drew back. "You are attending balls regularly now? The man who has sworn never to become leg-shackled? Surely you haven't had a change of heart."

"Absolutely not," Sophia said. "He has no heart to change. Besides, wife-hunting would interfere with his plot to ruin my life."

Crispin's unwavering focus shattered, and he turned to glare at Regina's sister. "I couldn't care less about your aims to snare a husband, and I have better ways to spend my time than scheming against you. You are not the sun every gentleman gravitates to, Sophia Darlington."

Sophia shrugged one shoulder. "And yet you seem unable to resist stalking me around the ballroom floor. He thinks he is being discrete," she said to Regina as if Crispin had suddenly lost his hearing, "but I see him staring daggers at my partners. More than one gentleman has made a quick escape at the end of the promenade, thanks to Lord Margrave's dark glowers."

Oh, dear. Sophia was truly put out with him if she'd reverted to his formal address.

Regina glanced at Crispin for confirmation that he had been following Sophia. Ruddy patches appeared on his face, and he snatched up the contract to scrutinize it more. "With Charles away someone needs to keep watch over you. *All* of you."

Xavier's eyebrow arched. "I am capable of caring for my betrothed and her family."

Crispin lowered the sheet of foolscap. "Who are you, exactly? You seemed to have appeared from nowhere to whisk the Darlingtons to Hyde Park for a picnic, and suddenly you and Regina are to be married."

Sophia bounded from the settee, eliciting a startled bark from Cupid. She hugged the dog and kissed his furry head to soothe him before nailing Crispin with a scathing glare. "It appears you not only follow me around the ballroom, but you've taken to spying on me at the park. How else would you know about our picnic?"

"I was riding, as I do every day. I happened to notice the lot of you as I was leaving."

The little dog whimpered and wiggled to break free of Sophia's arms to reach Crispin. He ignored the dog and returned to questioning Xavier. "How do you know Mr. and Mrs. Tucker?"

Regina grumbled under her breath, but Xavier simply lounged on the chair with an insolent slant to one side of his mouth. "Serafine Tucker is my sister. Are you well acquainted with my kin? Do speak with them if you require a personal recommendation, although it seems clear Miss Darlington is not seeking your blessing."

The muscles in Crispin's jaw bulged. "No, she isn't. She wishes to use my connections to secure a special license, but she cares nothing about my thoughts on her marriage."

Regina's frustration began to ebb. Uncle Charles, Aunt Beatrice, Regina, and her sisters were all Crispin had in his life. His desire to protect them while Uncle Charles was away was rather sweet. She placed a hand on his shoulder to express her thanks and friendship, but she held his steady gaze to let him know she wouldn't be swayed.

"Your blessing means a great deal to me. You must know I care, but I have always been of an independent mind. I have made my decision. Mr. Vistoire will be a good husband."

A whisper of doubt caused her heart to flutter, but she maintained her confident demeanor. How was one to know with certainty if a man would be a good husband until it was too late?

"I've *made* my decision." She smacked her palm against the desk to punctuate the finality of her choice.

Crispin's brow wrinkled "I heard you the first time." He dropped the contract on the desk. "It is a generous agreement. Your interests will be protected, if he signs the contract as it is."

Xavier rose from the chair, towering over Crispin and reached for the contract before snatching the quill and ink from the corner of the desk. The curling of his top lip communicated his disdain for Crispin and his insinuation. "I will sign the agreement if it meets with *your* approval, Miss Darlington. I ask for nothing in return."

He bent over the paper with the quill poised to sign his name, looking to her for consent. She gave a quick nod. He scribbled his name on the contract, then slid it toward her and held out the quill. Her hand shook slightly when she signed her name.

"Sophia." She passed the paper to her sister to bear witness and held her breath as Crispin followed suit after a lengthy hesitation.

"I will call on James Hillary next," Crispin said as he replaced the quill and stood. "I am aware of at least one occasion when he was able to expedite the approval of a special license. That was for his son, however. I cannot promise Mr. Hillary will grant my request."

Regina nodded. "We are grateful for whatever you are able to do."

"You are welcome." The viscount brushed past Sophia en route to the study door, pointedly avoiding eye contact with her. At the threshold, he spun on his heel to aim one more unnerving scowl at Xavier before jerking open the door and stalking away. The front door slammed a few moments later.

Regina gaped at her sister. "What in the world has Crispin in such a foul-temper?"

Sophia frowned. "I don't know what has gotten into him lately. He's as grumpy as an old toad."

"I had no idea toads were so emotive," Regina teased.

"I said they are *grumpy*—not performing Shakespearean plays. Have you ever seen a toad without a frown?"

She laughed and tweaked her sister's cheek. "Try not to be too harsh with Crispin. He misses Uncle Charles when he is away."

"We all do, but you won't find me lurking in corners plotting the dismemberment and death of others."

"You shouldn't say such things about Crispin, even in jest."

Sophia sniffed as if to say she was not joking.

Regina abandoned the topic. "Retrieve your gloves and bonnet. If you are still accompanying us to the Commons, we should hurry along. We have quite a task facing us this afternoon after we apply for the license."

She had updated her sisters on the recent development of the map while Aunt Beatrice had a private word with Xavier. Both conversations went much better than she'd anticipated. Aunt Beatrice hadn't asked for her pistol, and her sisters seemed more intrigued by the mystery of the map and who wanted it than indignant over Xavier deceiving them. There had been time to rummage through Uncle Charles's study before Crispin arrived, but many hiding places still needed to be explored.

Sophia pulled on her gloves in the foyer. "The library itself could take a few days to search. How long do we have?"

"Four days," Xavier said.

Regina turned toward him. "Now that we are betrothed, do you think the risk of Farrin sending in another man will be eliminated?"

"Perhaps once word reaches him."

"Can't you speak with him? Do you know where to find him?"

If Xavier had a meeting place, perhaps it would provide a useful clue to lead them to Farrin's employer.

"Farrin finds me when he wishes to speak. He says the streets have eyes and ears."

"Then we must herald our good news so the message reaches him. Lady Faldingworth's ball is this evening. We'll dance several sets, whisper in corners together, and tell everyone of our betrothal. That should earn a mention in the gossip rags."

Xavier caught her shoulder when she tried to sweep through the front door. "I'd prefer no one is under the illusion this is a love match."

Sophia gasped and Regina experienced his words like a physical blow.

"I simply mean I don't want Farrin knowing I actually care for you." He squeezed her shoulder and drew her close, soothing her hurt. "If the blackguard realizes my true feelings, I'm afraid you would become another target to control me, and I won't place you in any more danger."

"Gigi, you never said anything about being in danger if you marry." Sophia's blue eyes had grown to twice their usual size.

"I'm not in danger. There is no cause for concern." She held Xavier's gaze, daring him to contradict her in front of Sophia.

"I agree to one dance," he said. "Possibly two as long as the appropriate time has elapsed between sets. We may tell others of our agreement, but there will be no whispering in the corner." A sultry smile spread across his face. "And no slipping off to the gardens together."

A thrill swept through her at the reminder of their encounter in the Norwick's gardens. Xavier had accused her of wanting him to bed her and vowed to win her hand. She'd thought he was arrogant and deluded at the time.

Sophia cleared her throat, causing them both to startle. "I don't want to know what the secret smiles between you mean, but I agree with Mr. Vistoire. Placing yourself in danger is not an option."

Regina's smile widened. "Very well, Mr. Vistoire. I won't try to tempt you into taking a moonlit stroll or demand your attention on the ballroom floor. But I hope you don't expect me to congregate with the wallflowers while you pretend to barely know me. I would hate for anyone to think I am smitten with you and use the knowledge against *me.*"

"That might be the closest I will ever get to a profession of love from you, darling. I will take it."

Twenty-three

As soon as the hack rolled to a stop in front of his sister's home, Xavier spotted Farrin's men across the street. The larger one met his gaze through the carriage window and smirked. He was an ugly fellow with pocked skin and dead eyes that exuded hatred for anything with a heartbeat. Xavier knew his type. Most men were too intimidated to challenge brutes like him, and he probably enjoyed beating the hell out of the ones that did.

Xavier climbed from the hack and stood on the walkway until it drove away. With the street clear, he stalked toward the men. The brute's partner came forward to meet him at the edge of the street. Xavier wasn't intimidated. He could hold his own when allowed to square off with a man. Even the giant ones posed little threat with Xavier's speed. He stopped inches from the man's face.

"Tell Farrin I want to speak with him."

The ugly one sneered over his friend's shoulder. "Do we look like servant boys? We don't deliver messages for anyone."

Xavier ran his gaze over the men from head to toe and shrugged. "You look more like the post coach horses' asses, but I fail to see how your appearance is relevant. Give Farrin the message."

"Go to the devil," the smaller man spat.

The brute shoved his partner aside and rolled up his sleeves. "Make another demand, and I'll rearrange your pretty smile, you fop."

Xavier flashed his pretty smile and bit out each word to taunt him. "Give. Farrin. The. Message."

He ducked when the man swung for his nose, weaved to his left to come up behind his opponent and drive his own fist into the man's kidney. Xavier's opponent arched his back, howling in pain. Xavier punched him twice more in the same spot in rapid succession. The man's knees buckled, and he collapsed on the walkway, his body jerking with spasms.

The brute's partner charged him. Xavier bent low to slam his shoulder into the man's doughy middle and flipped him flat on his back on the cobblestone street. As both men gasped to catch their breath, Xavier retrieved one of his calling cards and flicked it on the ground where they lay. "If I have to ask once again, I will no longer be polite. I want to speak with Farrin."

He didn't want to take a chance that news of his and Regina's betrothal wouldn't reach Farrin. He would deliver the word himself and tell him to keep his men out of Wedmore House.

As he spun on his heel to return to his sister's side of the street, the neighbor's curtains fell back in place. He frowned. It appeared the town house to the left of Isaac and Serafine was no longer vacant. He'd discussed with his brother-in-law letting the town house from the owner, a widow who preferred a quiet life in the country and didn't appear to have the funds to pay board wages to keep up the house. It had seemed a perfect solution for everyone until he could convince his sister to return to New Orleans. Moving next door would have allowed his sister and her husband privacy while Xavier remained close enough to watch over them.

If he hadn't decided to alter his plans after his audience with Regina, he would be disappointed to have lost out to another tenant. Letting rooms at the Pulteney Hotel made more sense until after the wedding. Once he'd drawn Farrin's men away from his sister's home, Xavier would encourage her and Isaac to visit their American cousins in Brighton. Lisette was lying in wait with her first child and would likely welcome Serafine's company. The women had always been close like sisters.

Apparently, Lisette had met and married an Englishman when she and her younger brother Rafe traveled to London with Serafine to search for Xavier. After Xavier settled the score with Farrin and the man financing him, he would call on his cousins too. He was Rafe's guardian, and he should see to the boy's welfare, even though Serafine reported Lisette's husband loved Rafe as if he were his own child.

Xavier jogged up Serafine's front steps and closed the door behind him. Small footsteps pounded down the corridor.

Simon screeched with joy, and it was the sweetest sound he'd ever heard. The tot's wide smile made him forget about the confrontation on the street and the coming meeting with Farrin. Xavier scooped him into his arms and tossed him over his shoulder. Simon kicked and giggled all the way down the corridor as Xavier carried him back toward the drawing room. Serafine looked up from her knitting with an expectant smile. "Are congratulations premature?"

He shook his head. "Miss Darlington accepted my proposal."

Serafine cried out and launched from the settee to come place a kiss on his cheek. "It is sudden and unexpected, but I couldn't be happier for you."

Tears welled in her eyes. Xavier drew back in shock. His sister had never been demonstrative or sentimental, but she was beginning to resemble a watering pot lately.

"Tears and a kiss, Serafine? Are you under the weather?"

She puckered her lips and wiped the wetness from her eyes. "I'm perfectly well and capable of showing affection. I've even been known to cry occasionally."

Never in his presence. When they were children and he'd teased her, she'd turned to stone. Xavier used to call her Medusa and say she must have caught her reflection in the mirror. Even with his merciless pestering, she'd not uttered a sound or cried like he'd wanted. He had apologized a thousand times over once they were grown.

"I know you have feelings," he said with a smile. "But you must admit it is a *rare* occasion when you cry."

She beamed at him and circled her hand over her flat stomach. "Not when I am expecting."

Xavier's gaze darted to the discarded knitting on the settee—a tiny yellow bonnet—then back at Serafine.

Merde. He would be gray before the end of the week.

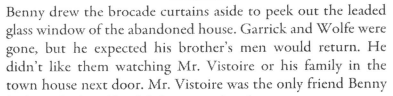

Benny drew the brocade curtains aside to peek out the leaded glass window of the abandoned house. Garrick and Wolfe were gone, but he expected his brother's men would return. He didn't like them watching Mr. Vistoire or his family in the town house next door. Mr. Vistoire was the only friend Benny had ever had, and he didn't want to lose him.

Nope, Benny didn't like the men loitering outside one bit, but he didn't know how to make them go away. Usually, he didn't have to worry about what to do. Tommy gave the commands. Benny followed them.

He knew he was born without smarts. His father had reminded him every day before he was sent to live in the country. Benny was an idiot, a dolt, a fool, an embarrassment, and a disappointment. Sometimes his father referred to him as a bastard, but when he'd asked his mother what the word meant, she'd slapped him and forbidden him from ever uttering the word again. He still didn't know what a bastard was, but he'd decided if he was one, he should never admit it.

Even his younger brother had come to realize Benny's faults, and when their father died, he'd assumed Father's role—including reminding Benny of the tragedies that would befall him if he ever left the farm or let anyone else know of his existence.

Mr. Vistoire was the only person who hadn't seemed to notice Benny was a dolt. His friend had spoken to him as if he were a man, not a child or a beast to order around. He'd told him about his home in New Orleans and his travels around the globe. He'd recalled stories from his childhood and discussed men like Galileo and Aristotle. Benny rarely understood those talks about the men with unusual names, but he'd kept his mouth shut so Mr. Vistoire would keep speaking. A voice aside from his own had been a welcome addition to Benny's silent and lonely existence.

When Mr. and Mrs. Hull were alive, life hadn't been terrible. The farm's caretaker and his wife had treated him with kindness, invited him to their table, and taught him how to fend for himself. Even though they hadn't quite thought of him as family, he hadn't minded. In Benny's experience, family was cruel, and the Hulls were vastly better than any family he could imagine. When they were gone, he'd mourned for them—just as he would grieve for Mr. Vistoire if Tommy ordered his execution.

A tremor wracked Benny's bulky frame, and he peered out the window to reassure himself that his brother's men were truly gone. The street was empty, but the command to kill Mr. Vistoire could come any moment, especially after the confrontation Benny had just witnessed.

He worried he wouldn't be able to protect his friend or the family his friend loved, but he promised to fight until he drew his last breath. And if he were allowed to become a ghost when he died—and he did hope that was possible, for he would enjoy walking through walls—he'd still fight for Mr. Vistoire.

Benny owed the man a huge debt. At first, he'd held Mr. Vistoire prisoner out of fear. Tommy's threats to have Benny skinned alive if he lost his prisoner had terrified him. His brother was known to order equally brutal punishments for others who'd displeased him. Later, Benny had an additional reason to keep Mr. Vistoire locked away. He enjoyed the other man's companionship. He'd given Benny a reason to wake every morning. Benny had been wrong to keep his friend from his family, but he would set everything to rights again.

He didn't know how, for he wasn't born with smarts, but he would muddle through the best he could. Benny drew the curtains aside to peer out again. Until he figured everything out, he'd just keep watch over his new neighbors.

Twenty-four

Regina, Evangeline, and Sophia assembled in a quiet corner of the Faldingworths' ballroom between sets, bowing their heads together.

"What did you learn?" Regina whispered.

Evangeline grimaced and touched her gloved fingers to her temple. "Nothing so far, but I've only spoken with two of Uncle Charles's associates. I was detained by Lord Reinhardt."

Regina hissed in sympathy. The gentleman was well known for his lengthy monologues on hounds, and the blight plaguing civilization, also known as the middling sort. Being caught by Lord Reinhardt was the unfortunate consequence of dropping one's guard. "Did you have any luck, Sophia?"

Her youngest sister shook her head. "My dance partners have been uninterested in antiquities, and even less keen on associating with anyone who is." She pursed her lips. "I must say it has been eye-opening. Any man unwilling or incapable of discussing a topic so dear to Uncle Charles and Evangeline could never win my hand."

Evangeline smiled and leaned her head against Sophia's in a show of affection. "Thank you, dearest."

Sophia's dimple pierced her cheek. "That is simply how I feel. No need to thank me." She gestured for Regina to deliver her own report.

"Your gentlemen don't want to discuss antiquities, and my partners prefer no conversation at all."

Typically, Regina declined to stand up with the scoundrels clamoring for her attention, but she had chosen to endure their tedious company for investigative purposes. She and her sisters were making a list of gentlemen who collected old maps. So far, they hadn't gathered a single name.

Evangeline waved for them to come closer. Regina and Sophia swayed toward her. "I have been mulling over the situation all evening, and I keep coming back to the journal I found in Uncle Charles's desk. I think his new project could be responsible for our dilemma."

Regina's breath caught slightly. "His study of the ancient assassins?"

"What assassins?" Sophia whispered.

Regina had forgotten Sophia was absent when Evangeline broke into their uncle's desk and found the journal about the fabled group of warriors called the Black Death.

"Uncle Charles has ventured into a new area of study." Regina glanced over her shoulder to ensure there were no eavesdroppers. "I promise to tell you later."

Uncle Charles was tightlipped with anyone outside of Wedmore House about his expeditions, and he swore the family to secrecy for fear another antiquarian would find the treasure before him. Regina nibbled her bottom lip, contemplating the reason he'd hidden the Black Death even from them.

Evangeline lowered her voice even more. "I have combed through everything Uncle Charles has recovered from a site, and I could recite his study findings verbatim. There is no ancient map in his collection, and none have been catalogued."

"It could simply mean whoever wants it is mistaken about its location," Sophia said.

Evangeline's blue eyes sparkled in the candlelight. "Or it could mean Uncle Charles has acquired a map to lead him to his next dig. Perhaps he has it in his possession, and his expedition is already underway."

A shiver snaked up Regina's back. Surely Uncle Charles wouldn't begin a dig without informing them. Any manner of calamity could befall him on an expedition, and they hadn't said their special good-bye.

The first time Uncle Charles left her and her sisters in Aunt Beatrice's care, Regina had clung to him, begging him not to leave. Another man might have brushed her aside and scolded her for such an unbecoming display of emotion, but not Uncle Charles. He'd told her a tale about how everything would be all right as long as she didn't wish him luck. Instead, they would wished each other the most ridiculous tragic ends they could imagine to trick the gods plotting mischief in whatever region he was set to visit.

May you fall face down in your plum pudding and die of happiness, Gigi.

Uncle, may the first woman you sight strike you *blind with her beauty and cause you to stumble into the Nile.*

They would exchange bad wishes until she'd doubled over with laughter, and the things that had frightened her seemed as silly as their make-believe endings. She had told herself that she had outgrown the ritual, but the quiver in her stomach suggested she hadn't.

Evangeline stood up straight, the excited light fading from her eyes. "It's time for the next set. Lord Nayland is practically galloping across the room in his haste to claim his dance with you."

Regina winced. She hoped her next dance partner was better behaved than her last three. The other gentlemen had been too bold by half and challenged her reflexes with their wandering hands.

"Instead of inquiring only about an interest in maps," Evangeline said in a hurried whisper, "question him about the Crusades."

Regina nodded to show she'd heard as Lord Nayland stopped in front of her and sketched a bow. "Miss Darlington, I believe I have this dance."

For show, she checked her dance card before offering a polite smile and allowing him to escort her onto the floor. She searched the crowd for Xavier, suppressing a sigh when she still didn't spot him. With his unusual height and dark curls, he was difficult to overlook.

Turning her attention toward her main purpose, she questioned Lord Nayland about his interest in ancient treasures, and asked if he knew anyone with a passion for cartography.

One side of his mouth slid up higher than the other when he smiled. "If discussing old broken pots and crumbling parchment stirs you, I could feign interest."

Regina gave him credit for honesty, although the way he raked his gaze over her made her wish poking one's dance partner in the eye wasn't frowned upon. Fortunately, the string orchestra began to play and provided her with an excuse to end their conversation.

Lord Nayland proved to be a decent dance partner. Aside from the occasional innuendo and his intense stare, his behavior remained aboveboard. By the time the quartet's ending notes floated on the humid air, she'd learned to ignore his unwavering gaze and was enjoying the fluidity of the movements.

Lord Nayland brushed a lock of dark blond hair from his forehead and drew her hand through the crook of his elbow. "You are a skilled dancer, Miss Darlington."

"Thank you, my lord." She glanced around the ballroom, hoping Xavier had arrived during the dance, but he still appeared to be missing. Lord Nayland urged her closer to his side. "If you are searching for your aunt, I saw her hurry outside a moment ago. I believe she might be ill."

Regina almost rolled her eyes at his blatant lie. Aunt Beatrice was at home under Joy's care and likely in bed at this hour. "How do you know she is ill, my lord?"

"She looked pale. Perhaps even slightly green around the gills." He tugged her in the direction of the veranda doors. "Please, allow me to offer my assistance. I will take you to her."

Regina planted her feet, dragging him to a stop, then smiled sweetly. "Heavens! I almost forgot Aunt Beatrice isn't here this evening. Auntie must have a mirror image trotting around tonight."

His pale blue eyes darkened to the color of the stormy sea. "You are without a keeper." Perhaps it was her imagination, but she would swear he'd licked his chops.

"No, my lord. Lady Seabrook is my chaperone, and she is keeping close watch over my sisters and me." She nodded toward Sophia's dearest friend's mother, a red-faced matron who had positioned herself in front of the veranda doors.

Lord Nayland waved and the woman's eyebrow arched in censorship. None of her charges were being whisked outside without going through her first. At a little under six feet tall, the lady's wrath caused many to tremble in fear. Lady Seabrook was Viking by heritage and only a fool would engage in battle with her. Her weapons might be mere words, but she could cut another down to size as effectively as if she wielded a sword and shield.

Lord Nayland's mouth set in a grim line, and she suspected he found the countess to be more bother than threat. He turned to Regina to lift her hand to his lips then bade her farewell. Lady Seabrook came forward as soon as he disappeared into the crowd.

"Was the baron bothering you? Should I request my husband have a word with him?"

Regina smiled in gratitude. "Thank you, my lady, but there is no need to trouble the earl."

"Especially when Miss Darlington's betrothed has arrived." Xavier's familiar accent created gooseflesh along Regina's arms, and she wheeled toward him with a thready gasp.

Lady Seabrook stepped forward to stand beside Regina and raised her quizzing glass to inspect him. "Miss Darlington is betrothed? To whom?"

Xavier flashed his easy smile. "To the lucky gentleman standing before you, my lady. I was smitten from the moment I saw Miss Darlington, and I am honored she has accepted my proposal."

Regina linked arms with him, savoring his warmth against her side. "Please allow me to make introductions. Lady Seabrook, may I present Mr. Xavier Vistoire, my fiancé?"

"Indeed." A rare sign of pleasure spread across Lady Seabrook's face, plumping her high cheeks. "What an unexpected and wonderful surprise. Does my daughter know?"

"We've told no one aside from family and you," Regina said. "It is all very new, so we haven't had an opportunity to share our happy news."

"May I help spread the word?" Lady Seabrook asked with a hopeful arch to her pale blond brows.

"We would be grateful, my lady," Xavier said. His dark green gaze bore into Regina, and he lowered his voice for her ears only. "Every blackguard in Town needs to know you are mine."

Twenty-five

Xavier pressed his clenched fist against his thigh and glowered at any man who dared to look at Regina as he escorted her to the refreshment room. Every bloody rake in attendance deserved a beating, and probably several others swarming about Town like locust did too. He would happily deliver facers to every one if doing so wouldn't spark questions from Regina that he didn't wish to answer. Even though she was aware the vermin were talking about her, she shouldn't have to know what they were saying.

When he had arrived at the ball, he stopped inside the great room's arched doorway to search for her. A group of men had gathered at the edge of the dance floor while the orchestra tuned their instruments between sets. As one would expect, they had come together to crow about their latest adventures—a successful run at the Hazard table, a reckless horse race through Hyde Park, a front row view of a boxing match. He recognized his old self in many of their stories, but he no longer cared about frivolous past times. Losing everything made him realize what was truly important. If he had family and friends, he was a wealthy man.

"How did you fare with the Fallen Angel?" one of the gents had asked another.

"One point for signing her dance card and another because it was a waltz. I almost earned five more for squeezing that luscious bum, but she blocked my attempt. She is quicker than I anticipated."

Xavier had jeered them under his breath, disgusted by their childish game.

A third man joined the conversation. "How many points will I earn for bedding her tonight?"

The others had guffawed and declared him fit for Bedlam. Xavier had intended to move further away so he need not listen to their obnoxious braying when he overheard something that made his blood boil.

A blond fellow with hair falling into his eyes had emerged from the pack. "It is my turn, and soon you will eat your words. Miss Darlington is as good as conquered."

Xavier wished he had punched the scoundrel then and there, but he hadn't wanted to focus attention on the men's sport. Now, he tried to shake off the memory and drew Regina closer. He would be damned if another man touched her. Any *conquering* would involve the two of them only, and it would be mutual. She was his. He was hers. And he was half mad with jealousy, which was a novel and unwelcome state for him.

Leaving her side only long enough to retrieve a glass of lemonade, he handed it to her. She wore an embroidered white muslin gown that most would describe as modest, but the sheerness of the fabric hinted at her peaches and cream skin hidden underneath.

"Thank you." She accepted the drink with a bemused smile. "Would you like to walk with me?"

He nodded sharply. She took a sip of her drink before leading him on a leisurely circle around the perimeter of the room. Several times, Regina slanted a glance at him from beneath her lashes that was likely unintentionally seductive, but it aroused him all the same.

"Do you have something you would like to discuss, Miss Darlington?"

"I'm uncertain engaging in anything besides banal chitchat would be wise considering we are now on display."

"What do you mean?" He tore his gaze from her to look about the room and realized several pairs of eyes were following them. "I suppose word of our engagement is making the rounds."

A pink blush infused her skin, and her blond lashes fluttered. "Yes, that would stir a bit of interest, although I suspect the way you have been devouring me with your heated looks has the gossips giddy."

"Was I devouring you, love? I hadn't noticed."

"You know exactly what you are doing, Mr. Vistoire, and I'd thank you to stop." She paused in front of a deserted alcove and frowned at him. "After your insistence that we not give the impression we have made a love match, I'm surprised by your predatory behavior."

Her rebuke sobered him. "Quite right." He cleared his throat and gazed out at the crowd as he wrestled his jealousy into submission. "I spoke with Farrin today, so he knows of our engagement. Nevertheless, I will strive to behave more like a gentleman to protect the secrets of my heart."

She gazed at him oddly as if she didn't believe he cared for her.

"Would you like to stand up with me for the next set," he asked, "or would you prefer to savor your lemonade?"

"I believe I have a prior commitment." She lifted her dance card to inspect it. "Yes, I've promised a quadrille to Mr. Quincy next, but I saved one dance for you as you wished."

Xavier extended his hand to take her lemonade. She passed it to him, and he placed both of their glasses on an end table inside the alcove. "May I see your dance card?"

She smiled sweetly and complied with his request. Instead of signing his name in the empty slot, however, he reached to untie the ribbon securing the card to her wrist, stalked to the nearest unlit fireplace, and tossed it in the grate.

She gawked as he returned to her side.

"For heaven's sake, I *need* that."

When she tried to march to the fireplace to retrieve the card, he seized her above the elbow. She pointedly scowled at his fingers loosely circling her flesh. He wasn't hurting her and she could easily free herself, but he gentled his touch anyway.

His mouth was tight when he smiled. "Dancing with these...*gentlemen* will give them false hope."

She glanced at the card teetering on the pile of birch logs. "But I promised."

Linking arms, he urged her away from the ornate gilded fireplace. She huffed but abandoned her dance card to walk with him.

"They will still claim their dances," she grumbled.

"And we will inform them of our betrothal."

She darted a sideways look at him, opened her mouth, then snapped it shut.

Having put enough distance between them and the fireplace, Xavier turned to face her. "Do you have more to say, Miss Darlington?"

"I—no." Her tongue flicked over her lips, leaving them moist and kissable. "Well, perhaps there is one item to discuss. I think I should honor my word to the gentlemen who signed my dance card."

His gaze narrowed on her fingers toying with the cameo locket around her neck. He couldn't make sense of her insistence on dancing with the blackguards. Not when she'd indignantly accused him of being no better than these rakes trying to seduce her. He suspected her changed position had nothing to do with enjoying their company. "What do you have up your sleeve, Miss Darlington?"

"I am barely wearing sleeves, Mr. Vistoire." She arched a haughty eyebrow as if daring him to contradict her.

Her stubbornness made him grind his teeth, but when he spoke, he did so with controlled politeness. "Perhaps my understanding of English adages is faulty, *ma chérie*. Allow me to clarify. What machinations do you have at work this evening?"

She sniffed. "If you are insinuating I am hiding something, you insult me."

Evangeline entered the refreshment room and stopped to look around. She spotted them then headed in their direction. Regina tried to discreetly send a signal to her sister with a quick slash of her hand through the air, but Xavier seemed to be the only one to notice.

"I have spoken with every aging lord in attendance," Evangeline said without pause. "None of them seem to know anything about Uncle Charles's newest interest. He hasn't written to his close associates either. The entire affair is peculiar. Did you learn anything from Lord Nayland?"

Regina sighed. "Evangeline, do you ever stop to consider your audience before speaking?"

Her sister blinked several times, looking back and forth between him and Regina. "I thought Mr. Vistoire knew about the—" She swept a quick glance around them and lowered her voice to a whisper. "He knows about the map already. I didn't realize the rest was to be kept secret."

"The rest?" Xavier asked as Regina groaned under her breath. "Let's move to the veranda where we can speak in private."

All three of them passed through the great room in silence and exited the house through a set of French doors. A few guests had wandered outside, but they appeared to be absorbed by their own business and didn't glance in their direction. He ushered the women to a vacant corner of the veranda.

Xavier crossed his arms. "I knew you were hiding something. Tell me about *the rest*, and what any of this has to do with Lord Nayland."

Regina's chin lifted a fraction. He expected an argument from her, but perhaps she realized if she didn't tell him what was going on, Evangeline would.

"We are compiling a list of men who might be interested in Uncle Charles's latest venture. Evangeline believes there is a possibility the map has no value in itself, but it could lead to the discovery of a fabled group of mercenaries that roamed the desert hundreds of years ago."

Regina's sister eagerly recounted what she'd learned from reading her uncle's notes and presented a credible argument to support her belief.

"The group's reach was further than the desert. As I said, there are reports of strikes occurring in Europe as well. If they actually existed and proof can be found, it will be a windfall for the antiquarian who finds it first. The discovery could be as momentous as the Rosetta stone. Uncle Charles will be famous," Evangeline concluded in a breathy voice.

Regina explained how they were talking with others about their Uncle Charles with the hope the name of a potential competitor came up in conversation. "At least it would allow us a place to start. We have nothing to go on now, and I am unwilling to take a passive approach when it comes to protecting our families."

Affection swelled like a wave inside him, washing over him. For as long as he could remember, he'd convinced himself he didn't care—not about family, others' judgments of him, or what became of him. He had professed love for his mother and sister when they asked, but the words had been obligatory and rote. Deep inside, he'd known it was true—he did love Mother and Serafine—but if his father caught him showing affection to either one, he called Xavier weak and punished him with the intentions of turning him into a man.

Xavier had learned during his exile that the true measure of a man was his ability to love without fear, and in this moment, he was sure he loved Regina. Unfortunately, they had an audience. He held his hand out, and she placed her smaller one in his.

He smiled. "We will keep our families safe together."

It wasn't the most elegant profession of love, nor direct, but he would have many opportunities to tell her, and he made a silent vow to tell her every day for the rest of their lives.

When they returned to the ballroom, Regina stiffened beside him. A lanky gentleman with stooped shoulders raised a hand in greeting then headed in their direction.

"Mr. Lawrence," Evangeline spat. "If he knows what is good for him, he will keep his distance."

What a coincidence. If memory served, Lawrence was the name of the weasel that had started the rumors about Regina.

"Pardon me, ladies." Xavier intercepted him and spun him around in the opposite direction. "Might I have a word with you, sir?"

The man threw a look back over his shoulder as Xavier escorted him from the ballroom. "I was coming to congratulate you and Miss Darlington on your betrothal."

"How thoughtful," Xavier drawled. "We are touched, I assure you." He tightened his grip on the man's arm. Nodding his thanks to the footman for holding the door, Xavier practically dragged Lawrence into the dimly lit corridor leading to the card room. The quartet's music grew muffled as the footman closed the door behind them.

Lawrence stumbled as he tried to keep up with Xavier's determined strides. "Is there a problem, sir? Have I done something to offend?"

Xavier located an empty drawing room, steered the man inside, and secured the door. The wall sconces had been lit in preparation for any guests wishing to find a quiet place for conversation.

Xavier shrugged off his jacket and laid it over the back of a chair. "Do you expect me to answer, or should we dispense with the pretense that you are ignorant to what you have done and get on with it?"

Lawrence gulped. "Get on with it?"

"It is within my rights to defend my betrothed's reputation. I could issue a challenge, but my days are quite busy lately. I would prefer to see to the matter now."

"Just one moment." The man held up his hands and patted the air as if signaling Xavier to calm himself. "Let's talk about this."

Until that point, Xavier had kept his anger locked away, but it was close to breaking loose. He sensed the quickening of his heart; his hands curled into fists.

"I—I see you have heard about the misunderstanding involving Miss Darlington. I promise, I never touched her."

"If that is true," Xavier said through gritted teeth and stalked toward him, "why did you lie about kissing her?"

Lawrence slowly backed away. "Well, I did mention there was a misunderstanding, did I not? A blunder on my part, to be more accurate. I never meant any harm to come to her. Please, allow me to make amends. I will do anything."

Xavier stopped his advance. "Anything?"

"Of course," he said, nodding vigorously. "Anything you ask."

"Recant. Tell your friends you fabricated the tale."

The man recoiled. "Recant? I'm afraid I cannot do that. I would become a laughing stock. They already deride me for being shy, and there was that time I fainted at Madame Montgomery's brothel."

"So you tried to improve your standing among the gents by slandering an innocent lady." Xavier shook his head and began rolling up his sleeves. "You are aware I have no other options.

Do you have a preference on which eye I blacken first, or should I start with bloodying your nose?"

Mr. Lawrence's face drained of color. "Are you serious? I have never been involved in a round of fisticuffs."

"You won't like it. That much I can guarantee." Xavier sighed. "I did hope for a fair fight, but a man must do what he must for his lady."

He took a step forward with his fists raised and Lawrence cried out, "I will do it. I will recant."

Xavier dropped his fists by his sides. "Very well. If I hear another word of this nonsense about Miss Darlington, you should expect a visit from me, and next time, I won't be as forgiving."

Lawrence thanked him and scrambled for the door.

It was just as well Xavier hadn't needed to punch the blighter. If he'd dirtied his attire, he would have been forced to leave early, and he was looking forward to his and Regina's first dance together.

Twenty-six

Regina was pleased when Aunt Beatrice woke at her usual time and was well enough to join her and her sisters in the library after breakfast. She and Evangeline dragged a wingback chair close to the window so their aunt would have brighter light to work on her knitting. The late morning sunlight wouldn't help her to see any better, but she sighed with pleasure as she sank into the chair. Cupid dutifully sat at her feet, looking at her in expectation.

"Warmth at last. I have been freezing all morning," she said and patted the chair cushion in invitation for her dog to join her. Cupid leapt onto the chair, wedged his small body between Aunt Beatrice and the chair arm, and settled in for a nap.

Evangeline carried a stack of books to the library table to add to the other towering stacks. "Auntie," she teased, "you would ask for a blanket in hell."

"Evangeline, language!" Aunt Beatrice made a tsking noise, but her eyes twinkled with amusement.

Sophia, who had claimed a spot on the ladder, tossed a smile over her shoulder. "Shouldn't she be sent to bed without supper? I could eat her dessert, so it doesn't go to waste."

"You always were a plotter," Evangeline grumbled, but it was all in good fun.

Regina chuckled and grabbed a book from one of the towering stacks crowding the sturdy table. There was just enough space for one of them to flip through the books in search of the map. She fanned the pages before turning the book upside down and shaking it.

Aunt Beatrice looked up from her knitting. "What in heaven's name are you doing, Regina?"

"Clearing the dust from the pages."

"Why isn't Mrs. Cox cleaning the library?"

"Dust makes her sneeze, Auntie," Sophia said as she passed a book to Evangeline who was standing at the foot of the ladder.

"A maid with an aversion to dust? I have never heard of such a thing."

It took a moment for Aunt Beatrice to realize Sophia was joking. "Oh, Sophia Anastasia Marietta Jane." Aunt Beatrice snorted. "*Jane*? Whatever was your mother thinking when she chose names for you girls?"

Regina laughed. Only Aunt Beatrice would oppose a normal name like Jane. "If I recall, Papa insisted his mother's name be included somewhere."

"Such an unreasonable man," Aunt Beatrice said with a pitying shake of her head and returned to her knitting.

Regina hardly thought allowing Mama free rein to name her and her sisters was the act of an unreasonable man. Smitten and indulgent? Absolutely. Also a testament to how much their father had loved their mother. And she had loved him, so each of her daughters bore the name Jane in addition to a Christian name shared with an angel.

"Was Mama always interested in angels?" Sophia asked. "Sometimes I drag out her charts just to see her handwriting."

Aunt Beatrice's face softened. "Not when she was a girl, but your mother and uncle were curious children. She was as likely to be caked in dirt as Charlie was. The two of them were always traipsing around the countryside in search of buried treasures."

Evangeline returned to the table with a load of books in her arms. "I never knew Mama was interested in antiquities. It must be in my blood."

"Oh, yes. She was heartbroken when Charlie left on his first expedition and your grandparents made her stay behind. Her interest in angels began after he returned and brought back his first find. It was a piece of a sculpture depicting an angel. She was intrigued by the fact he'd uncovered it in India."

The front bell rang, interrupting their reminiscing.

"I will see who it is." Evangeline placed the stack of books on the table and left to answer the door.

"Are you expecting Mr. Vistoire?" Sophia asked as she descended the ladder.

"Not until this afternoon. He has taken rooms at the Pulteney Hotel and is moving his belongings this morning."

Aunt Beatrice muttered her approval. "The man is thinking ahead. You'll need a place to spend your wedding night."

Grabbing another book from the pile, Regina ducked her head as heat flooded over her, fearful if Auntie saw her face, she would know Regina and Xavier hadn't exactly waited for their wedding night.

Her aunt chuckled. "You young girls fluster too easily."

Evangeline returned with Crispin in tow before Aunt Beatrice said anything else embarrassing. "Look who I found lurking on the front stoop. Lord Margrave."

Cupid's head popped up at the mention of his favorite visitor's name.

Crispin's gaze darted toward Sophia. "I wasn't lurking. I have come with a purpose."

Sophia shrugged as if she didn't care why he was at Wedmore House, but she abandoned her task to sit in a chair and fold her hands in her lap.

"The special license has been granted." He pulled a folded paper from his jacket and brought it to Regina. "I took the liberty of speaking with Vicar Burnett, and he has agreed to perform the ceremony tomorrow morning at nine."

Regina's stomach pitched. "Tomorrow? That is sooner than I expected." She'd hoped to find the map and remove it from

Wedmore House before she and Xavier were expected to retire to the hotel.

"I will cancel with the vicar if you have come to your senses," Crispin said. "Perhaps you would like more time to become acquainted with your betrothed."

She smiled as sweetly as possible while grinding her teeth. Most ladies knew much less about their future husbands than Regina did about Xavier, but she couldn't very well contradict Crispin without admitting to matters that were none of his concern.

"You are a dear friend." Regina accepted the license and cupped his hand between hers. "Tomorrow will be grand. Thank you."

"It was my pleasure." His grim expression said otherwise. "Do you mind if I sit a moment?"

"Not at all," Aunt Beatrice said. "You are always welcome at Wedmore House."

He grabbed a library chair from the table and sat, tipping his head to the side to study the piles of books. "What are you doing to Wedmore's library?"

"Dusting the shelves," Sophia said with a slightly defiant edge to her tone.

"I see." His brow furrowed, and he took a deep breath, releasing it in a slow stream. Considering he and Sophia had been at each other's throats the last time they'd gathered, he was likely trying to control his temper. "Miss Sophia, this morning at the club I heard you have developed an interest in cartography."

Sophia sat up straighter. "At your club? How could that be?"

"Your suitors were discussing it. They seemed perplexed by the possibility anyone would find the subject fascinating, much less a lady."

Sophia bristled. "What does being a lady have to do with anything? Am I supposed to have wool between my ears and care only about gowns and bonnets?"

A grudging smile spread across his face. "Not all ladies have wool between their ears. I've always found Miss Darlington and Miss Evangeline better conversationalists than most gents."

A scarlet flush climbed Sophia's face. "My *sisters* are intelligent." She surged to her feet, appearing ready to storm from the library. "And I'm just another dotty chit with nothing on her mind besides marriage."

"I never said you were dotty." Crispin grabbed her hand when she tried to bolt. "You are just as intelligent, I'm sure of it. But you must admit, you rarely engage in conversation with me, so it is difficult to form an opinion about what is between your ears."

"Is it any wonder I avoid you when you insist on insulting me?" She tried to jerk her hand free, but he held tight.

Aunt Beatrice glanced up from her knitting, appearing not the least bit unsettled by their display. "Please don't quarrel, children. It is growing tedious."

Sophia gawked at their aunt.

"Do they argue often, Auntie?" Evangeline asked.

"Only every time they cross paths."

Sophia glared at Crispin. "And only because he has a knack for being annoying."

"I didn't come here to insult you," he said with an impressive modicum of decorum. "I was hoping to call a truce. Wedmore wouldn't want us arguing like we have been."

Sophia's angry glower began to slip. "I am sure you are correct, and I don't want to disappoint Uncle Charles. He considers you as close to a son as he will ever have." She sighed, her shoulders slumping as if she was defeated. "Very well. I promise not to argue with you anymore."

He smiled and released her arm. "I hope you will still challenge me occasionally. Otherwise the Season would become exceptionally dull."

"We can't even agree on not arguing." She released an airy chuckle and plopped back into her seat.

"Yes, but we do have a common interest," he said. "Cartography. When I travel, I chart the lay of the land."

Regina came forward. "I never knew that about you. How long have you drawn maps?"

Crispin shrugged. "As long as I can recall. I used to copy old maps when I was a child. Then I drew maps of our house and neighborhood."

"Did you ever draw any for Uncle Charles from your travels?"

"A couple of times, maybe. Why do you ask?"

Regina waved off his question. "Curiosity. We were discussing Mama and Uncle Charles earlier. It is fun to discover new facts about others."

His strong brows lowered over his hazel eyes. For one tense moment, she worried he would question her further. Instead, he swung his attention back to Sophia.

"There is a noon lecture at the museum on travel routes used during the Crusades and the men who charted the terrain. Given your interest in such subjects, I thought you might like to accompany me."

"We accept," Regina blurted.

Crispin's jaw muscles bulged, and when he smiled, it was more a gritting of teeth than an expression of pleasure. "You should join us as well, Miss Darlington."

"I would be delighted." She flashed an innocent smile, fully recognizing the sarcasm in his voice and choosing to ignore it. "Thank you."

"Aren't your forgetting someone, Regina?" Aunt Beatrice piped up. "You are expecting Mr. Vistoire."

"Not until much later."

"Be that as it may, you are not an appropriate chaperone for your sister, at least not until after your wedding." Her aunt folded her knitting with the needles tucked inside and bent forward to drop it in her sewing basket, waking Cupid again. "I will resume chaperone duties."

"Auntie," Regina said, "Dr. Portier recommended you rest for the next few days."

"I will have plenty of time to sleep. I am attending a lecture."

Further protests proved futile, so Regina conceded. "Very well. Evangeline and I will finish cleaning the library while you are gone. In the meantime, I can assist Sophia into a fresh gown."

Regina linked arms with her youngest sister and hauled her from the chair. When they reached Sophia's chambers above stairs, Sophia placed her hands on her hips. "While you and Aunt Beatrice were debating who should perform chaperone duties, no one thought to ask if I would like to go to the lecture."

Regina swept to Sophia's wardrobe and flung the doors open. "You must go. The man who wants the map could be at the lecture." She snatched a green walking dress from a peg then presented it to Sophia for her approval.

She shook her head. "The blue one, please."

Regina exchanged the green gown for the blue and brought it to the bed. "I am sorry, Soph. I realize Crispin tries your patience, but one of us should be at the museum today. You needn't question anyone. Just take note of the speaker and who attends his lecture."

Sophia dropped on the side of the bed, rested her elbows on her knees, and propped her chin in her hand. "I understand that I must go, and I will, but what if Margrave asks *me* a question I cannot answer? I know nothing about maps."

"You can pretend to trip. He will forget what he asked while he is seeing to your welfare."

Sophia's blond eyebrows lifted. "And what if we're sitting?"

"I don't know. Uh, *drop* something."

"Like what?"

Regina swung her head side to side searching for an object Sophia could take with her that wouldn't be out of the ordinary. She spotted a folded handkerchief with delicate pink roses stitched at the corner on the bedside table and grabbed it. "Drop this."

Regina shook the flimsy muslin square in front of Sophia, and she grabbed it. "Fine, but I might be dropping my handkerchief all afternoon."

"Then perhaps Crispin will be too winded from retrieving it to ask anymore questions."

Sophia giggled and hugged the square to her chest. "Now I want to drop it more than necessary. A silent Margrave would be music to my ears."

Twenty-seven

Later that morning, Xavier's sister followed him to the foyer of the town house she shared with her husband and son. "I still don't understand the reason you are letting rooms at the Pulteney. We have plenty of space and we enjoy your company."

Xavier placed his valise beside the door and decided to change tactics. "You will have less space once the baby arrives. I'm sorry, but I need quiet and privacy."

Serafine winced, and he wanted more than anything to recant. Hurting his sister was not part of his plan to protect her, but she wasn't accepting his decision to move to the hotel.

He softened his voice. "I enjoy your company as well, Sera. I'm not setting up house across the sea. Once you return from Brighton, you may visit whenever you like. Simon and Isaac are welcome as well."

"Perhaps we should postpone our holiday until after your wedding."

"Lisette needs you more than I. Our cousin will give birth any day, and she is likely frightened out of her wits. She has always looked to you for guidance. You should be there for her and Rafe."

Rafe was Lisette's younger brother, and he'd been the center of his sister's attention since their mother died in childbirth. An infant in the home would take some adjustment.

"The boy might feel ignored for a while after the baby arrives," he said, "and your presence will bring him comfort."

She bit her bottom lip, as she seemed to grapple with her choices. "I suppose you are right about Lisette needing me," she said at last, "but I would like to be here for you, too. I wanted to be present for your wedding."

"I understand. I wish I could have been here for your wedding. I'm sorry I missed your special moments."

And all the smaller ones in between.

A lump formed in his throat, and Xavier placed his arm around Serafine's shoulders. Too much time had been lost between them already, and now even more was being stolen. But a temporary separation was preferable to losing each other forever.

"Please go to Brighton. Miss Darlington and I won't marry for several weeks, and you would miss out on the birth if you waited."

He hated lying to his sister, but he wanted her far from London when the time came to challenge Farrin.

"What if my bride and I honeymoon in Brighton?" he asked. "Our family would have an opportunity to become acquainted with Regina, and I would like to meet Lisette's husband and welcome the new babe."

A bright smile lit Serafine's face. "That would be lovely." She gave him a brief hug then stepped away as if she needed to release him quickly or she would never let him go. "Do you promise to come to Brighton?"

"I do. And do *you* promise to set off at dawn? You have a long journey ahead."

"I will see that she makes good time." Xavier looked up to see Isaac descending the stairs. Serafine's husband came to slip his arm around her waist. "It is time to let your brother go. You will reunite soon."

"I know." Tears shimmered in her eyes, and she leaned her head against Isaac's shoulder. "Do you swear we will see each other again?"

"Yes." Xavier's voice cracked. "This is a temporary separation. Remember, I am not going anywhere."

After his discussion with Regina's aunt, he'd come to a decision. The family house in New Orleans held too many unpleasant memories. He didn't want to raise his children in a home tainted by anger and despair. England would become his home, where his bride would be happiest and his kin would be close.

He retrieved his valise. "We will see you in Brighton."

Serafine allowed him to walk out her door this time. The hack he had ordered was waiting in the street. He glanced around the neighborhood in search of Farrin's men, but he only spotted an old woman in a hooded cape moving in his direction, a footman approaching the door of the house on the corner, and a few ladies out for a stroll. The street had been clear of Farrin's thugs all morning, but Xavier had no doubt he was still being watched. A prickle of unease lifted the hair on the back of his neck.

The coachman opened the carriage door and placed the steps for him. "May I take your case, sir?"

He handed it to the man and grabbed the door to steady his climb when something tugged at his jacket. He startled and turned to discover the old woman clinging to him. The hood blocked her face from view. *A beggar in need.*

The coachman's boots thudded against the cobbles when he hopped from the carriage. "Move away, wench."

"Xavier," she mumbled and lifted her head.

He gasped at the sight of her—her eye was swollen shut and her lip was split. "Claudine? What happened? Who did this to you?"

Her chin quivered. "The duke."

Xavier cursed under his breath and darted his gaze around the neighborhood to see if she'd been followed. Madame Parma had compared Claudine to a bird in a gilded cage. The Duke of Stanhurst wouldn't allow her far from sight.

"Are you certain you were not followed?"

"No one pays attention to old women. I wasn't followed."

He took in her tattered attire, recalling how he had mistaken her for an elderly woman moments earlier. The way she'd slumped forward, as if her back were bent from years of bearing heavy loads, and her wobbling walk had convinced him at a glance. She had always been an excellent actress.

Xavier placed his hand on the small of her back. "Climb inside. I will take you someplace safe."

He considered providing shelter at the Pulteney Hotel and quickly discarded the idea. She might be recognized, which would make the duke's task of tracking her easier. He knew of only one place where she would be given safe haven.

Once he had her settled in the carriage, he spoke quietly with the driver. "My destination is Conduit Street. Wedmore House."

The driver gave a sharp nod.

Xavier climbed into the carriage, pulled the curtains, then joined Claudine on the bench. The carriage lurched away from Serafine's house and rattled over the uneven street.

He swiveled toward Claudine. "Will you allow me a closer look at your face?"

She flinched, pulling the hood lower to hide. "I'm embarrassed for you to see me this way."

"You have no reason to feel embarrassed. You are not to blame for what has been done. Stanhurst should be ashamed to show *his* face. I only want to examine your injuries. Will you allow me?"

She inclined her head slightly and didn't move as Xavier removed the hood. Her chestnut hair hung in tangled waves around her shoulders. He was careful to maintain a blank expression as he inspected her battered face, but his hands shook with repressed rage. She would heal, and those who looked on her would consider her beautiful. Most would never see the scars she carried inside, but they would be there.

"Stanhurst must answer for what he has done. I will call on him and he will answer to me."

"No!" Claudine grasped his hands, clinging as if he might walk out of the moving carriage to confront the duke. "You can't go to him. He wants you dead."

He smiled, hoping to help calm her nerves. "We have something in common. I want him dead too. Although I will settle for gravely wounded."

She didn't return his smile.

"Tell me what happened," he prompted. "What precipitated his attack?"

"One of the actresses spoke with you at the theatre. She knew you'd come looking for me." Claudine pulled a handkerchief from her sleeve and gingerly dabbed at the tears when they slipped onto her cheeks. "She thought she could ingratiate herself with the duke by claiming I was being unfaithful. She wants Stanhurst to toss me aside, so she can assume my position."

"I can't believe Madame Parma betrayed you." The leading lady's compassion for Claudine had struck him as genuine. She had played him for a fool.

"It wasn't Lia. She is a loyal friend." Claudine sniffled. "Zoe is a young upstart with high ambitions. She has no idea the price she would pay if Stanhurst made her his mistress."

The pixie. Stanhurst would delight in squelching the girl's high-spiritedness, just as he'd taken joy in robbing Claudine of her confidence. Knowing the young actress was responsible for Claudine's current state made it difficult to feel sympathy for her, however.

"Zoe will have to fend for herself," he said, "but you are never returning to Stanhurst. Is your friend still in Vienna?"

"I don't know. The duke's servants hold the post until he inspects it. If Sarah has written to me, I've never seen her letters."

Xavier felt his nostrils flare, but he kept his temper in check. Cursing the Duke of Stanhurst wouldn't help Claudine. "My betrothed and her family will provide you safe haven for now. We can write to the theatre owner once you are settled. If your friend has moved on, he should know where she was headed next. Then we'll write to that theatre and continue sending letters until we find her."

She shook her head. "Searching for her would take too long, and I couldn't impose. Please accept my congratulations on your betrothal, though."

He leaned against the seatback with a smile. "Thank you. Regina is the most magnificent young lady I have ever known. She is also kind and tenderhearted. I imagine she will insist you stay at Wedmore House."

Claudine grimaced. "I didn't seek you out so you could assist me. I came to warn you against Stanhurst. When he called at the town house last night, he kept ranting about how he should have killed you himself instead of trusting others to do it."

Xavier's breath caught in his lungs. Could the duke be responsible for his imprisonment? "Did he say anything else?"

"No."

"Are you sure? Think about it a moment."

"I don't think there was anything else. His ramblings were nonsensical most of the time. He talked of finding out about Vienna and that you were assisting me, but I already knew he had discovered our plans. He told me the morning we were supposed to leave. That is how I learned the servants are loyal to him." Her brow furrowed. "Xavier, what happened to you? The duke said you left without me, but I couldn't believe it was true."

"It was a lie. I'd been winning at the gaming tables, so I made one last trip to the Den the night before our departure." He'd wanted to return home wealthier than when he'd left and prove his sister's worries about gambling were for naught. He had won at Hazard that night and lost over two years of his life.

"I hadn't arranged for a carriage to come at a certain time, because I hadn't wanted to be forced to leave if I found myself in the middle of a lucky streak. I remember a biting wind whipping through the alley, and how glad I was that I would be home soon where the winters are milder. I'd overindulged. I wasn't listening for footpads, and I couldn't see anything in the dark. I don't recall much after leaving the Den, other than I experienced a blinding pain at the back of my head. I was in and out of consciousness, and every time I woke, I was traveling in a carriage. I was held prisoner until several days ago."

"This had to be the duke's doing, only I think he never meant for you to survive." Fresh tears wet her cheeks. "I am sorry. I never should have accepted your help. Can you ever forgive me?"

"There is nothing to forgive, Claudine."

He opened his arms, and she fell into his embrace with a sob. He held his friend as she cried tears she'd likely been storing inside for years. She was spent by the time the carriage arrived at Wedmore House.

"Could I take a moment to speak with Regina alone? She isn't the type to require smelling salts, but I don't want to catch her by surprise."

Claudine tried to wipe away evidence of her tears with the damp handkerchief. "You should send me on my way. I am afraid of causing trouble for you."

Xavier opened the carriage door and stepped down without waiting for the coachman to set the stairs then turned back to address her. "You are not returning to the duke. Now, please wait here. I won't take long."

As he started toward the front door, it flew open and Regina greeted him with a brilliant smile. Instinctively, he blocked her view of the carriage interior. Regina drew up short, her smile falling away. He'd hoped to prepare her and absorb some of the shock of seeing Claudine's battered face.

"I've brought an old friend with me," he said. "She has been hurt and needs tending."

He cautiously moved aside, so Regina could see into the carriage. Regina covered her mouth with her hand.

He cleared his throat. "This is Claudine Bellerose. I'm afraid she has nowhere to go. Could I bring her inside?"

"Yes, of course." Regina came forward as Xavier helped Claudine from the carriage. She placed her arm around the actress and guided her inside Wedmore House. As soon as Xavier closed the door behind him, she called out for her sister.

Evangeline appeared in the corridor outside of the library and hurried toward them with a rustling of skirts. Her eyes widened as she drew near. "Good heavens. Who is this and what happened?"

"This is Claudine, an old friend to Mr. Vistoire."

Evangeline skidded to a stop. "Oh?" She drew out the word, glancing warily at Regina, perhaps seeking direction on how she should react to Xavier bringing a strange woman into their home.

Claudine's chin quivered again as she seemed to fight against tears. "I am sorry. I shouldn't have allowed Mr. Vistoire to bring me."

Regina frowned at her sister. "Of course you should have. Forgive us if we have given offense. We are simply surprised, because we were unaware Mr. Vistoire knew anyone in London aside from his sister."

"Claudine is an actress," Xavier said. "We lost touch, but she sought me out today to warn me that someone wishes me ill."

Regina arched an eyebrow. "Evangeline, please show Claudine to the guest room, while I ask Cook to put the kettle over the fire."

"Come this way, miss." Evangeline ushered Claudine toward the staircase. "Are you able to climb?"

"*Oui*, if we move slowly."

Regina's sister linked arms with the actress. "Take as much time as you need. Once we have you settled, I will find a clean gown for you."

He stood guard as the women ascended the staircase, holding his breath every time Claudine tottered and Evangeline fought to rebalance them both. When they reached the landing without incident, he exhaled with a noisy whoosh then turned to Regina.

"I should see to the kettle," she said, "but when I return, I would like to understand what is going on."

Several moments later, she bustled back into the foyer. "Cook will prepare a pot of tea and a pitcher of fresh water to clean her cuts." Regina tried to whisk past to lead him to the drawing room, but he captured her around the waist and pulled her to him for a chaste kiss.

"I haven't delivered my belongings to the hotel yet, and I would like word of my move to reach Farrin before sundown. Serafine and Isaac will be leaving early tomorrow morning. Could we discuss Claudine when I return?"

She frowned. "I am more interested in discussing who wants to harm you."

"Claudine's benefactor made threats against me, but there is no need for worry." Stanhurst was a coward who only hurt those who couldn't defend themselves. He had enlisted others to do his dirty work last time, and Xavier would be watching over his shoulder now. It seemed highly probable Stanhurst was responsible for his troubles with Farrin, but Xavier would like his suspicions confirmed.

"Have you had any luck finding the map?"

"No," she said with a sigh. "But we haven't finished searching the library. You should continue on to the hotel. We will watch over Claudine while you are gone."

"*Merci.*"

Regina's lashes fluttered as if she couldn't understand him.

"Thank you," he said, thinking perhaps his French had confused her.

She laughed. "I know what you said. I'm simply trying to understand why you are thanking me."

"Many ladies wouldn't acknowledge a woman of Claudine's background, much less welcome her into their home. Thank you for not turning her away."

"It never entered my mind," Regina said with a shrug.

"I know." He cupped her face, his fingertips nestling into the luxuriously soft hair at her nape. Tenderness filled his chest, bursting through in his smile. "This is why I love you."

Her eyes widened, and she stared at him with her lips parted. His profession hung between them for several labored breaths. His gut clenched. He hadn't planned to tell her that he loved her. At least not now, and not like this.

"Um..." She glanced toward the stairwell then back at him.

He decided to spare them both. "I should be going."

She grasped his forearm as he turned toward the door. "May you find a gold coin in the street and be run down by the post coach."

He blanched. "I beg your pardon?"

"It is a ritual." A furious blush made her cheeks glow. "Before my uncle leaves on a journey, I wish him bad luck to trick the gods into keeping him safe. It is a silly child's game. I'm sorry."

She placed a peck on his cheek then hurried for the staircase. Lifting her skirts, she dashed up the stairs. He smiled. Her expression of love wasn't what he'd expected, but it delighted him all the same.

Twenty-eight

Regina soaked a cloth in the washbasin, wrung out the excess water, and worked up a decent lather with the soap. Neither she nor the actress had spoken since Evangeline left to retrieve a clean gown. Regina realized she was being an abominable hostess, but she couldn't shake off her embarrassment from earlier.

No lady with her wits about her should ever wish the man she loved to be flattened on the street, but that was the problem. The ability to think clear whenever he was near had become an impossible task. Furthermore, the realization that she did in fact love him frightened her.

Evangeline whisked into the room with a simple pink muslin dress draped across her arm. It didn't seem like the most flattering color for the actress, but it was clean. "I found this in Sophia's wardrobe. I think it is most likely to be a fit."

"*Merci.*"

Evangeline pulled the chair away from the desk and dropped onto it. She tipped her head to the side. Regina saw the blunt question coming, but she was powerless to stop it. "What is the name of the rat who did this to you, and do you want us to bloody his nose on your behalf?"

Claudine's smile seemed slightly grotesque with her swollen lip. "*Merci*, but no. It is best if you avoid Stanhurst."

"A duke," Evangeline said then whistled. "They are nearly untouchable."

The Duke of Stanhurst was a distinguished man with graying hair and a frosty glare that could leave a person feeling the cut direct as if it were a tangible thing. His reputation for a callous disregard for others was well known, and most tried to avoid him if possible. His son Lord Geoffrey had inherited his black heart.

"How long has the duke been mistreating you?" Regina asked.

"Close to the beginning. I suppose we enjoyed a few months of harmony before I angered him enough to strike me."

Evangeline leaned forward. "What could you have possibly done to warrant him striking you? He sounds mad."

"I wore the Earl of Ventnor's favorite color. I didn't know it was his lordship's favorite since I had never made his acquaintance, but when he complimented my gown that evening, he mentioned a preference for blue. On the carriage ride home, Stanhurst accused me of trying to entice the man."

"Well, that answers my question. The duke is fit for Bedlam."

Taking a deep breath for fortification, Regina approached Claudine with the wet cloth and lowered beside her on the edge of the bed. "Xavier said you sought him out to issue a warning. Do you believe the duke truly means to harm Xavier?"

"I'm uncertain." The actress accepted the proffered cloth and thanked her. "Stanhurst often speaks out of turn when he is on a tear, but I was unwilling to take a chance with Xavier's life."

"Yet, you risked your own." She studied the actress. Like her sister, Regina was dubious about Claudine's previous association with Xavier. "How is it you and Xavier know one another?"

"Your betrothed is a good man, or at least he tries to be. Two years ago, we met at the theatre after a performance. He was the only person to see beyond the act I put on for onlookers, or perhaps everyone knew the truth about the duke and simply didn't care that I was miserable." She sighed, her shoulders drooping as if she was weary of trying to hold herself upright. "Whatever the case, Xavier offered his assistance to help me escape from London. I had an actress friend in Vienna willing to take me in. I could have found work on the stage once I arrived, but Stanhurst kept every coin I made. I had no means to travel until Xavier came forward."

"What happened? Did you change your mind?"

"Xavier never arrived the morning we were to board the ship. I believed the duke when he said Xavier had decided I was too much trouble and left without me. I should have known something was amiss, but Stanhurst was especially cruel to me when he learned I wanted to leave him. I only discovered today that Xavier was being held prisoner all that time."

Evangeline angled a narrow-eyed glance in Regina's direction. "Has the duke ever mentioned a man named Farrin?"

Claudine startled. "Not for a long time. Mr. Farrin dined with Stanhurst at the town house several times, but as I said, it has been a few years. How do you know Mr. Farrin?"

"He is responsible for Xavier's imprisonment." Regina gently nudged Claudine's arm. "You should clean your cuts so they don't fester."

Claudine carefully circled the cloth over the abraded skin stretched across her cheekbone. "The servants are in Stanhurst's pockets, and one of them informed him that I was packing. That is how he knew I was sailing that morning, but he implied he'd had a conversation with Xavier about leaving me behind, and we know that is a lie. I'm certain the duke played a part in Xavier's disappearance. Do you believe he hired Mr. Farrin to see to the deed?"

Or made false claims to insure Xavier was no longer a threat to the duke losing his mistress.

"Why do you stay with him?"

Claudine's gaze dropped and ruddy patches appeared on her cheeks and neck. "I have nowhere to go, and even if I did, I'm rarely left alone."

"You may stay here as long as necessary," Regina said.

Evangeline reached a hand toward Claudine, and the actress met her halfway. They linked fingers and held on to each other. "No one deserves to be treated in such a manner. I am glad Mr. Vistoire brought you to Wedmore House, and I agree with my sister. You should remain here until you have a safe place to go."

Claudine's sad smile tugged at Regina's heart. "Thank you both for making me feel I have someone to confide in again," the actress said. "The worst of this ordeal has been the loneliness. It was easier to let friendships fade than face Stanhurst's temper. I would give anything to stay, but if I'm not home by sundown, the duke's servants will send word to him. Stanhurst will believe I am with Xavier, and I'm worried for him."

"Well, I regret to inform you that we won't allow you to go back," Regina said. "Xavier can hold his own against the duke. You have warned him and he will be cautious." Her heart floundered in her chest. The words were for her own reassurance as much as for Claudine's.

The actress pressed her argument, but in the end, she didn't stand a chance against Regina and Evangeline. Eventually, she acquiesced.

"Splendid," Regina said with a clap of her hands. "Let's wash your hair before you change into a new gown."

Once the actress's chestnut brown locks were clean and combed, Evangeline assisted her into the pink gown. Regina and her sister stepped back to inspect Claudine. Her injuries were still a shocking sight, but she looked more comfortable and at ease.

"Come with me," Regina said. "My next task is to teach you how to defend yourself."

Regina led her to the large room where she practiced Wing Chun and spent the next half hour teaching Claudine simple moves to ward off an attacker, so she could make a fast escape. She proved to be a quick study.

Since they had no way of knowing how long Claudine would be a guest at Wedmore House, Regina decided it was best to inform Aunt Beatrice about their visitor sooner rather than later. The three women retired to the drawing room to wait for Aunt Beatrice and Sophia to return from the lecture at the British Museum. Evangeline took the time to tell Claudine about their unusual living situation and unconventional kin.

"Your great-aunt sounds delightful," Claudine said.

When Sophia and Aunt Beatrice returned at half past two that afternoon, Crispin said his good-byes at the door, much to Regina's relief. She didn't know how she would explain Claudine's presence or appearance, and she worried he might accidentally let word slip that the actress was staying as their guest. Aunt Beatrice and Sophia entered the drawing room arm-in-arm.

"I am done in to a cow's thumb," Aunt Beatrice declared. "I couldn't catch a wink the entire lecture with that old man elbowing me in the side every time I nodded off."

"That wasn't a man, Auntie. It was Mrs. Walton."

Aunt Beatrice snorted and waved her hand in the air. "Oh, yes. Margaret Walton née Paulson. The poor dear was one of six daughters, and any one of them could have passed for a boy. If their mother had dressed them in short pants, no one would have been any wiser."

"Until their wedding nights," Evangeline said.

Aunt Beatrice frowned. "I suppose I hadn't considered the moment of consummation, but point well made."

Regina smiled at Claudine sitting on the settee across from her. "You were warned."

"We have a guest?" Sophia's voice held a note of wariness as she studied Claudine's battered face.

"Allow me to present Claudine Bellerose," Regina said. "She will be staying with us for a time."

"She is an actress," Evangeline added.

Aunt Beatrice gasped, her face alight with pleasure. "Oh, I do love the theatre. How marvelous to have an actress lodging with us. Welcome, Madame Bellerose."

"*Merci*, Madame Allred."

"And she is *French*." Aunt Beatrice's whisper was meant for Sophia's ears, but it carried in the small room. "Everyone calls me Aunt Beatrice, dear. I insist you do as well. I look forward to visiting over dinner this evening unless you are expected at the theatre."

Claudine was perched on the edge of the settee with her hands folded in her lap. "No, ma'am. I am not expected on stage this evening."

"Splendid. Now if you will excuse me, it is time for my afternoon rest."

Sophia glanced back and forth between Regina, Evangeline, and Claudine with a puzzled wrinkle to her brow. "Let me see you settled above stairs, Auntie."

Aunt Beatrice continued to chatter as Sophia led her away. "An actress at Wedmore House. Can you imagine? She must have arrived in a hurry. She is still in stage make-up."

Regina apologized to Claudine. "Our aunt's eyesight is failing, and she has never been known to censor what she says. We have always loved her forthright manner, but it doesn't suit everyone."

Claudine smiled. "She is genuine and gracious. Two fine qualities for a lady to have."

"She could talk someone into old age," Evangeline said, "and she will have many questions about the theatre. If you need rescue, mention the weather, and we will intervene."

"I could discuss the theatre for hours. Perhaps your aunt will need rescuing."

Regina grudgingly admitted Claudine didn't fit the image she'd always held of actresses from watching them flirt with gentlemen in the Grand Saloon. The woman was surprisingly humble.

Claudine covered a yawn with her fingertips. "Excuse me. Recent events have taken a toll."

"If you would like to retire to the guest room, we won't be offended," Regina said. She was eager to question Sophia about the lecture, and there were still a few shelves to clear in the library.

Claudine agreed a rest would be appreciated and declined Evangeline's offer to assist her on the stairs. She and Sophia met at the doorway as Regina's sister returned from tucking in Aunt Beatrice. The actress exchanged a brief greeting with Sophia before going.

Regina bounced up from the chair. "Let's talk in the library while we finish searching the books."

Her sisters followed in her wake and set to work right away.

Regina climbed the ladder to begin grabbing books from the shelves. "How was the lecture?"

Sophia took up position at the table to fan through the books. "The lecture was surprisingly interesting and well attended. There were at least two dozen members in the audience."

"Oh, that is a lot of people to remember."

Sophia lifted a book from the pile on the table and rattled off a long list of names with impressive speed. "I'm not including Margrave, Auntie, and myself."

"Your recall never ceases to amaze me. How do you do it?"

"I pretend to host a dinner party," Sophia said with a shrug. "I created a seating chart in my mind. One must be careful when seating guests. I certainly wouldn't want Lords Corby and Ledbery in close proximity to one another. They chattered the whole lecture and were quite distracting. Oh, I did forget one. Lord Geoffrey was present."

"How was Margrave?" Evangeline accepted a book from Regina and added it to the stack in her arms.

"As brooding as ever, but I didn't mind as much since he kept Lord Geoffrey in his place. Margrave claims he is fulfilling his promise to Uncle Charles to keep watch over me this Season."

"Has he heard from Uncle Charles?" Regina asked.

"No. Apparently, our uncle isn't writing to anyone. None of his colleagues at the lecture have heard from him either." Sophia grabbed another book to flip through. "Uncle Charles spoke with Margrave before leaving England, although I don't know why our uncle would specifically request Margrave watch over me and not all of us."

With arms laden, Evangeline shuffled toward the table. "Perhaps because it is your first Season, which leads me to believe he had no intention of returning. He is close to discovering something monumental. I know it. All this time searching for a map is a waste of time. Uncle Charles has it with him." She dropped the books on the table with a bang. "He is seeking evidence of the Black Death's existence."

Sophia stuck out her tongue and made a gagging noise. "Every time you mention that name, I think of rats."

What if Evangeline was correct? This could be a waste of time, and they didn't have much left.

Regina descended the ladder to join her sisters at the table. "Do you really believe the man who hired Farrin is interested in proving the Black Death is not a myth?"

"Every antiquarian's dream is to uncover that which everyone else believes is a fantasy." Evangeline's wide blue eyes sparkled. "It would be like discovering Atlantis was a real city or finding the Holy Grail. I know others are interested, or they will be once they realize the group is not a myth."

"How can you be sure?" Sophia asked.

"There were rumors the leader of the Black Death kept a fortress in the mountains. Uncle Charles never named his source, but he was allowed to examine a letter from one of the source's ancestors. Only one person, a French knight, spoke of having ever seen the stronghold. He said the battlements were barely visible among the clouds, and the castle walls were at least twenty feet thick. In the noble knight's estimation, the fortress was impenetrable."

"Do Uncle Charles's notes indicate which mountains or where to search?"

"The broad area, yes. If he was able to identify the exact mountain, he must have the information with him."

Regina tapped the tip of her finger against her chin as she digested the information. Xavier needed a map to use as leverage to find out who was responsible for the threats against their families, and Regina wanted to it removed from Wedmore House. Farrin probably wouldn't know a fake from the legitimate one. As long as he collected his fee, why should he care where the map led? If it showed a location within the general vicinity of where the group might have settled, it shouldn't alert the buyer to the map being a forgery either. Although, even if the buyer did recognize it for a fake, perhaps it would achieve what Xavier wanted. It could draw the rat out of hiding.

"I have an idea."

Twenty-nine

After Xavier settled into his rooms at the hotel, he visited the print shop to order calling cards that reflected his change in residence. And since it was vitally important to give the impression he was permanently entrenched at the Pulteney, he stopped at the closest coffeehouse to engage in discourse with several groups over a two-hour span, dropping his name and telling everyone he'd just taken rooms at the hotel. He was easily the most obnoxious popinjay in the all male crowd, which would ensure at least a few would mention him outside of the establishment.

Once he was satisfied he'd done his best to advertise his whereabouts, he made his way back to Wedmore House to check the progress on finding the map. He'd also promised to inform Regina of what had transpired with Claudine earlier, although he expected she'd gathered the story from the actress already.

Cupid greeted him at the door, his sharp yipping muffled by the thick wood. When no one answered his repeated knocks, he let himself inside and snatched the dog in his arms before the little rogue had a chance to defile his trouser leg. "You are a scamp and an incompetent butler, my friend. I think you would allow anyone to walk in the door."

As a precaution, Xavier turned the lock and went in search of the ladies of Wedmore House. He found Regina and Sophia huddled around Evangeline at the table in the library. Their aunt and Claudine were missing, and he suspected both ladies were resting above stairs.

Sophia tapped her finger to the paper in front of Evangeline. "There is a sandy plain here, and then the mountain range runs toward the west and south coasts."

His pulse skipped. "Did you find the map?"

The women startled and whipped their heads around to gawk at him.

"Xavier Vistoire." Regina wrinkled her nose at him. "You scared us."

"My apologies. No one came to the door when I knocked, except my little friend here. You really should remember to lock the door."

"Mrs. Cox and Cook have gone to the market," Sophia said.

He set Cupid on a chair by the window and approached the table so he could look over Evangeline's shoulder. As he'd hoped, the Darlington sisters were discussing a map, but the quill in Evangeline's hand puzzled him. "What do you have happening here? Are you altering the map? Where did you find it?"

Regina's smile was much too sweet. "I will tell you all about it. Just one moment, please. Was there anything else, Sophia?"

Her sister shook her head. "We've captured everything. I am certain."

"Very good. Please proceed Evangeline."

Regina's sister sanded the paper and waved her hand over the top with a dramatic flourish. "I give you Uncle Charles's map." She pushed from the table and stood, allowing Xavier a better view of the drawing.

He scrunched his brow as he read the title scrawled across the top of the roughly drawn map. "Sinai Peninsula."

Regina handed him the map. "Evangeline has perfected our uncle's hand, so even if Farrin's buyer is familiar with Uncle Charles, he won't guess it is a forgery."

"What are you suggesting?" He dropped the map on the table and crossed his arms.

She imitated him, crossing her own arms and notching her chin. "I'm suggesting a solution to keep my family safe. We have searched every hiding spot in Wedmore House and found nothing. Only three days remain to uncover something that isn't here. It is time to alter our strategy."

Sophia linked arms with Evangeline. "Perhaps we should give the two of you a moment alone." Before he or Regina could respond, the ladies hurried for the library door.

Color had risen in Regina's face, and her eyes had assumed the feverish gleam that came when she was agitated or excited. "I want Farrin to call off his men, so we have to make him believe the map is not at Wedmore House. This is a business venture for Farrin. As long as he produces a map for his buyer, he will receive his reward. He has no way to know it is a fake, and we doubt the buyer does either."

"You don't know that for certain."

"It is a gamble, but I see no other choice. You can withhold the forgery for information just as well as the real one."

Xavier pinched the bridge of his nose to stem the pressure building behind his eyes. Perhaps she was right about Farrin not knowing details about the map, but he would know what area of the world it should depict. If the blackguard realized he was being duped, he wouldn't hesitate to kill every one of them.

"How do you know the Sinai Peninsula is the right place?"

She explained Evangeline's belief that someone else wanted access to the map Charles Wedmore was using to pinpoint the location of his next big discovery. "Uncle Charles's notes indicate the Black Death originated in Egypt. He has reliable evidence they had a fortress in the mountains of Sinai. He has done extensive study, and Uncle Charles is rarely wrong about these sorts of things. Sophia saw a map of the Third Crusade at a lecture today. Our map might not lead anyone to the Black Death, but it is an accurate depiction of the area. There are no mistakes."

"And you trust her memory?"

"Explicitly when it comes to matters like this. You would as well if you'd grown up with her. She never forgets anything she sees."

"I understand your desire to protect your family," he said. "I want it as well, but there are three more days to search. Couldn't we give ourselves at least one more day to be certain?"

"No. Lord Margrave arrived with our special license this morning, and he arranged for a vicar to come at nine o'clock tomorrow. We could reschedule, but I'm afraid I don't want to wait."

He blinked. A smile eased across his face as he realized her meaning.

She plopped into the chair her sister had vacated and gazed up at him with a look of misery that made his heart ache. "I'm sorry about what I said about the gold coin and post coach. I didn't mean—"

"I know what you meant, Regina." He snagged a chair to sit close and playfully squeezed her knee. "And I'm certain there will be some days when you will want to be rid of me. That seems to be a common sentiment among those who know me."

Her throat convulsed as she swallowed. She turned her palms toward his to link fingers. "I don't want to be rid of you. Quite the opposite. I was afraid if I admitted to loving you, perhaps I would never have the chance to tell you again."

"I will never leave you. I don't have the willpower." He leaned toward her. The faint notes of her citrus and spice soap teased him. "You have become part of me. I cannot walk away without losing a piece of myself, even though I know you don't deserve the burdens that come with marrying me."

"Your burdens are mine and mine are yours. That is how it is with marriage. Farrin and Stanhurst are temporary complications." One side of her mouth twitched as if she might smile. "You, on the other hand, will be saddled with my kin forever."

He opened his arms to her. "I adore your family."

She left her chair to sit on his lap and laid her head on his shoulder. She sank against him with a sweet little sigh. He wrapped his arms around her to savor the soft feel of her body curled against his and touched his lips to her hair.

"I adore *you*, Regina. A lifetime together will never be enough, but I will take whatever gift I'm given. I want to hold you like this forever. I want to wake to your smile and spend our days verbally sparring with one another, or physically if you wish it—although I will need lessons if I hope to hold my own."

She lifted her head. "Lessons in bantering or Wing Chun?"

"I suspect both." He kissed her forehead then rested his cheek on the top of her head when she laid it against his shoulder again.

"I've been thinking a lot about fatherhood today," he said. "I will be a better father to our children than my own was to me. I want to be part of their lives from the beginning. I want to cradle them against my chest while they drift to sleep, secure in the knowledge they are loved. I'll teach our children to skip rocks on the lake, how to sit a horse, to hunt and fish—"

"You would teach our daughters these things, too?"

"Of course! Why wouldn't I? If my wife knows hand-to-hand combat, her daughters are more than capable of mastering each of these tasks and more."

"I do love you," she murmured and wiggled even closer, the heat of her skin penetrating the barrier of clothes between them. "I love you so very much."

He hadn't realized what a balm those words would be to his soul, but now that she'd said them, he wanted to hear them again and again.

"I think Uncle Charles will heartily approve of you."

"He has my gratitude, as does Aunt Beatrice. I credit them for the courageous woman you are. I want our daughters to be like you."

She shook her head, her hair making a shushing noise against his jacket. "I'm not courageous."

"You are the bravest person I know."

"I am afraid," she said.

Xavier urged her to sit up to allow him to look into her face. "What frightens you? No one is going to hurt you. I promise."

"It is a promise you cannot keep. Love can only end in heartbreak. This is the lesson I learned from my parents. One day, everything can be perfect, and the next the ones you love are never coming back. I've managed to keep everyone else at a distance, because it is safer. But I can't do it with you. I love you, Xavier, and I am frightened of losing you."

"You aren't going to lose me. I will still be chasing you when I'm an old man, and you'll be wishing I would leave you alone."

"Never." She twined her arms around his neck. "Promise you will be careful. Claudine fears the duke will come for you once he realizes she is gone."

"Stanhurst is a coward who hurts those who cannot fight back."

"But he brought Farrin into your life—into *our* lives—and now we are entangled in this mess with Claudine and the duke too."

Xavier stiffened. "Do you believe Stanhurst has a connection to the map? What did Claudine tell you?"

Regina's eyes flared. "I— No, she said nothing. It didn't occur to me that Stanhurst might be involved with the map. I figured he was responsible for your disappearance. Do you think the duke is Farrin's buyer?"

"Farrin would need a giant set of brass ballocks to defy the duke's wishes and then use *me* to make a profit off him. If Stanhurst leveled charges against me to get me out of

Claudine's life, I'm sure he expected Farrin to kill me. The duke has powerful friends in Parliament. Farrin would be foolhardy to test his reach. I think it is unlikely Stanhurst has any interest in the map."

"Maybe Claudine can tell us if he collects antiquities. She already admitted to knowing Farrin. He dined with the duke several times years ago, which is rather damning. I have no doubt Stanhurst tried to get rid of you."

"We will speak with Claudine after dinner. The duke's connection with Farrin and now his resurgence could be a coincidence, but I wouldn't want to be caught unaware. I suppose I have one last gamble in me."

He tried to grab the paper, but Regina jerked it out of his reach.

"You are not facing Farrin and his men alone. Not this time."

"You are not accompanying me." He grabbed for the map once more and she hopped from this lap, dancing out of his range.

"Yes, I am." She folded the paper into a small square and shoved it into the bodice of her gown. "I will keep it safe in the meantime."

He allowed a wicked smile to slide across his face. "You know I am not afraid to fish around for it." Slowly, he stood and took a step toward her.

Her lips parted in surprise. "Don't you dare come any closer."

"Or what?" He prowled toward her as she scurried backward. "Are you going to unman me before our wedding night? I do hope you will ponder the consequences and reconsider."

A red blush rose in her cheeks. "I would never do any such thing. It is improper to even suggest it."

She backed into a stack of books and lost her footing. Xavier pounced, catching her around the waist and pulling her toward him before she tumbled. She clung to his jacket, a breezy laugh escaping her. "Thank you. That could have been disastrous."

"Allow me to check you for injuries." He skimmed his hands along the curves of her waist and brushed the undersides of her breasts.

She grumbled and tried to twist away, but as soon as he grazed her nipple, she held still. He circled the pad of his finger around the erect bud, avoiding contact until she began to whimper and lean into his touch. He rewarded her with a light pinch then twirled the nipple between his thumb and fingers.

She closed her eyes with an exaggerated sigh. Her head lolled back, exposing her neck and chest. Pushing the yellow muslin from her shoulder, he placed a kiss on her dewy skin and nibbled along her collarbone. Her pulse fluttered beneath his lips. The soft little noises coming from her were as erotic as hell, and he was losing sight of his original purpose.

The folded paper blocked full access to her other breast. He reached into her bodice, grasped the edge, and leisurely pulled the map from her gown. Tossing it over his shoulder and not caring where it landed, he grinned. "Now you are all mine, Miss Darlington. There is nothing to keep me from touching you wherever I like."

"Regina," one of her sisters called from the corridor. "I have been sent to retrieve you and Mr. Vistoire for dinner."

"One moment, Sophia." Regina jerked her gown to cover her shoulder as Sophia appeared at the threshold. Regina cleared her throat. "We will meet you at the table."

"Um, all right. I will let Aunt Beatrice know. Take your time." Sophia turned on her heel and left.

"Oh, law." Regina held a hand to her head and squeezed her eyes shut. "Do you think she saw us? I won't be able to look in her direction without dying of mortification."

"She saw nothing." Xavier offered Regina the reassurance she needed. Sophia might have stumbled across them, but he would have been obstructing her view. He pointed to the dust stains on Regina's gown to distract her. "Would you like to change before dinner? I will inform everyone that you will be joining us soon."

"Yes, thank you." She dropped her hand to her side. "This settles it. We are spending our wedding night at the hotel. Otherwise, I'll be wearing a sack over my head to avoid looking at anyone."

Xavier chuckled and held his hand out to her. "A simple request that I am happy to grant. Will you allow me to escort you to the stairs?"

She placed her hand in his, and he drew her from the room. At the foot of the stairs, he kissed her cheek. "I will see you in the dining room, love."

Holding the hem of her skirts out of her way, she practically ran up the stairs. When she disappeared from sight, he returned to the library, grabbed the map from the carpet, and tucked it inside his jacket. He was willing to take a risk with his own life, but he would never risk Regina's. Any meeting he arranged with Farrin would be with him alone.

Thirty

When Xavier returned to the Pulteney Hotel after dining at Wedmore House, he discovered word of his move had reach Farrin. One of the blackguard's regulars—the dead-eyed gent with pocked skin—was posted on the walk outside the hotel. He stepped into Xavier's path as he neared, blocking the entrance.

"Come with me," he growled and tried to seize Xavier.

He evaded the man's clumsy grab and raised his fists. "In case you have forgotten, you did not fare well in our last scuffle."

The brute hesitated, lowered his arm, and took a step back.

"Yes, that is much better." Xavier didn't relax his guard even though the man seemed to heed his warning. "Tell your boss I have what he wants. I'll be at the coffeehouse in an hour."

He nodded in the direction of the coffeehouse on the corner where he'd been earlier. The patrons would be engaged in lively debate even at this hour, which meant more witnesses, and the close proximity to the Pulteney Hotel provided Farrin with less opportunity to nab him along the way.

Xavier couldn't resist taunting the man for allowing another to control him. "Your master will need to leave you on the street. Dogs are forbidden inside."

The other man snarled then snapped his jaws before grinning like a Bedlamite.

"You are an ill-mannered mutt," Xavier grumbled. "Go fetch your master. I will not wait if he is delayed."

The beast ambled away.

Xavier visited his rooms to retrieve the firearm his brother-in-law had provided for him before making his way to the coffeehouse. Isaac's lack of questions about the need for a weapon and his brief commentary on the matter had been appreciated.

"Watch yourself," he'd said.

As planned, Xavier arrived at the coffeehouse first and chose a place at one of the less crowded tables. He sat on the bench facing the door so he could see Farrin when he arrived. Iron candleholders hung from the arched ceiling, bathing the room in a golden glow that matched the jovial mood of the men. Their voices melded together and rolled over him like the rumble of thunder. The gent next to him slapped the table, tossing his head back with braying laughter. Even in a room crammed with men, no one seemed to notice Xavier was there, which was not reassuring.

He reflected on the conversation with Claudine after dinner. She'd been able to shed a little light on the relationship between the Duke of Stanhurst and Farrin. Xavier and Regina were certain Stanhurst had given him up to Farrin. One evening Claudine had overheard the men talking over brandy and cheroots, but hadn't known what to make of their conversation.

Stanhurst congratulated Farrin on being named commander of the Regent's Consul. I didn't pay much attention to anything beyond that point. I figured they were discussing one of those ridiculous secret societies men are fond of joining.

From what Xavier had seen of Farrin's men, they were not pampered gents who wished to play at intrigue. They were trained in inquisition and subterfuge, which pointed to the group having a much more subversive purpose.

Despite Stanhurst's likely involvement with Xavier's disappearance, he did not seem to be linked to the map. Claudine said she'd never known him to have an interest in antiquities, but his son was an avid collector. She reported that Lord Geoffrey had joined the duke and Farrin for dinner a few times, and while Stanhurst had retired to his study to read, Lord Geoffrey and Farrin spoke of Lord Geoffrey's latest interests.

Did you ever hear Lord Geoffrey speak of the Black Death? Regina had asked. Claudine confirmed the men had seemed fascinated by the topic, and she had always excused herself since discussions of plagues were not pleasant after-dinner topics of conversation.

It seemed the duke and his son had been in bed with the devil, and perhaps Lord Geoffrey still was.

Farrin entered the coffeehouse alone with ten minutes to spare. He scanned the area until he locked eyes with Xavier. His expression was blank as he sauntered toward the table. Xavier took in the plainness of his gray jacket and the beaver hat pulled low on his head. Farrin didn't want to be recognized, which provided Xavier with an advantage.

The blackguard slid onto the bench across from him, frowning when the man beside him elbowed him in the side without seeming to notice. He skipped any pleasantries. "Hand it over."

Xavier aimed a humorless smile in his direction. "I'm afraid you have mistaken the purpose of our meeting. I am not here to kowtow to you. I have a proposition."

"Is that so?" Farrin leaned across the table and bore his teeth. "What do you think you can do if I refuse to hear your proposition?"

Xavier pushed his jacket aside to reveal the holstered firearm. "I could shoot you now and be rid of you, or perhaps the Duke of Stanhurst will handle the matter when he arrives. He is your partner, is he not?"

Farrin blanched and threw a wild-eyed look behind him. Power rushed through Xavier's veins. He had Farrin by the short hairs, and the other man knew it. "I don't take your meaning."

"I believe you understand perfectly." Xavier drummed his fingers on the table. "I wonder, did you receive payment for doing his bidding, or were you simply expected to obey a man of superior status?"

Farrin quivered, clenching and unclenching his fists.

"I do hope it was the latter," Xavier said. "The duke is a vengeful old crow. Can you imagine what he would do to a man who duped him *and* stole his money?" Xavier tsked and shook his head. "Although I fear the man who betrayed him would face a most unpleasant outcome even if larceny was not involved. Angering a wealthy and influential duke is never wise, sir. One often finds himself at the end of a hangman's noose, although he is rarely guilty of the crime of which he has been convicted. Of course, Stanhurst isn't the type of man who would stoop to lies to rid himself of his enemies."

Farrin glowered as Xavier took a gulp of coffee. "Show me that you have the map, and we will negotiate."

Xavier was deliberately slow to set down the cup and withdraw the folded sheet of paper from his jacket pocket. He brandished it and tucked it back into his jacket without revealing what was written on it.

"How do I know you have the real map?"

"You are looking for the Black Death, are you not?"

Farrin's Adam's apple lurched. He eased back on the bench. "You are mad. The Black Death, indeed. Why would anyone care about the bubonic plague?"

"Perhaps Stanhurst will have an answer."

"What do you want from me?"

"I want to know who hired you to retrieve the map."

It could be coincidence Lord Geoffrey had been present at the lecture about the Crusades, and that he'd spoken to Farrin of his interest in the ancient group years earlier. Xavier didn't want to erroneously believe Lord Geoffrey was responsible for placing Regina's and his families in danger while the true culprit remained a threat.

The muscles in Farrin's jaw bulged beneath his pale skin. "We've never met in person. He sends anonymous letters and money."

Xavier didn't believe him for a second. If Farrin revealed his buyer's identity, he could forfeit the financial reward coming to him.

"If you wish to protect your buyer, I understand. Although you should be more concerned about protecting yourself."

Farrin's rust-colored eyebrow hitched up.

"The duke appears to have been delayed, but I can't imagine it will be much longer." Xavier narrowed his eyes. "A name for the map."

"I will consider your proposition." With one more glance over his shoulder, Farrin rose from the bench and strode toward the back of the establishment. Likely, he would make use of an alley exit.

Once Xavier was convinced Farrin was gone, he left the coffeehouse to return to his rooms. He moved at a quick pace, keeping watch for Farrin's men and listening for the sound of his squeaky carriage. Xavier arrived at the hotel without encountering either, and a thorough look around the street reassured him that Farrin's men were no longer stationed outside. But he wouldn't be able to sleep until he knew Serafine was safe. He hailed a hackney coach to take him to his sister's home.

"Wait here," he said to the driver. "I will only be a moment."

He walked up and down the deserted street several times without finding any signs of danger to his family. Eventually, he returned to the carriage and gave instructions to carry him to Wedmore House. He repeated the same routine until he was satisfied Regina and her family were safe.

The sky was streaked with pink when he returned to the hotel. The Pulteney was abuzz with staff as they went about their morning tasks. Upon reaching his door, he withdrew the pistol from the holster and searched his rooms. They were empty and nothing had been disturbed. When he determined all was well, he collapsed on the bed for a couple of hours sleep before he needed to ready himself for his wedding day.

Joy was placing the last pin in Regina's hair when Sophia bounded through her chamber door.

"Mr. Vistoire has arrived," she said. "Aunt Beatrice will keep him company while you finish your toilette."

Regina's heart performed a clumsy flip. "He is here *now*? He isn't due for another twenty minutes." She had hoped for more time to mentally prepare herself for their wedding night, or perhaps she hadn't wished to think about it at all before they spoke their vows. Her trepidation was not due to a lack of enthusiasm, however. Rather, she worried that she might be too eager for his attentions, which she had recently discovered no proper young woman should ever be.

Sophia crossed the room to place her hands on Regina's shoulders and leaned down to meet her gaze in the mirror. "He is early. I believe that is a good sign."

Regina smiled at her sister. "It is a good sign he arrived at all, no?"

"There." Joy stepped back to view her handiwork. "Not a single hair is out of place."

"Everything looks perfect from this angle," Sophia agreed. She moved to stand beside the looking glass, ran her gaze over Regina, and applauded. "Brilliant work!"

Joy beamed. "Will there be anything else, miss?"

"No, thank you, Joy," Regina said. "You've truly outdone yourself today."

The maid bobbed a curtsey before heading for the door. Once Regina and her sister were alone, Sophia whistled. "You look marvelous, Gi. Mother's diamonds suit you well."

Regina turned her head from side to side to admire the stunning teardrop jewels crowning her head. "This headpiece was a gift from Papa during their courtship. Mama's parents wouldn't allow her to accept it, because they thought it was too extravagant. He saved the gift and presented it to her on their wedding night."

"How romantic." Sophia sighed. "And you've chosen the perfect gown."

Regina felt truly beautiful in the lavender chiffon. She moved to the looking glass so she could get a full view of her gown and hair together.

Sophia picked up the thin book lying on Regina's side table. "*A Proper Lady's Guide to Marriage: an Essential Handbook for New Brides*," she read aloud. "Please don't tell me you read this rubbish."

They had found it earlier in the week when they were searching Uncle Charles's library.

"I couldn't sleep last night," Regina said. "I thought I might learn something of value to help prepare me for tonight."

"It is written by a *man*." Sophia brandished the brown leather bound book. "I assume the thin volume is reflective of the author's knowledge on the subject."

Regina chuckled, appreciating her sister's unusual candidness. "He could have stopped writing after the first paragraph. *I* should have stopped reading it."

Sophia sank on the edge of the bed and flipped the book open to the first page. She sat in silence for a moment then wrinkled her nose. "He makes the marriage bed sound as appealing as snuggling with bedbugs. Consummation is a duty to be endured? The marriage bed is for begetting an heir, and no enjoyment is to be had by either party?" She slammed the book closed and tossed it over her shoulder. "Well, you know what they say, those who fail to please are always the first to criticize those who succeed."

Regina laughed. "No one says that."

"They should, because it is true."

"And how would you know what is true when it comes to matters of the heart?"

Sophia grinned. "Aunt Beatrice told me, and before you ask how our spinster aunt has knowledge of such matters, I don't know. But I believe her."

"That settles it." Regina stood and approached the bed to grab her gloves and don them. "If Aunt Beatrice said it, then it must be true."

Although she was teasing her sister, she too trusted their great-aunt over a stranger. Besides, it was too late to follow advice from the essential handbook for new brides. She already enjoyed Xavier's touch, and she didn't believe it possible she would ever find it unpleasant.

By the time she was ready to join the wedding party below stairs, her nervousness had abated mostly. Sophia stopped her outside the drawing room and tossed her arms around her neck. "I'm sorry Mother and Father aren't here to see you marry, Gigi. If they were, I believe they would tell you how very proud they are of you for keeping us close and taking good care of Auntie and Uncle Charles. I know Evangeline and I are proud to call you our older sister."

Regina hugged Sophia in return then cradled her cheeks. "Now, tell me the truth. You drew the short stick and were stuck with the task of giving me the talk."

Sophia laughed. "I did not. I volunteered. How did I do?"

"You were perfect, dearest."

They embraced once more before entering the drawing room. Xavier stood as she stepped through the threshold. His mouth hung partially open as if he'd been in the middle of speaking and forgotten his words. She suspected she appeared just as stunned by her first glimpse of him. He wore a double-breasted coat the color of rich wine and ivory trousers that could have appeared ostentatious on anyone else, but with his coloring and long, lean body, he was nothing less than striking.

He came forward to take her hand and draw it through the crook of his arm. "Miss Darlington, you look even more lovely than usual."

She wanted to return the compliment, but she felt everyone's eyes on her and shyness overtook her. She could be bold and strong, but showing her softer side with onlookers made her feel too vulnerable.

Sophia joined Aunt Beatrice on the settee. Evangeline and Joy had claimed two chairs. As agreed last night, Claudine was staying above stairs in the guest room to keep her presence at Wedmore House secret.

The vicar stood in front of the fireplace, waiting to perform the nuptials. Crispin, who was acting as a witness to their marriage along with Aunt Beatrice, had taken up position behind the settee.

Vicar Burnett held out his hand palm up, inviting Regina and Xavier to come forward. "Shall we begin?"

He led them through their vows, and before his words pronouncing them husband and wife sank in, Regina was signing her name to the parish registry. Xavier accepted the quill from her, dipped the tip in the inkwell, and scrawled his name on the page. While still bent over the book, he aimed a sideways glance at her. "The deed is done, Mrs. Vistoire, and I am a lucky man."

A small jolt passed through her at the sound of her new address.

The wedding party, minus the vicar who had other responsibilities to attend, retired to the dining room for a small breakfast. Regina hadn't swallowed her last bite before Aunt

Beatrice was shooing her upstairs to change her gown, so she and Xavier could be on their way. Evangeline and Sophia accompanied her to her chambers and helped pack a valise for overnight.

"We will be back tomorrow," she promised.

Evangeline rolled her eyes toward the ceiling and shook her head. "Enjoy your newlywed status. There is no need to rush back. We will be all right."

"I would feel better if we stayed together at least until the troubles with Farrin and Claudine are settled." She nibbled her lip as she contemplated the wisdom in leaving even for one night. "Perhaps we should stay—"

"Go," her sisters said at the same time.

Sophia closed the valise and lifted it from the bed. "You only get one wedding night, and you are *not* spending it at Wedmore House." Without further debate, Sophia marched out the chamber door with Regina's belongings. Regina resigned herself to spending the night away from her beloved family and trailed behind her.

A hackney coach was waiting outside when they reconvened in the drawing room. Crispin had already gone, and Claudine had come out of hiding. Cupid was sprawled on her lap, basking in the joy of a good belly scratch, and Aunt Beatrice had returned to her knitting. After taking a deep fortifying breath, Regina said good-bye to her family and accepted her new husband's escort to the coach.

Once she was settled on the bench, Xavier climbed in beside her and drew the curtains. The door closed, and he gathered her to him and captured her lips with his. He gently nipped her mouth several times before cradling the back of her head and deepening the kiss. A smoldering fire lit in her lower belly as her breath rushed from her lungs. He leisurely swept the tip of his tongue across her mouth, and she parted her lips on a sigh. His tongue brushed against hers in a loving, seductive stroke that left her tingly all over. He eased back, breaking contact, but seemed to have second thoughts and pressed his lips to hers for one last lingering kiss.

"Sweet Mary, Mother of God," he muttered then leaned against the seatback and drew her against his chest. She rested her head on his shoulder and covered his heart with her hand. It knocked beneath her palm, strong enough to be felt even through layers of clothing.

"What happens now?" she asked.

He chuckled, jostling her slightly. "It is still morning, and you are a new bride. I don't wish to be thought of as uncivilized, so I will refrain from answering that question. Would you care to take a stroll once we reach the hotel?"

She sat up. "No, I meant what happens with Farrin. How will we reach him to let him know we have the map? I assume you took it to the hotel last night. It was missing when I returned to the library."

His posture grew rigid. "I never agreed to allow you to meet Farrin."

"I wasn't asking for permission. You need me and I am coming with you. I refuse to sit around worrying while you meet with him alone. What if he takes you again?"

"There is no reason to worry. I met with him last night. I expect he has gone into hiding for a time to avoid a confrontation with Stanhurst."

Regina felt like she'd been hit with a boulder. "You met with him last night? Xavier, anything could have happened to you, and I might have never learned your fate." Tears blurred her vision, and she pressed her hand against the ache in her chest. How could he disregard her wishes so easily?

"Regina, please don't cry."

His request made the tears come faster.

He cradled her face between his palms and gingerly swiped away a tear with the pad of his thumb. "I am frightened too.

Losing you would kill me, especially when I would be responsible. I brought this mess into your life. It is my duty to clean it up."

"No, Uncle Charles is responsible." Trying to will her tears to stop, she caught them with her fingertips and dampened her glove. She was not a sentimental ninny, and she didn't want to be seen as one. "I'm sure he did not intend to place us in danger when he began his research, but this is his doing. You are in this mess because of him, so if I apply your logic, *I* should be cleaning up the mess."

Xavier released her and frowned. "That is nonsense."

"Yes, it is. I am glad to hear you admit it. From now on, we will face our troubles together."

He removed his hat and shoved his fingers through his curls with a breathy chuckle. "Fair enough. We will put our heads together from now on."

She was encouraged by his agreement.

"However," he said with his green eyes darkening and boring into her, "if I am ever faced with a choice between placing you in danger or risking my own life, I will always choose to save you."

"You have no concept of the word partnership."

One dark eyebrow lifted. "That is where you are wrong, *ma chérie*. I insist my better half stays alive."

"And I intend to see that my stubborn half does the same."

Thirty-one

Xavier had taken rooms toward the back of the hotel due to the almost constant rattle of carriages along Albemarle Street. Noise from the busy thoroughfare grew muffled as one of the hotel's footmen led Regina and Xavier along the dim corridor with her valise in hand. Once inside the apartment, Xavier directed the footman to take his bride's belongings to the bedchamber and paid him a shilling before he left.

Regina wandered around the space, inspecting her new surroundings. She had barely spoken since their tiff in the carriage. While he understood the reason for her upset, he maintained that he had made the correct decision. Regina was too good for the likes of men like Farrin, and Xavier wanted to keep her ignorant of the evil that existed in her own backyard.

"Does this meet with your approval?" he asked as she trailed her fingers over the surface of the marble topped sideboard then checked her glove for dust. She wouldn't find anything out of place—the maids kept the rooms spotless—but her satisfaction mattered a great deal to him.

"It is nice," she murmured before moving to the impractical gray silk sofa and plumping a tasseled pillow. She paused to sniff the vase of pink phlox on the side table. "Nice."

He suppressed a sigh as she wandered past him to reach the bedchamber without looking at him. He stood in the doorway and leaned against the jamb. She walked with a rigidness to her back and limbs that seemed almost painful. He couldn't decide if she was still angry or simply nervous to be alone with him. Either way, he needed to do something to change the tide, or their first day as husband and wife was going to be a chore for both of them.

"Did you pack your trousers?" he asked, nodding toward the valise sitting beside the wardrobe.

She spun away from the water closet door. "Pardon?"

"I asked if you packed your trousers. The ones you were wearing the night I found you punching a helpless bag of sand."

"Of course, not. It is our wedding night, and trousers hardly seemed appropriate."

He came forward with a smile, eager to see her in whatever flimsy nightrail she'd chosen, but now wasn't the time. "I never did learn what that sandbag did to earn your disfavor, but it must have been something dastardly. Perhaps he misled you?"

She nailed him with a look that would turn him to stone if she had that power.

"Did he refuse your help and act on his own without regard for your feelings?"

"Yes, that is exactly what he did." Her hands landed on her hips. "And then he had the gall to bait me. Does any of this sound familiar?"

He grinned as he sauntered toward her, stopping with only a couple of inches separating them. "You want me to say I was wrong for meeting Farrin without you."

Color rose in her cheeks. "Yes," she said through gritted teeth.

He shrugged one shoulder before moving to the wardrobe and casually opening the doors. "There is only one way to settle this." He dug inside until he found a pair of buckskins that would be the least likely to fall around her ankles and one of his shirts. He turned back toward her and lifted the pants. "We will settle this like men."

She rolled her eyes, clearly thinking he was teasing.

He tossed the clothes on the bed and came to stand before her. "I will help you undress, then I want you to put these on.

We will spar and if you best me, I will apologize for delivering the map without you."

Her jaw dropped. Gently, he placed his hand on her chin, closed her mouth, then turned her back to him to untie the sash around her waist.

The sash came loose, but she held it in place with her hands covering her stomach. "You cannot be serious."

"Hmm, but I can." Grasping the end of the bow holding her dress together in the back, he tugged. "Don't you want me to admit I was wrong?"

"Well, yes." She tried to spin around, but he caught her shoulders to keep her facing forward and leaned his head close to hers. He closed his eyes and inhaled. Her exotic scent left him feeling slightly intoxicated.

"Then *make* me apologize, madame." He brushed a kiss across the rim of her ear. "Unless you believe you are incapable of besting me," he whispered.

She trembled, her body suddenly searing hot. "I *will* make you apologize." Jerking away, she pulled the gown over her head then faced him with defiance flaming in her gorgeous amber green eyes. Her chest rose and fell with each rapid breath, and his gaze was drawn to her décolletage. Her ivory skin was flawless, and her corset made her modest breasts look plump and irresistible.

"Should I help you loosen your corset?"

"I don't need your help." She ripped at the corset strings and when she had them untied, she wrestled open the fastenings down the front. "Just like you don't think you need mine."

With her corset lying defeated on the Aubusson, she removed her petticoats and chemise. All reserve and shyness had fled, and she stood before him bare except for her stockings and slippers. His magnificent bride brimmed with audacious courage, and damned if she didn't look like she really wanted to bloody his nose.

He chuckled. "I'm beginning to feel overdressed."

"That is not my problem." She snagged the shirt from the bed to pull it over her head. The hem hung to her knees. She hitched her chin, challenging him. She was as provocative as hell, and it required every ounce of his willpower not to scoop her in his arms and toss her on the bed.

He rubbed his clean-shaven jaw, studying her while she held his gaze without blinking. "Put on the pants," he said.

"Take off your jacket."

"You didn't say please." Not that he cared. He was already shrugging out of his jacket then reaching to untie his cravat. When he'd shed both pieces, he held his arms at his sides, inviting her inspection.

She pointed, flicking her finger up and down from his neck to his waist. "And your waistcoat."

Her eyes widened when he didn't stop with his waistcoat and tore his shirt over his head.

He smirked. "If you can forego pants, I can do without a shirt."

"What you wear or don't wear has no bearing on the outcome of our match." Fiddling with a strand of hair that had come loose when she'd disrobed, she averted her gaze. "You do not intimidate me."

"*Bien*." Lying was not her forte, but her lack of skill in this area made her even more desirable. "Follow me and let us clear the air."

He didn't wait to see if she would argue. He returned to the sitting room and began pushing furniture to the perimeter. Once he had an area clear, he squared off with her.

She crossed her arms, cocking a hip. "You don't actually expect me to fight you. It is our wedding day."

"You are angry. Why shouldn't we clear the air?"

"I never said I was angry."

"Perhaps not with words, but your body betrayed you." He assumed a boxing stance, teasing her. "Come on, Regina. You know you want to draw my cork, so do it."

She shook her head.

He playfully took a swipe at her. She deflected the blow and scowled. "Stop."

"If you can manage two good hits, I'll stop." He danced around her, hopping on the balls of his feet.

"Two strikes and you will admit you were wrong and offer your apology?"

"No, that will take three." Grinning, he grabbed for her. She grasped his wrist, pushed him off balance, and drove the heel of her palm toward his nose. She stopped short of punching him.

He hissed. "So close. Better luck next time."

The spark in her eyes flamed. "That counts as a strike. Two more and you lose."

"I said three good hits and you never touched me. Sorry, sweetheart."

"You are as mad as a March hare! I'm not going to hit you."

He continued to hop from foot to foot, circling her. "Very well. Three good hits from me, and you must admit you are angry."

"I am not."

He shot his left hand out and lightly smacked her bottom. She gasped, frozen by what he could only surmise was shock.

He winked. "That is one for me."

When he tried to whack her other bottom cheek, she leapt to the side with a cry of outrage. "Xavier Vistoire, you better stop right now."

"Make me." He repeatedly attempted to grab her bum, but she kept spinning as soon as he made contact, so he tickled her sides instead.

She squealed, wiggling to escape his eager fingers and laughing so hard she couldn't form full sentences.

"You better—"

"I am going to—"

Whatever had caused her aloofness earlier was forgotten in that moment. Her full belly laughter was infectious. She thrust her arms up between their bodies then chopped downward, breaking his hold, and dashed for the sofa. He gave chase. She leapt onto the cushions, almost tipping over until she flung her arms to her sides and regained her balance. The low table pushed against the sofa created a barrier.

"What are you going to do now?" she taunted.

"I will not be thwarted by a table." He grabbed for her and she slapped at his hands, still laughing.

With a growl, he jumped on the sofa, too. She screamed and ran over the table to escape. Her feet hit the floor. Xavier chased her around the room, his fingertips grazing the muslin shirt, but she was too fast. When she raced into the bedchamber, however, he had her trapped. Still, Regina wasn't ready to surrender. She barreled toward the door and Xavier snagged her around the waist, lifting her feet off the floor.

They stumbled into the wall. Her body became wedged between his and the yellow wall covering, and she stopped struggling. Her cheeks had taken on a rosy glow, and her hair was mussed. They were panting. Her luscious breasts were flattened against his chest. He was hard and hungry for her, but her smile held him entranced.

"You are beautiful, love." He wrapped his hand around the nape of her neck, the fine silky strands of her hair caressing his skin.

Her hands skated over his chest, slowly and sensually exploring every muscle. She licked her lips, preparing for his kiss. And he wanted to kiss her. He wanted to bed her now, but he owed her something first.

He brushed the hair from her forehead, unable to look away from her. "You could have struck me. You were faster, but you did not take the opportunity."

"I didn't want to hurt you. I *never* want to hurt you."

"I wasn't trying to hurt you either, Regina. I'm sorry I disregarded your wishes about meeting with Farrin, but you *are* my better half. Monumentally better. You are kinder, more thoughtful, smarter..."

She shook her head.

"Yes, you are. The last two years of my life were miserable, but at the end of the nightmare, I found you. You are a reward I'm uncertain I deserve, but I am grateful for every moment with you." In the chaos of his existence, she was his haven. His hope. His one true love. "You are definitely too good for men like Farrin. Perhaps I am stubborn, or I am possessive, but I don't want him to have any piece of you."

"He cannot have any of me, because I belong to you, Xavier. My heart and mind. My—" Her breath hitched. "My body."

A need as essential as breathing flooded his veins, and he couldn't deny himself any longer. His mouth crushed against hers. She moaned, twining her arms around his neck and drawing him closer. Their tongues swept across one another in an erotic dance, and he tasted a trace of mint from the tea she'd had at breakfast. He leaned into her, pressing her against the wall, but it still wasn't close enough.

Fisting the hem of her shirt, he dragged it up her body and over her breasts. He sucked in a sharp breath when her bare skin touched his, branding him with her heat.

He pulled back just enough to admire his lovely wife. Daily exercise kept her slender and strong with a tapered waist and flat stomach, and her breasts were on the smaller size, like plump peaches. She was unlike any woman he had ever seen, and she was perfection in his eyes.

He grazed his fingers along the swell of her breast then the underside before cupping his hand around her. His darker complexion contrasted with her ivory skin—different on the outside yet perfectly matched. Deep inside, he had known she was meant for him the moment he woke to discover her tending him.

"I love you," he murmured and placed a tender kiss on her lips.

She caressed his cheek then kissed him in return. "I love you, too."

Her nipples were like pale pink rose buds, perky and begging to be licked.

"*Dieu, je te veux.*"

He grabbed her arse and lifted her higher, bracing her against the wall. She wrapped her legs around him. Bending his head to taste her, he circled her sweet little bud with his tongue before taking her in his mouth. She arched her back and buried her hands in his hair, her nails glancing his scalp and sending his blood pounding harder through his veins. He lavished attention on her breasts, alternating between them until she was writhing and making the most arousing noises.

Unable to wait any longer, he carried her to the bed and set her on the edge. Slowly, he peeled the shirt over her head then removed her slippers, leaving her stockings undisturbed.

A soft gasp reached his ears. Regina's lips were parted and her attention was locked on the bulge in his trousers. For a fleeting moment, he expected her to turn away and halt their love making, but she didn't.

He stood still, not wanting to frighten her. With eyes lit with curiosity, she allowed her gaze to travel over his body as he'd done to her. He grinned, pleased with her boldness.

"I should have guessed you would be no shy maiden in the bedchamber."

"Oh!" Her eyes snapped up to meet his. They clouded over.

He bent forward so they were forehead to forehead. "I love your curiosity and courage, Regina. I wouldn't want you to be any other way."

She released her breath and smiled. "Then it is acceptable that I want to see all of you?"

"*Absolument.*" He reached to unfasten the front fall of his trousers.

Wedmore House was filled with ancient artifacts depicting the male form, but the sight of Regina's husband in living, breathing bronzed flesh was a true masterpiece. Despite his reassurance that her ogling was permissible, heat swept into her face. She was hot all over, tingling in her breasts and between her thighs. She ached for his touch, but she was not so courageous as to ask for it.

He dropped beside her on the bed to tug off his boots and stood to slide his trousers over his hips and firm thighs. His green eyes smoldered then flamed as she continued to marvel at him. He stroked himself as if he was unable to resist the feel of skin against skin, yet holding back from touching her until she was ready.

She gave a small nod. He exhaled, smiling.

"Move higher on the bed, goddess."

As she scooted toward the pillows, he prowled toward her on hands and knees. Her heart trembled in her chest before slamming against her ribs. She laid her head on the pillow and he covered her body. His biceps tensed as he held his weight off her. Power and strength coursed through him, but his kiss was gentle.

She placed her hands on his chest to explore the chiseled muscles beneath his hot skin. A sparse dusting of soft dark hair spread across his chest. Leisurely, their mouths moved together, tasting one another. The sound of their sighs mingled, filling her ears, and as he trailed kisses down her neck and along her collarbone, her sighs became low moans.

When his lips brushed her aching nipple, she arched, her body begging for more. He didn't deny her, taking her in his mouth and suckling until she was restless and shifting on the bed. Settling beside her, he continued his loving attention to her breasts and placed his hand on her thigh. A strong pulse fluttered between her legs, and her breath caught.

Xavier lifted his head and slid his hand up her thigh. "I want to see you when I touch you."

She held his gaze as his hand moved agonizingly close, yet not close enough. Her hips lifted from the bed seeking satisfaction, and he covered her mound with his palm, rubbing in a small circular motion that wrenched another pleasurable moan from her. His eyes darkened until she couldn't see even a hint of green any longer.

She felt slick and hot, just as she had been the day she'd surrendered to him on the settee. He caressed her skin, coaxing the fire inside her to flame brighter, hotter. It slowly began to consume her as he stroked her, the intensity building with each loving touch. His fingers explored her body, slipping into her and then sweeping across her pleasurable spot until she was panting hard, and still she couldn't catch her breath.

Her release was as powerful and shattering as an explosion, and she cried out repeatedly as wave after wave of pleasure shook her. As the last quiver of her body faded, she dissolved into the bedding, sated but longing for more. She reached for her husband, her hand curling around his neck to pull him to her for another kiss. A brief peck and a whispered request, "Make me your wife, Xavier."

Xavier's blood roared in his ears, and he position himself above Regina. He trembled with the effort of restraining his urges. He wanted to be deep inside her, thrusting hard and holding her tight, but that would come in time. Now she needed tenderness, and he needed her forever.

He placed his lips to hers—nipping and teasing her mouth with his tongue until he sensed the shift in her. She grasped his shoulders and pulled him toward her. He allowed the tip of his cock to slide inside her, fighting to hold back until her body relaxed beneath his. Then he forged a little deeper. He took her slowly, allowing her time to adjust to him. She hissed when he broke through her body's resistance, but she wrapped her arms around his back, holding him when he was fully seated inside her.

She was tight and wet, and he was dying a slow death by not being allowed to move. "Regina, I am losing control. Forgive me."

Her eyes widened and she loosened her grip. He withdrew and eased back into her. She gasped, closing her eyes with a pleasurable smile playing about her lips. After several moments, she tentatively began to move with him.

"Yes." He grabbed her arse to guide and encourage her, but she required little of either. Her responsiveness captivated him and he lost whatever loose grip he'd maintained on his control. He drove into her, coming hard with three thrusts. As he recovered, he stayed inside her. He cradled her face and kissed her, then rolled to his back and gathered her to him. She laid her head on his chest and walked her fingers over his skin. He smoothed his hand over her hair.

Now that he could think clearer, he was worried about his lack of restraint. He cleared his throat. "Did I hurt you?"

She shifted to rest her chin on his chest and smiled with a sparkle in her eyes. Her coiffure was beyond repair and a rosy pink stained her cheeks. "Do I look injured?"

He grinned. "You look well-shagged."

"Well-shagged indeed." Her smile widened to show a flash of white teeth. "Is it improper to wonder when we can do it again?"

"Probably," he teased. "Thank God I didn't marry a proper wife"

Thirty-two

Regina rolled off Xavier and collapsed on the bed to catch her breath. The sky beyond the windows had grown dark a couple of hours earlier, but she didn't want to succumb to sleep. Even though she was tired and a little sore, she wanted to hold on to the thrill of making love a little longer. She hadn't expected to become so lost in her husband.

"How is it you were able to charm me into staying in bed most of the day?" she asked.

He twined his fingers with hers on the mattress between them. "I believe this last round was your doing."

She laughed, turning her head to see his profile in the dark. "I liked it better when I could see you."

"Duly noted. I will light the lamps before you ravish me next time."

Her stomach growled.

He chuckled, released her hand, and pushed up to sit on the side of the bed. "I suppose I should feed you if I expect you to keep pace with me."

They had fed each other bites of sandwiches and fruit at teatime, but they'd soon forgotten about their hunger and abandoned the tray to race each other back to the bedchamber.

Xavier stood. "Wait here and I will bring a lamp." He walked into the great room and a few moments later, the flare of a flame brightened the room. When he returned, he held the lamp high, raining golden light over his nude body. She sat up in bed and smiled, remembering the wicked acts they had engaged in earlier.

He playfully shook his finger as he placed the lamp on a chest of drawers. "Stop looking at me like that, Regina Vistoire, or I will never leave our bed."

She wouldn't be opposed, but her stomach growled again and she was forced to admit she had grown ravenous. "Very well. You may leave it briefly, but only because I'm famished."

She swung her legs over the edge of the mattress and searched the floor for Xavier's shirt. In their haste earlier, it had been wadded into a ball and tossed in the direction of the bedside table but missed its target. She bent to retrieve it from under the table and pulled it over her head.

Xavier found his pants and pulled them over his hips. "I will ring for a meal."

Neither was fit to dine in public now, nor did she want to endure a long dinner hour hiding that she was the most gratified bride in London. She spotted a leg of the buckskins sticking out from under the bed and snatched them en route to the water closet. "I will be setting myself back to rights."

"I like you out of sorts." Xavier caught her around the waist and placed a kiss on her forehead. She leaned into him, savoring his warmth and masculine scent. When they released each other, Xavier grabbed a candle, removed the lampshade, and lit it. "For you, madame." He replaced the candle in the holder and passed it to her.

"Thank you." She rose on her toes and placed a peck on his lips. "Please hurry back. I cannot be certain, but I think I am missing you already."

He smirked, appearing rather pleased with his effect on her. "I am only going to the sitting room."

She let herself into the water closet and closed the door. The candlelight seemed brighter in the small space, and she caught her reflection in the looking glass. "For pity's sake," she mumbled. Her hair was a mess.

She could hear Xavier moving about in the bedchamber as she combed her fingers through her hair. When she'd accepted her efforts were for naught, she picked up the white porcelain pitcher on the washstand and poured water into the basin. Xavier announced he would be back shortly, and she teasingly wished him a safe journey.

She dropped a cloth in the basin and was wringing the water from it when a loud bang caused her to jump.

"Where the hell is she? Claudine!"

Regina's heart stopped.

"She is not here, Stanhurst. Get out!"

Good Lord. Claudine had warned them against the duke, but Regina hadn't expected Stanhurst to come to the hotel where any number of people might recognize him.

"Claudine! Where is the whore?"

"Madame Bellerose is not here." Xavier sounded calm—much calmer than she felt with her heart trying to beat its way through her breastbone. Her husband's lack of excitement only seemed to agitate the duke. He bellowed for his mistress.

"Lord Geoffrey, are you going to allow your father to cause a scene?" Xavier asked.

Regina mouthed a curse. Stanhurst had brought his son.

"He does as he wishes," Lord Geoffrey said. A crash came from the sitting room.

"Claudine! I know you are hiding. Show yourself and I will forgive you."

"I already said she isn't here."

"Shut your bloody mouth, you lying bastard. Claudine, come out. No one will be hurt if you show yourself now."

The only liar in the room was the Duke of Stanhurst. Regina had witnessed the aftermath of what he had done to the poor woman, and if she had any say, he would never see Claudine again.

"Don't make me drag you out by your hair!" Something smashed against the wall.

Regina pulled on the buckskins. Stanhurst needed to know he couldn't come to their rooms and harass her husband. And he certainly couldn't kick up a fuss and use foul language with a lady present.

"Stop!" Xavier barked. "You can't go in there."

Regina tugged on the water closet door to find Xavier blocking the doorway to the bedchamber with his body.

"Remove yourself, Vistoire. My father only wants the woman. Set her free and you will not be harmed."

"The duke is mistaken," Xavier said. "I have no prisoners here. I am *alone*."

The warning in her husband's tone was clear. He wanted her to stay hidden.

She peeked through the crack in the water closet door.

"Step aside, Vistoire."

Xavier's back stiffened and he raised his hands in the air. "For God's sake, put away the pistols before one of you puts a hole through the wall. We can resolve this peacefully."

Oh, law! They were armed. What was she supposed to do now? She eased the door closed, trying to recall what items were in the bedchamber and if any of them could be used for a weapon. In truth, she hadn't been paying attention to her surroundings earlier, and she probably wouldn't reach anything before the duke or Lord Geoffrey overtook her.

The duke yelled for Claudine repeatedly, his voice growing louder as he entered the bedchamber. Scrambling to extinguish the candle, Regina almost knocked the holder off the washstand. She caught it before everything tipped and blew out the flame. The water closet was plunged in darkness, but as her eyes adjusted to the scant moonlight streaming through the window, she could distinguish the outlines of the washstand and chamber pot.

The banging continued. Drawers slammed and glass shattered, which made no sense when Claudine was clearly too large to hide in a vase.

"What the hell is this? A bloody valise?" The duke seemed incapable of speaking in a volume below a bellow. "These are women's clothes. She *is* here. Claudine! I am going to blow a hole in you the second I find you, you ungrateful bitch."

"No one is getting shot. Put down the pistol." The thread of panic underlying Xavier's command caused her to tremble.

She was torn between fighting off the duke and his son at her husband's side and going for aid. Deciding the odds of saving Xavier were greater if she sought assistance, she unlatched the window and rose on the tips of her toes to lift the sash to its highest position so she could fit through the opening.

The duke's yelling grew louder.

The window ledge was too high for her to just climb out, so she jumped, hauling her torso onto the windowsill. Her legs dangled and the wood casing pressed hard into her belly. She had no leverage to push herself to freedom, and her arms weren't strong enough to lift her body weight. Rocking from side to side, she swung her legs toward the adjacent wall and got a foothold. She braced her feet against the wall and wiggled into a seated position on the windowsill. The duke hadn't discovered the water closet yet, but based on the loud crashes and shouts outside the door, he wasn't giving up until he searched every inch of the space.

Carefully, she climbed to her feet and inched onto the building's ledge. She hugged the wall, the cold stone gouging her cheek. Her fingers ached from gripping tightly to the edges of the blocks. One strong wind could blow her over the edge. The two-story fall to the alley might not kill her, but she would definitely be maimed.

"Upon my honor, Madame Bellerose is not here."

Xavier shouted when the water closet door flew open and the window lit up. Regina held her breath. Her legs quivered. If the duke looked out the window, he would see her.

"She isn't here, Stanhurst," Xavier said, "but I will take you to her. She has caused me enough trouble. You may have her."

Regina's heart dropped to her stomach. If Xavier left the hotel with Stanhurst, she wouldn't know where to find him, because she knew with certainty he would never take the duke to Wedmore House. Nausea welled up inside her when Stanhurst agreed.

The window darkened again, and she shuffled back toward safety. Climbing inside the building proved easier. She lowered to the water closet floor as quietly as possible and pressed her ear to the door. The rooms beyond were silent. She crept into the bedchamber and ascertained she was alone. Xavier had left the lamp burning.

She raced to collect her slippers, grabbed the sash from her gown to help keep Xavier's pants from drooping on her hips, and extinguished the lamp. After she shot into the corridor and dashed down the stairs, she burst through the front door of the hotel to the accompaniment of scandalized gasps from people on the walkway, but she couldn't care less about offending anyone.

The duke's carriage was pulling onto the street, becoming swallowed by the flow of traffic. Regina spotted a hackney coach across the way. She darted into the well-traveled thoroughfare, weaving between carriages when they were at a standstill, and reached the opposite walkway without incident.

"You there," she called out to the coachman. "I need a coach. It is urgent."

A broad-shouldered man stepped in front of the carriage door, blocking her access. He was young with a face that teetered between handsome and average, but his cocky smile brimmed with the confidence of one who thought highly of himself. "Let me see your blunt, *miss*." He ogled her attire. "You are a miss, are you not?"

She huffed. "I haven't time for nonsense. Step aside."

He planted a hand against her shoulder when she tried to push around him. "Not until you tell me how you intend to pay."

She sputtered. "I assure you that you will receive compensation when I reach my destination. I give you my word."

"Your word means nothing. What else do you have to offer?" His wolfish grin caused her stomach to plunge.

"Surely, you are not suggesting—" A tap on her shoulder interrupted her line of thought. She turned to discover a veritable giant standing behind her.

He smiled politely and tipped his battered hat. "Mrs. Vistoire, would you please move aside?"

"How do you know who I am?" she asked, too shocked to object when he took hold of her shoulders and walked her a few paces away.

"Mr. Vistoire is my friend." He returned to the carriage and punched the young man without warning. The poor man dropped on the walkway, holding his nose and moaning.

"Jamie?" The coachman leaned out of the driver's box to check on his partner, and the large man with unnaturally purplish-red lips snagged him by the collar and dragged him from his seat. When the coachman protested, the brute kicked him in the backside and sent him sprawling on the ground.

He held his hand out to her. Regina backed away, her muscles tensing in preparation of running as fast as her legs would carry her.

"They are going to kill Mr. Vistoire," he said. "We have to go if we are going to save him."

Regina hesitated. It was madness to go anywhere with this stranger, but something inside her urged her to take his hand.

Perhaps it was the lack of malice in his eyes, which was in conflict with the violence she'd just witnessed. But she was desperate to reach her husband so she trusted her instincts.

She scrambled onto the box. The carriage tilted violently with his added weight when he climbed up beside her, and she grabbed for anything to keep from sliding toward him.

"There was a ducal coach that just left the hotel," she said. "Did you see which direction it went?"

"Yes, ma'am." He released the brake and snapped the reins. The team darted onto the street, barely missing the coachman who tried to jump in front to stop them. "They are headed to the docks."

"How do you know?"

She gasped when they almost collided with a Berlin. He maneuvered them through a break in the traffic, and they barreled past two more carriages. She gripped the edge of the seat until her fingers ached.

"I heard the duke tell his coachman," the man shouted over the rattle of harnesses and roar of wheels and hooves.

He drove the team like the madman she had first judged him to be, racing around corners. At one point, she would have sworn they were on two wheels.

"Who are you?"

"Benny. Mr. Vistoire is my friend."

Benny! Xavier's gaoler. What had she done?

He snapped the whip over the horses' heads, and the team tore down an empty street. Buildings flew by in a blur, and it was too dark to make out landmarks. The wheels hit a hole in the street, bouncing her in the air. Benny shot his arm out and grabbed a handful of her shirt to save her from flying off the box.

Her hands and legs shook from the close call.

"Hang on, ma'am. I took an oath to protect Mr. Vistoire's loved ones, and he is smitten with you."

Against her better judgment, she clung to him. She wanted to ask how he knew anything about her relationship with Xavier, but instead she asked, "What oath? Xavier never mentioned you pledging an oath to him."

Benny grinned, revealing gaps where he was missing a few teeth. "He doesn't know about it. I said it when I was watching over his family. Can't be seen or Tommy will have me flayed."

Regina's eyes widened. Surely, he was exaggerating. "Who is Tommy?"

"My brother, and he gets real angry when I forget to call him by his new name, so don't say anything when we get to the docks."

An alarm sounded in Regina's mind. "Why would your brother be at the docks? What does he have to do with the duke?"

"I don't have all that sorted out, ma'am, but I followed my brother last night after he met with Mr. Vistoire."

"Your brother is Farrin?" Regina's head began to spin and pins of light danced in her vision.

Benny glanced at her. "You don't look well. Are you going to faint?" Before she could say she was all right, he palmed the back of her head and thrust it between her knees. "Keep down until it goes away."

She flailed her arm, trying to knock his meaty hand away, but she couldn't reach it and slapping his shins had no effect. Oddly, the dizziness receded, and she realized he was still talking.

"I kept a watch on my brother all night. He met the duke's son this morning in the park. They were talking about the duke and Mr. Vistoire."

"Let me up," she commanded. "I am not going to faint."

He released her, and she sat up slowly, pushing her hair away from her face.

"How were you able to eavesdrop at the park? What are you, a spy?"

He flashed his gap-toothed smile. "No, ma'am. Truth is, no one pays attention to an idiot. And I wore a disguise."

She didn't even want to know what disguise a man of his size could possibly wear to go unnoticed. "What did they say?"

"They want to kill the duke and blame Mr. Vistoire. The duke's son will shoot Mr. Vistoire and say he was defending his father. But if I know Tommy, he probably plans to kill all three."

"That is not reassuring, Benny. Not reassuring at all."

He shrugged. "We will stop him. They aren't far ahead of us now."

With their wild race through the streets, she wouldn't be surprised if they arrived at the docks first. "How are we going to stop them? They have pistols."

"We will think of something together."

"Together," she mumbled. "Once this is behind us, would you talk to my husband about togetherness? He is unfamiliar with the word."

"Whatever you want, ma'am."

She smiled at his agreeableness. "In the park, did either man mention a map?"

"The one that leads to the assassin group? Aye, then Tommy told the duke's son to shut his mouth or he'd cut out his tongue." Benny slowed the team and pointed ahead. "See, I told you we would catch them. That is Tommy up ahead."

Regina squinted at the indistinct carriage in the distance. "How can you tell?"

"The back wheel of his town carriage wobbles."

Now that they were no longer careening down the streets, she released Benny's arm and scooted to create a little distance between them. "Are you telling the truth about wanting to help my husband? You were his gaoler."

She didn't exactly expect honesty from him, but she needed to ask.

"Yes, ma'am. I am real sorry for what I did. I was lonely and Tommy said he would kill me if I set him free, but it was wrong to keep him from his family. I owe Mr. Vistoire. I will die for him, or you."

Thirty-three

An eerie creaking carried on the night air as Xavier was forced to walk ahead of Stanhurst and his son at gunpoint. Water slapped against the sides of the ships, and the flow of the River Thames created a constant rushing sound.

The stench of dead fish assaulted his sensibilities. He covered his nose and mouth. Darkness blanketed the area, making it difficult to see anything besides the dark bulks of the ships moored along the quay, which would aid him once he escaped.

He glanced at the river and discarded it as an option. Even if he managed to swim out of range of their pistols—which would be a difficult feat fully attired—he would likely contract dysentery.

"You said you know where Claudine is," Stanhurst snapped. "The docks are deserted."

"She is onboard one of the ships, the *Eleanor*. I don't know where it is moored. We will have to look for it."

Xavier set his sights on the rows of warehouses standing in the distance. They would provide places to hide and perhaps he'd find a weapon. He just needed to create a distraction, so he could make a run for shelter then find his way back to Regina.

The burning in his gut returned as he recalled the moment Stanhurst had jerked open the water closet door. Xavier had been terrified the duke would mistake Regina for his mistress and discharge his weapon, but she had saved herself. Stanhurst hadn't noticed the open window, or if he had, apparently it hadn't occurred to the duke that a woman would use it to escape. A sour taste rose in the back of Xavier's throat. Had she climbed back inside safely?

They were nearing the warehouses and his means of escape. He glanced back over his shoulder. "I suppose it didn't occur to you to bring the carriage lamp. It would make finding the ship easier."

The duke growled in frustration. "Retrieve it," he barked at Lord Geoffrey. "The whore is going to pay for her betrayal."

A low chuckle from behind them caused Xavier's hair to stand on end. He knew that laugh.

"Isn't shagging you punishment enough?"

Stanhurst spun toward Farrin. "What the devil are you doing here? You are a traitor to the King. This man is a *spy*, and you allowed him to go free."

The night hid Farrin's face, but Xavier could hear the sneer in his tone. "You are a liar and coward. You don't even have the liver to do your own killing."

Xavier eased toward the warehouses, his muscles tensing to run.

"Did you find the map?" Farrin asked Lord Geoffrey.

"It wasn't at the hotel. Maybe he hid it at his sister's house."

"What bloody map?" Stanhurst swung toward his son, and Xavier sprinted for the warehouses.

Farrin cursed. "You take care of him and I'll give chase."

A shot echoed on the air.

Xavier ducked, but when he realized he wasn't hit, he kept running. Reaching the first warehouse, he darted for the back of the buildings. A second shot rang out, which definitely wasn't meant for him. He didn't slow his pace. Tripping in the dark was preferable to a lead ball through the back.

"Xavier!" He thought he heard Regina calling his name, but that was impossible.

Footsteps pounded after him, heavy and approaching fast. Xavier darted between two warehouses, trying to lose his pursuer. The man followed.

Xavier spotted a door on the right. Reaching it, he tugged on the handle. It was unlocked. A strong hand snagged the back of his jacket. Xavier twisted toward his opponent and nailed him with a left uppercut to the gut.

The man released him and doubled over. Xavier drew his fist back and slammed it into the thug's jaw. He followed with a left hook. His opponent crumbled on the ground.

"Xavier!"

He startled, turning in the direction of his wife's voice. "Regina!"

"Xavier, where are you?" She sounded close, but he couldn't see her.

"I am here."

"Where?"

He stepped over the man and followed her voice toward the back of the warehouses. She appeared in the opening between the two buildings. Xavier intercepted her, gathering her close and burying his face in her hair.

"Thank God, you are all right," he said. "Come on. We have to go."

He captured her hand to pull her along behind him. She was slower than he had anticipated given how fleet of foot she had been when he'd chased her around the hotel.

"Farrin is here," he said. "We must hurry."

"I know. Where is Benny? He was trying to catch you to tell you we'd come for you. We have a coach waiting."

Merde! He skidded to a stop. "That was Benny? What are you doing with him?"

"He appeared from nowhere outside the hotel. He said he would help me rescue you."

Xavier didn't know how to make sense of this news. Benny had always been his opposition. He was Farrin's henchman. Xavier gently took her by the shoulders. "He didn't hurt you, did he?"

"No, of course not. He cannot drive a team worth a pence, but he got us here in one piece."

"I see." Xavier dragged his fingers through his hair. "He is lying by the warehouse door. I didn't know who was grabbing me."

Regina gasped. "What do you mean he is lying by the door? Is he hurt?"

"He is unconscious."

"For heaven's sake, did you render him unconscious?" She tugged her hand free. "He is here to help us." She started to go back the way they had come, but he captured her wrist.

"Benny is too large to move. Please, let's get you to safety, and I will come back for him."

She jerked free again. "We are staying together. I would rather be in danger with you than frightened out of my wits wondering what has happened to you."

Xavier considered her position and agreed not knowing her fate earlier had been a special type of hell. He nodded sharply. "When there is no more danger, we will come back for him."

They heard the scuff of a boot at the same time. Their heads snapped in the direction of the sound.

"Mr. Vistoire," Farrin called from the darkness. "My generosity is at an end. I want the map."

Xavier and Regina broke into a run. Farrin cursed and chased after them. Xavier guided Regina down a narrow passage between warehouses. At the end of the building, she cut right. "This way. The carriage."

Xavier followed her. They sprinted alongside the water. A carriage light flickered in the distance. Just a little further past the warehouses, and they would be on the street.

Farrin burst onto the quay in front of them, and they froze. He lunged for Xavier. Regina shot out her leg, kicking Farrin in the chest. He caught her foot and flipped her to the ground. With a guttural growl, Xavier tackled him. The impact rattled his teeth. He scrambled for position with Farrin trapped beneath him. He drew back his fist. Farrin blocked his punch and slammed him in the nose in a move Xavier would have expected from Regina. He held his nose and stood, staggering. Farrin used his leg to sweep Xavier's legs out from under him. He fell on his side with an oof.

Regina jumped between him and Farrin. She blocked three strikes and almost managed to land a hit to his eye, but Farrin was fast. He seemed to know what Regina was going to do before she did. Crouching low, she twirled and tried to kick him off his feet. He leapt over her leg and sprang forward to grab her by the hair. She cried out, clawing at his hand.

Xavier bounded from the ground and raised his fists, but Farrin was using Regina as a shield. "Release her!"

Farrin shoved her into Xavier and they both fell. His body cushioned hers.

"Enough of this child's play," Farrin snapped and pulled a knife from his boot. He brandished it; moonlight glinted dully off the blade. "I am going to carve up the wench and make you watch."

He took a step toward them. Regina slammed her foot into his knee. A loud crack preceded his howl. He hopped on his uninjured leg, shouting obscenities.

Xavier climbed to his feet and hauled Regina up beside him. Farrin grasped the blade, drawing his arm back to hurl it. Xavier shoved Regina behind him. A bellow came from between the warehouses—much like a warrior's cry as he rode into battle. Farrin jerked toward the sound. A large man streaked across the quay and took a flying leap at Farrin. They crashed into the water.

"Benny!" Regina hurried to the edge of the quay. "Where are they? I don't see them."

She shouted Benny's name.

Xavier joined her in searching the inky water, but the men had disappeared. He couldn't even tell where they had sunk below the surface.

"Oh, Xavier." Regina clutched his arm. "Is there nothing we can do?"

He tucked her against his side, offering comfort. She was trembling. "I am sorry, love, but there is nothing when it is so dark."

They stood at the edge of the quay, staring into the water longer than any man should be able to hold his breath.

"Benny said he would give his life for you," Regina murmured. "I wish it hadn't come to that."

Xavier hugged her close to kiss her temple. "Let's get you to the carriage, and I will come back to see to the duke and his son. I suspect they will both require an undertaker's services, but I want to be certain."

"Farrin and Lord Geoffrey planned to shoot you both and blame you for the duke's death."

As he and Regina turned away, a splash and loud gasp came from the water. Regina rushed to peer over the side. "It is Benny. Find a rope or pole."

In an act of ungodly strength, Benny slapped the quay, hooked his fingers over the edge, and hauled himself from the water until he could brace with his palms. When he kicked his leg over the side, Xavier grabbed him and helped pull him onto the quay. He flopped on his back, panting like Cupid after a run.

"Where is Farrin?"

Benny didn't answer. Xavier crouched beside him and shook his shoulder to get his attention. "What happened to Farrin? Is he alive?"

Benny shook his head. "He wouldn't let me help him. I tried to save him, but he wouldn't let me."

Xavier sat back on his haunches. He couldn't quite believe Farrin was gone, and there was no more danger.

Once Benny had recovered enough to walk, the three of them headed back to the carriage. Xavier saw that Regina was settled inside, but he was hesitant to leave her in Benny's care.

"I will be all right," she reassured him. "Benny has sworn an oath to protect you and everyone you love. He has proven himself tonight, wouldn't you agree?"

Xavier was still uneasy about Benny's shift in loyalties, but he had saved his life. And more importantly, Benny had protected Regina, the woman who gave his life meaning. In the end, he decided trusting Benny was preferable to leaving Regina alone.

Xavier found the duke and Lord Geoffrey near the water, and just as he'd expected, the duke's days of terrorizing Claudine were finished. Xavier was unsure how he would explain their untimely demises to the local magistrate, but he couldn't leave without possibly incriminating himself in their murders.

Xavier returned to the carriage and had Benny drive to the closest tavern. The magistrate and undertaker were summoned, while he and Regina shared a meal with Benny. When the magistrate arrived, he listened to Xavier's accounting of the evening's events.

"Two murders and the murderer drown," the man repeated. "Sounds like you told us all we need to know. I bid you a good evening."

Apparently in Wapping, a dead duke and his son didn't cause much of a stir.

It was after midnight when Benny delivered Regina and Xavier to Wedmore House to insure that Regina's family was safe. Benny set the brake and climbed down from the box.

"You do not need to see us inside," Xavier said when the man tried to follow them.

Benny nodded. "Yes, sir. I will be here when you wake."

"Here?" Xavier pointed to the walkway. "As in here on the street?"

"I should be close in case you need me."

Xavier sighed. "For pity's sake, you cannot sleep on the street."

"Return the coach and make your way back here," Regina said. "I'm afraid the guest room is already occupied, but we have an extra bed in the carriage house."

"Just for tonight," Xavier added so Benny didn't get up his hopes that he would become a permanent guest at Wedmore House. "We will find you better accommodations tomorrow."

Benny flashed a wide grin at Regina. "I told you we were friends. Mr. Vistoire is a good man."

Regina returned his smile then gazed up at Xavier. "He is the best kind of man, Benny."

Xavier and Regina slogged up the stairs after sending Benny on his way. She checked on her aunt and sisters, waking them briefly to inform them that she and Xavier were there for the night.

Sophia sat up in bed. "Is everything all right?"

"Yes, dearest. We have no more cause for worry. Go back to sleep and I will tell you about it tomorrow."

When she joined Xavier in her bedchamber, she limped to the bed and fell back on the mattress with her eyes closed.

Xavier came to stand over her. "What will your aunt and sisters think when they realize I brought you home limping?"

She aimed a sleepy smile at him. "They will think I am a very lucky wife."

He chuckled and crawled on the bed beside her. "I am the lucky one. Even though you pushed me down the stairs and crowned me with a fire poker the first time we met."

"I did *not*." She lifted to her elbow and pretended to glower. "I told you, Cupid made you fall."

"Oh, sure. Blame the dog."

"You are impossible," she said and rolled her eyes.

He flipped her on her back, pinning her arms against the mattress. "Impossible not to love." He rained kisses all over her face. "Say it, Regina Vistoire. You love me. Say it."

She was laughing and wiggling on the covers as he continued his barrage of kisses, but she managed to blurt, "I love you!"

He stopped teasing and cradled her face. "I love you, too."

Epilogue

It had been three weeks since Regina and Xavier's eventful wedding night, and Wedmore House was immersed in chaos. Regina hugged Cupid against her chest to keep him from darting out the door as two newly hired footmen carried trunks to the carriage under the new butler's direction.

"Did you pack my riding habit?" Evangeline asked Ann, the lady's maid they had hired to travel with them to Brighton and then on to Athens to find Uncle Charles.

"Yes, miss. As well as your riding crop and compass, the large stack of books from your bedside table, your magnifying glass, the trowel and brushes you keep in the battered box under your bed, and two extra nightrails. Have I forgotten anything?"

When the new maid mentioned nightrails, Evangeline blushed and her gaze shot toward Xavier, who had just come inside from overseeing the loading of her trunks.

It was a reminder to Regina that although her sister was blunt around her, Sophia, and Aunt Beatrice, she was still an innocent.

"You have been very thorough, thank you," Evangeline said. "I should check the library once more, I think."

She dismissed Ann and bustled from the foyer with her head down. Regina smiled and scratched Cupid behind the ears. Xavier ambled over to her. "Your sister seems to have packed the entire contents of her bedchamber."

"I think she hopes Uncle Charles will allow her to stay behind when we return."

A few days after her wedding, a brief letter from Uncle Charles had arrived reassuring everyone at Wedmore House that he was in good health. The markings indicated he had sent it from Athens. Unfortunately, in his letter, he indicated he didn't know when he would return to London. There was a matter to settle before he could return home. Evangeline was convinced he was on the verge of an important discovery, and she wanted to be part of it.

He had wished Sophia a successful debut Season and promised to return no later than Christmas. Regina's youngest sister had been disappointed that a marriage contract must wait, but she couldn't change the circumstances.

Uncle Charles had closed his letter with a message for Regina. *May Cupid surprise you in your sleep and drown you in kisses.*

Xavier held his arms out to take the poodle when Regina's efforts to contain him were losing effectiveness. "Would you like me to try to calm him?"

"By all means." She surrendered the unruly little rogue.

Xavier cradled Cupid in his arms to scratch his belly and murmur to him in French. "*Tu es un petit bâtard.*"

Regina laughed. "He is going to think that is a term of endearment when you say it so sweetly."

"It is." Cupid's tongue had flopped out of the side of his mouth and his eyes were closed. He was content for the moment. "Did Benny leave already? He is typically harder to get rid off than a case of gout."

"He takes his new duties very seriously," Regina said. "Claudine plans to go to the playhouse this morning, and Benny insists he must escort her."

Xavier shook his head. "That woman has more patience than I do."

Benny had been underfoot since the night at the docks, proving he was as loyal as a hound. Regina didn't mind his presence, but Xavier often grumbled that a bit of privacy for newlyweds would be appreciated.

After the duke's death, Claudine moved back to the town house. The duke had signed it over to her after an especially volatile evening in a bid to earn her forgiveness. She had sold some of the jewelry he had bestowed on her in place of apologies over the years to support herself.

Upon her return, Claudine had turned out all of the duke's servants and hired replacements. She'd taken on Benny as well, and because Xavier had asked Benny to take good care of Claudine, the man had become the actress's shadow. He probably drove the other players at the small playhouse Claudine had recently joined batty, but no one would be giving her trouble.

With the last of Evangeline's trunks loaded on the carriage, Sophia and Aunt Beatrice joined them in the foyer to say good-bye.

Sophia tossed her arms around Evangeline's and Regina's necks to deliver one giant hug to both. "If you find Uncle Charles in Greece, first give him my love, then bind his hands and feet and tote him back to London. Christmas is too long to wait."

Crispin arrived in time to overhear Sophia's comment. "Christmas will arrive before we know it, and what exactly are you waiting for?"

Sophia sniffed. "*I* am getting married."

Crispin looked like he might swallow his tongue. "You've received a proposal? The Season has just begun."

"Well, I haven't received an offer yet, but Lord Ingram has hinted he might."

He scoffed. "Putting the cart before the horse again, I see."

"I am confident I will receive an offer soon." Sophia squared off with him, hands on her hips. "Perhaps *more* than one, you boor."

"Sophia," Aunt Beatrice gently scolded. "Be kind to Lord Margrave. After all, he is curtailing his usual activities to escort us about Town the remainder of the Season."

Sophia tossed her hands in the air. "Splendid. He will scare away every suitor. I am doomed."

Regina and Xavier exchanged a knowing look. They were predicting Sophia would receive her offer of marriage, but it wouldn't be from Lord Ingram.

"On that hopeful note," Xavier said, "we should be going."

Regina kissed Aunt Beatrice's cheek and thanked Crispin for watching over her aunt and sister during their absence. Once they were settled in the carriage and underway, Evangeline smiled sympathetically at Xavier.

"You had no idea the family you were acquiring when you married my sister. They are mad." Considering Evangeline was wearing goggles that made her eyes four times larger than normal and gave her the appearance of a bug, she might have thought to include herself among the madhouse residents.

Xavier squeezed Regina's hand and smiled at her. "I acquired a lovely family, but even if I hadn't, a little madness is a small price to pay to be with the love of my life."

Coded Message

Received in London 21 May 1820
rlrutxsliupwkewejfwgtxrlhlmotzrgmvaexlumuuimyddxfxrro
trtgetnmwhxqkroketgvpgfihwzrvbsrsdlvztdeehvwaiprvbeonecv
mkvprkwwmhtozqolignfqimhprydkdbtvib

Deciphered Message
Charles Wedmore has continued to evade capture, but I
have finally tracked him to Greece. My mission is coming to an
end at last.

Loyal servant to the King,
Sir Jonathan Hackberry

Acknowledgments

I would like to thank my good friend Lori for her encouragement and enthusiasm from the start of this adventure. She helps me to remember to have fun along the way, and I appreciate her more than mere words can express. I'm also grateful to my husband for helping me work through plot issues. Some of my favorite scenes are often the result of one of our brainstorming sessions.

Thanks to my good friends and fellow authors Heather Boyd, Julie Johnstone, and Ava Stone for their guidance and generosity throughout this process. They are the best.

I would also like to recognize reader Nicole Laverdure and thank her for her assistance with Xavier's French. I ran most of the phrases by her, but not all, so any mistakes made are my own.

Lastly, I want to thank my editor Karen Dale Harris for her excellent feedback and investment in this new series. Working with her was a pleasure.

You might also like...

The Dangerous Duke of Dinnisfree
by Julie Johnstone

Justin Holleman, the Duke of Dinnisfree, is used to being wanted—in bed, for missions, and even dead. He's protected his country more times than he can remember, gaining enemies along the way, but he failed to defend himself from the past that hardened his heart. Instead, he became an expert at shutting people out. Yet now, in order to save the king, Justin needs to let go of his old ways and let someone closer to him than ever before. He approaches the mission with his classic cold calculation, but his fiery new ally upends his ordered world and entices him at every turn. Suddenly he's in danger of compromising his assignment and losing his heart, two things he swore never to do.

Desperate to protect her parents from poverty, among other things, Miss Arabella Carthright unwittingly becomes a pawn in a dangerous political battle when she agrees to aid an enigmatic stranger. Having learned long ago to count only on herself, she's surprised when time and again the duke actually aids *her*. But when his true assignment becomes clear, Arabella realizes the man she's come to care for poses the greatest threat to those she loves.

As Justin and Arabella face their feelings and their web of deception falls away, they must decide how high a price they are willing to pay for love and loyalty.

ABOUT THE AUTHOR

RITA-nominated historical romance author, Samantha Grace, discovered the appeal of a great love story at the age of four, thanks to Disney's "Robin Hood". She didn't care that Robin Hood and Maid Marian were cartoon animals. It was her first happily-ever-after experience, and she didn't want the warm fuzzies to end. Now that Samantha is grown, she enjoys creating her own happy-endings for characters that spring from her imagination. *Publisher's Weekly* describes her stories as "fresh and romantic" with subtle humor and charm. Samantha describes romance writing as the best job ever.

Part-time medical social worker, moonlighting author, and Pilates nut, she enjoys a happy and hectic life with her real life hero and two kids in the Midwest. To learn more about Samantha's books, visit her at: http://samanthagraceauthor.com/index.html

Also by Samantha Grace

Novels
The Beau Monde Bachelors
Miss Hillary Schools a Scoundrel (book 1)
Lady Amelia's Mess and a Half (book 2)
Miss Lavigne's Little White Lie (book 3)
Lady Vivian Defies a Duke (book 4)
The Rival Rogues
One Rogue Too Many (book 1)
In Bed with a Rogue (book 2)
The Best of Both Rogues (book 3)
Kissed by a Scottish Rogue (book 3.5)
Novellas & Anthologies
Danby Family
Twice Upon a Time
Charming a Scoundrel